CONFESSIONS OF THE VERY FIRST ZOMBIE SLAYER

(that I know of)

For information on subsidiary rights, please contact the publisher at rights@jollyfishpress.com. For a complete list of our wholesalers and distributors, please visit our website at www.jollyfishpress.com.

For information, address Jolly Fish Press, PO Box 1773, Provo, UT 84603-1773.

THIS TITLE IS ALSO AVAILABLE AS AN EBOOK.

Library of Congress Cataloging-in-Publication Data

Titchenell, F. J. R., 1989–
Confessions of the very first zombie slayer (that I know of) / F.J.R. Titchenell.
pages cm
Summary: "Fifteen-year-old Cassie Fremont must brave through the zombie apocalypse in an almost impossible journey across the country to find her missing friend"—Provided by publisher.
ISBN 978-1-939967-30-5 (paperback)
[1. Zombies—Fiction. 2. Voyages and travels—Fiction. 3. Horror stories. 4. Youths' writings.] I. Title.
PZ7.T522Co 2014
[Fic]—dc23

2014007381

Printed in the United States of America

10 9 8 7 6 5 4 3 2 1

For Matt, my husband, best friend, and personal clown, who first taught me the joys of zombie slaying.

CONFESSIONS OF THE VERY FIRST ZOMBIE SLAYER (that I know of)

F.J.R. TITCHENELL

JOLLY FISH PRESS
Provo, Utah

CHAPTER ONE

WHY THEY CALL ME THAT

When you think about it, there's no way Mark was really the first case. First one broadcast on American TV, sure, but not the first altogether.

On average, nearly 300,000 people die every day, and that stat is from before all this started, so even if you narrow down the beginning to a window of just five seconds, that's about eighty-three "first" cases. Eighty-three stories like mine. Some of them have to be technically earlier, a lot of them are probably more interesting, and a few might even be dumber, but the faces on the front pages of the last newspapers ever printed were Mark's and mine, so I guess we're as good a place to start as any.

So here's how the zombie apocalypse started for me.

It was during Boy Scout Troop 146's annual spring break camping trip. I'd spent weeks begging Rory and Lis, the twins who acted as my official best friends and only real girl friends, to sign up all the girls they could for Venturers so we'd have a crew big enough to go along with the guys.

Now I wonder whose face would have been on those papers instead of mine if my friends hadn't helped.

At the time, though, I was just glad to be there—so glad that I didn't even mind being sidelined with them and their army of satellite friends, making a campfire brownie oven out of tinfoil while the boys set up the tents. I didn't even mind the word I heard whispered behind me when I excused myself to say hi to Mark.

"Slut."

It's okay. Really. In girl talk, "slut" translates roughly to "my crush's crush," which isn't so bad, if you think about it. Besides, it was pretty common knowledge how many guys I'd gone all the way with.

Zero, if you're wondering.

My romantic conquests up to that point had consisted of precisely two counts of catching and hanging onto a boyfriend for more than three consecutive weeks, and one of them didn't really count.

Still, considering that this was a little over three years ago when I was only fifteen, even *I* had to admit that I wasn't off to a terrible start, and the secret wasn't in my frizzy hair or freckles or flat chest, that's for sure.

It was something I'd started doing on a whim, almost by accident. One afternoon, I'd just decided that I was going to start listening to all the stupid, pointless shit the boys said.

Simple? Sort of. I found out pretty quickly that if you're going to listen, you have to listen *hard.* Smiling and nodding doesn't cut it. You have to listen until you know why a Needler is a noob weapon and where Boba Fett made his debut appearance (Hint: It's not Episode V). Then listen harder. And then keep listening.

That's not my real secret, though.

My real secret is that I liked it.

Not just the attention from the boys, not just the envy of the girls. I liked the things the boys taught me. In fact, to this day, I read comics when there's no one around to impress. I still have my own proudly assembled Magic: The Gathering deck in the bottom of my bag, carefully sealed against weather damage and, after everything that's happened, I still feel liberated by the harmlessness of a paintball's sting, as long as I'm wearing my helmet.

I've got kind of a thing about helmets ever since Mark didn't wear one.

I'd noticed Mark at Rory and Lis's youth group two months earlier. Rory had noticed him back when they had been in the same daycare. Yes, I knew that. In my defense, that adds up to a *lot* of chances she'd had with him already, a lot of moments when she could have left the brownie oven or whatever she was doing and run to meet him at his mom's approaching SUV instead of me. She was so pretty. It should have been easy for her.

Yeah, it's not much of an excuse, but it's all I've got.

"You *have* to see what I brought!" This was how Mark greeted me, in a hushed, breathless tone, with an over-the-shoulder goodbye to his parents. I remember how he brushed off his sister's overenthusiastic parting hug and hurried off with me instead.

He steered us away from camp, behind a sumac thicket, in a way that told me it was something we'd have to get as much fun as possible out of before Kim, the troop leader, confiscated it.

I was right. He pulled something metal out of his bag.

"Beautiful, isn't it?"

It was. The nearly-new paintball gun his older brother had sold him before leaving for college was almost unrecognizable. Mark had cut the barrel short and sanded it so smooth it almost looked like it had been molded that way. He had switched some parts with a gun we'd broken the week before, so it could hold a bigger CO2 cartridge, and the paint job looked like it had taken hours, smoky metallic silver with just the right amount of grime in the crevasses. I was almost afraid to touch it.

"How does it shoot?" I asked.

Mark grinned. I loved the way he grinned, the frictionless spread of his lips over his perfectly even teeth. He held the gun out like a ceremonial offering. "Ladies first."

I'm not sure which I was more excited about, getting to fire that gorgeous weapon first, or getting to chalk up a few more points on the scoreboard between Rory and me I always pretended not to keep.

I didn't accept right away, as badly as I wanted to. It would have been wrong not to voice the warning, though I knew we would both ignore it.

"Kim will *kill* us if she gets a look at this."

We were allowed to play paintball during designated downtime, as long as no one fired at non-players, animals, property, cars, and so on, but modified guns were always iffy territory, and anything this realistic-looking was out of the question.

Mark grinned wider as he dug an older, unaltered gun out of his bag for himself.

"Gets a look at what?" a voice over my left shoulder said.

It made me gasp out loud and twist around to block Mark's masterpiece from view, but it was only Norman, my real best friend. Our other best friend, Hector, stood to his right, smirking at me a little. I stepped back to show off the gun.

"Sweet." Norman breathed reverently over it.

"Two-on-two battle?" Hector suggested nonchalantly to Mark. "You and Cassie, me and Norm, last team with a member standing wins lunch when we get back to civilization?"

Mark glanced at me for approval and then nodded. "Get your stuff. We'll wait. Just be quiet about it."

Norman brushed this off. "Nah, consider this your head start."

He was running for the tents half-a-second later. Hector stayed long enough to shift a meaningful gaze between Mark and me, shooting me a wink before following.

When I flicked off the safety on the sawed-off gun and started deeper into the dry, California live oak forest with Mark already hovering protectively closer to me, I made a mental note to thank Hector with lunch eventually, no matter who won.

The game started quickly after Mark arrived. He didn't even have time to drop his duffle in one of the boys' tents. We just stashed it in that sumac bush for later before rushing to claim the high ground. None of us dressed specially, unless you count stripping to our undershirts to keep our uniform shirts clean. If we'd taken more time, I don't know if Mark would have worn a helmet. I don't even know if he'd brought one. I always imagine one stuffed forgotten in the bottom of his bag like mine.

We were perfectly positioned by the time Norman and Hector caught up with us, me in the fork of a tree, Mark camouflaged uncannily in the bush below me, both with a clear shot at the whole hillside sloping down in the direction of camp. The ground was carpeted with bone dry leaves for yards in every direction.

We could hear them coming a mile off.

The new toy in my hands was itching to be played with, but I waited for Norman to get bored with the opening moves, like always. He was a good shot, though he was never as interested in winning as he was in making sure every game culminated in the most epic bloodbath possible.

"Oh, Cassie!" he called in the universal melody of taunting, climbing up toward the high ground where he knew we'd be. "Come on, Mark. Come and get me. I'm not that scary."

Mark was close enough that he probably could have shot Norman, but he waited, too. The shot would be clearer once Norman took a few more steps to the left.

Somewhere off to the side, I caught the more subtle movement of Hector skirting the back of the hill.

"Cass-ie!"

Norman kicked a pile of dead leaves and, at the same moment, I squeezed the trigger and cocked the gun again as quickly as I could, my fingers tingling from testing its impressive power for the first time.

The splatter of green only struck Hector's shoulder. I thought I was losing my touch for a moment. Then I decided to blame the shortened barrel instead. My timing, at least, was right on the money, and Norman whipped around in a full circle, trying to figure out where the shot had come from. He'd been listening too hard to himself.

He didn't look up at me.

No one ever did.

The moment Norman's back was fully turned, Mark burst out of his hiding place and fired two shots right between Norman's shoulder blades.

Norman turned to look at him with an expression of exaggerated shock, staggered a few steps forward, and collapsed, moaning like a second grader acting out a Shakespearean death scene. Even though I could only see the back of his head, I could tell Mark was rolling his eyes. I'd made the mistake of stopping to watch Norman a few times, but I knew enough by then not to let the theatrics distract me from what Hector was up to.

He had frozen for a moment after I hit him, trying to decide whether or not to drop, too. There had been some debate about that recently. The way we played, you're dead when you lose three points. Head or center mass is three points all at once, limb shots are one point each, but we'd argued over what the shoulder counts as. Norman always asked where the fun was if you couldn't even survive the most classic survivable shots. Hector maintained that it shouldn't be a classic survivable shot in the first place because the carotid artery runs right through it, and that we were better than every stunt choreographer ever for knowing that.

The most recent compromise we'd reached when we shared the house rules with Mark was that it counted for two points, so after a moment's indecision, Hector took cover behind the thickest nearby tree and angled his gun toward Mark's oblivious back.

I could have let him pick Mark off, and I'd still have won. He would have had to abandon his cover to get a half-decent shot at me, and I'd get a better shot at him first, but that kind of strategy doesn't exactly scream, "trustworthy partner material," so I felt my way back to my footholds instead and slid down the trunk, holding the sawed-off to my chest to avoid scratching the masterpiece paint job.

Hector fired once before I reached the ground and missed. While he was scrambling to get off another shot before Mark could turn to retaliate, he hardly noticed me sprinting around the other side of the tree. This time there was no arguing the lethality of my aim.

Mark threw his gun down with a cheer.

"Whatcha got a taste for?" I asked Mark. "'Cause I'm thinking sushi."

"I don't think you qualify yet," Norman said, moving for the first time out of his death sprawl.

"Hmm, the bet did say the team with *a* person left standing," Hector agreed.

I caught on and smiled at Mark, grinned, maybe not as smoothly as he would have himself, but just as slowly and broadly. I savored the ominous sound when I cocked the sawed-off once more.

Mark grinned back nervously, tried once to retrieve his own gun, realized he had tossed it too far out of reach, cursed under his breath, and bolted into the woods.

There's a reason they call it "the Chase." The whole boy/girl thing, I mean. It's the most suitable term I've heard for it. It *feels* like a chase. Sometimes you're chasing, sometimes you're being chased, and sometimes you can't tell which, but it doesn't matter because both sides put you in that same slow-motion zone where all the really sharp memories come from, the ones that remind you why you bother sitting through the boring parts of life.

That's the zone I was in that day, sprinting through the trees after Mark. The Chase. No waiting, no plan, no idea what I would do if I caught him, or if I didn't.

Norman and Hector only tried half-heartedly to keep up with me. I could still hear their breathless chanting, "Fin-ish him! Fin-ish him!" when I cornered Mark against a poison oak covered hillside, but I couldn't see them anymore.

"Fin-ish him! Fin-ish him!"

Even in the absence of the proper safety equipment, even with the sawed-off's extra pressure and the added closeness allowed by the shortened barrel, I'm sure it was a freak thing that happened.

One moment, Mark was trying to feint his way around me, jerking one way and then running the other, his eyes sparkling with focus. The next, he was crumpled, motionless, at my feet, a trickle of dark red cutting its way through the neon green splatter my shot had left on his temple.

As near as I can tell, it was somewhere between those two moments that the rules changed, not just for Mark and me, but for the whole world.

"Mark?" I asked this in a forced, cheerful tone. It's a silly old habit, trying not to sound too worried too fast, but it's a hard one to break. Even now, I approach the freshly dead as if they might be trying to make a fool of me, though I could sense the difference the very first time. This was nothing like Norman's scene-stealing game forfeits.

"Mark?"

Like a good little Boy Scout groupie, I knelt beside him and grabbed his wrist, feeling along the thumb side of the tendon with my first and second fingers. For all the jokes about the living dead the troop had made on first aid day, when we had learned how to take each other's pulses through considerable trial and error, we had eventually gotten the hang of it. I knew exactly where that little beat of pressure was missing from.

"Mark!" I stopped trying to hide my panic, hoping that someone would somehow call a stop to this horrible exercise before I had to figure out what to do next.

I couldn't remember whether CPR had ever restarted a heart that had stopped due to brain damage, but I couldn't think what harm it could do either, so I leaned over and started feeling for the right spot on his chest.

I know from later experience that the stillness after the fatal shot must only have been about thirty seconds. That first time it felt almost like the forever it should have been.

I had barely begun to throw my weight forward and count "one" when the hand I had just grabbed reached out and grabbed me back.

Mark sat bolt upright, spilling me off of him.

He was still dead; there was no question about that. I could see it in his eyes. When they locked on mine, they had that flat, thoughtless, inanimate quality I'd seen once before. When my first dog's terminal cancer had finally gotten too bad to live with, I'd been allowed to hold her paw while she was put down. After that, I never forgot what death looks like. When it comes to eyes, there's no mistaking it.

But then again, he was *moving*. Whatever was left of Mark had a vice grip on my left elbow, and his fingers were stretching toward my throat.

I leaned forward to meet him, clasping his hand to the soft, sensitive side of my neck, kissing his hungrily half-open mouth, moved to blissful tears by the awesome power of this love that had overcome death itself, and . . .

Oh, wait. No, I didn't. That's what I would have done two years earlier. Maybe.

See, one of the many side effects of keeping best friends like Norman and Hector, and sharing their books and movies and games, is that I don't actually think of corpses as sexy. I certainly don't think of them as safe.

So here's what I really did: I grabbed the beautiful sawed-off with my free hand, turned it around, and slammed the butt of it repeatedly into the already dripping bruise on the side of Mark's forehead. I didn't stop at the weird, inhuman throat scream he gave. I didn't stop when the plastic shattered. I didn't stop when Norman caught up and choked out some shocked gibberish from somewhere behind me. I didn't stop until I had the gooey pieces of what had been Mark's cerebellum in my hands.

Since Norman's the one who gave me that instinct, I count that as the first time his friendship saved my life.

Oh, and it was also the first time, or at least one of the first eighty-three times, that the dead returned to attack the living.

I guess that's a pretty big first, too.

CHAPTER TWO

I KILLED HIM. TWICE.

I'd like it to be known how deeply, sorely tempted I am to take advantage of the leisure and hindsight available to me to come up with a witty one-liner, something like "and stay dead," only much cooler, and pretend it's what I said next.

It's not like there are a lot of people who know the same things I know about what happened. A hundred years from now, who's to say it didn't go down exactly however I decide to say it did? But I'm not going to do that.

Let's get this straight right now.

I, Cassandra Emily Fremont, the very first zombie slayer (that I know of), do solemnly swear that this memoir, written for the benefit of any generations of human beings that may someday, possibly, hopefully, follow mine, and in stark contrast to all pre-apocalyptic history books I'm aware of, will contain nothing but the pure and whole truth of the events it details, to the best of my knowledge, no matter how painful, private, embarrassing, or inescapably lame.

Sound fair?

Good.

Unfortunately, with Mark down for the count again, it means that instead of dry action hero humor, you're going to be treated to this loving description of me majorly losing my shit. I mean, beyond the skull-crushing, brain-mashing kind of shit-loss I'd already committed.

Enjoy.

"Cassie?" Norman's voice was fragile and lost and only reached the thinnest outer surface of my awareness.

I don't think there were any actual words in my first response. It was this garbled screech, constricted by the urge to vomit. I scraped the tissue that had once controlled Mark's most basic, vital impulses off my fingers, smearing lumpy streaks of blood down my jeans, which didn't make the whole not-vomiting thing any easier.

"Oh, dear God." That was all that slipped out of Hector when he found us, but it was more than I'd ever heard him say involuntarily. It took him more than twice as many breaths as usual to summon the calm, reasonable tone he always used whenever there was no possible excuse for anyone to be calm or reasonable. "What happened, Cass?"

I knew it was vitally important for this question to be answered accurately and efficiently, so I really tried to process and order my thoughts thoroughly enough to communicate them that time. I didn't quite succeed. My next set of jumbled syllables fit together something like this:

"Mark dead . . . then not . . . but still was . . . dead again . . . had to, had to, I had to!"

"Okay." Hector tried to calm me, retrieving the remnants of

the sawed-off in exactly the same hovering way you reassure a cornered animal before throwing a canvas bag over its head. "Okay, you had to."

"I had to!" I repeated, trying to bury my face in my hands before I remembered the blood on them.

With me unarmed, Norman worked up the nerve to drop his own gun and put an arm around me instead, which seemed to make Hector decide it was safe to retreat toward camp. I formed one more word while he could still hear me, the essential word of both defense and warning.

"Zombie," I said.

Neither of my friends answered me, but I could tell by the moment of complete stillness that they had both heard.

I don't blame Hector for reporting me to Kim, or Kim for calling the cops. What else were they supposed to do? I don't blame Rory for screaming much worse things than "slut" and chucking briquettes at Norman and me until she had to be restrained. She couldn't hit the broad side of a Sandcrawler anyway.

I've seen corpses walk, skyscrapers crumble in disrepair, and the busiest freeways lie vacant at 8:30 on a Monday morning, but those forty-five minutes it took to get a full emergency response to our nice, secluded campground were the most surreal of my life.

Mark was dead. I had killed him. Without the zombie factor, it was the kind of big deal that adults always handled quickly, behind drawn curtains, leaving us to squabble over carefully portioned scraps of information—with so few of them and so many of us stuck with so much evidence for so long, it couldn't work that way this time.

Kim tried at first to stop people from seeing the body, but

by then everyone had gathered too close, ready to snap up the precious details while they could. Once they had seen it, they had all the knowledge anyone had on the matter, and then no one seemed to know what to do. Some stayed, not too close, watching. Others spread as far away from the mess as they could, busying themselves with whatever could be packed up. No one would be staying in the tents or making brownies in the fire pit that night. Lis went off somewhere out of sight to throw up. She wasn't the only one.

Norman didn't speak, just kept me wrapped tightly in all there was of his slight frame, simultaneously cradling me and pinning my arms to my sides, ignoring the film of paint, blood, and grey matter covering us both. Hector and Rory settled on either side of us, sentinels, whether for our protection or everyone else's, I couldn't tell.

No one tried to separate us, even though Norman had no particular authority to handle the situation. It wasn't as if there was any specific, applicable protocol to observe.

Really, I can't question the way anyone handled things, except maybe me.

I got a whole lot more warning than a lot of people do when they're about to be arrested. You'd think I'd have used it to try to escape before the cops arrived, or at least come up with the most plausible possible excuse.

"It wasn't me, it was a cougar! I was trying to beat it away!"

I'd watched way too much *CSI* to try that one.

"When we were alone, he attacked me and I . . . was really, really mad about it!"

That's probably about the best I could have done, but I didn't give it more than a passing thought.

All I did during the wait was bury my face in Norman's curly brown hair, trying to make the comfortingly familiar scents of his shampoo and sweat blot out the rusty bite of blood, breathing very slowly until the worst of the hysteria had passed.

Norman is the guy I started listening to first, back when I was all about dating strategy. He wasn't the target (a little too much of a goofball even for my tastes), and he'd only ever had eyes for Rory anyway, but since I'd had a thing for Hector in those days, I'd figured we could use each other to get closer to what we wanted.

It hadn't gone exactly according to plan. Rory would barely look at him. Maybe that part shouldn't have surprised us. I'd never, ever say that anyone was too good for Norman, but Rory and Lis did have a special kind of hotness written into their identical DNA that set them a little way apart from most people, even by Oakwood High's pretty rigorous hotness grading curve.

And Hector ended up stringing me along for almost a month before taking me aside to "ask a serious question."

I was hoping for, "Be my Valentine."

I got, "Could we still hang out if I told you I was gay?"

Yeah, he's the one who doesn't really count.

Oh well, it hurt, but there really isn't a more sincere version of "it's not you, it's me" out there, so I got over it, and the three of us had been pretty much inseparable ever since.

The process of accepting the beginning of my zombie-slaying years wouldn't have been easy under any circumstances, and it would have been impossible to get through it as quietly or non-destructively with anyone else at my side.

By the time we heard sirens on the access road, I'd been able to settle on one simple fact.

Here's where it starts getting kind of cool again.

"I'm okay, guys."

This was the first thing I had said after the Z word, just as the two dark blue uniforms came into view, when Norman's grip on me tightened in anticipation of being severed.

I could hear the leftover constriction in my voice, but it was so steady that Norman actually looked at me like he knew me for the first time since the paintball game.

"Would it be hopeless optimism," he asked, "if I said we'd be laughing about this someday?"

"Probably." The smile felt strange on my face, but it convinced him enough of my lucidity that, after an extra hug of a squeeze, he let me walk unaided into the authorities' waiting arms.

"My name is Cassie Fremont," I said, loudly enough for all the witnesses to hear even though at least ninety percent of them knew that much already. "And I'm very, very sorry, but I killed Marcus Cates. Twice."

Then I turned around and held my hands out behind me.

I have to admit, I was hoping for a slightly stronger reaction than the one I got. Most of the crowd was silent, and that part was fine, they were in shock, after all. The first officer to reach me—Aleman, her nametag said—just frisked and cuffed me without batting an eye, without saying any more than, "You're under arrest."

I could feel Norman regretting letting go of me even before he spoke.

"And by that she means, 'I want a lawyer.'"

"Don't need one," I said.

"Doesn't need a court appointed one," Norman corrected. "Because her mother—"

"Works in the completely unrelated field of entertainment law—"

"And has connections—"

"That I also don't need because I killed him!" I shouted over him.

"Lawyer!" he repeated.

"Once by accident," I explained, "once on purpose because he was still already dead anyway, and he would have killed me if I hadn't!"

"Sorry, her accent's kind of thick." Norman said this with a completely straight (if very pale) face, in the same plain, unflavored Hollywood accent we both shared with everyone else on that campground. "But I distinctly heard her say, 'lawyer.'"

Aleman escorted me to the waiting squad car without a word.

In fact, it was a long time before anyone said anything to me after that.

Here's the simple fact I had settled on: what had happened to me was real, or at least, it was impossible for my brain to distinguish from reality. No matter how much I thought about it, as awful and weird as it was, there was absolutely nothing about the memory to indicate a trick of the mind. It was as solid and certain as any other, and that could only mean one of two things.

1. Zombies were real.

Or,

2. I was completely, hopelessly, irrefutably insane.

Either way, my plan was the same.

In the first case, people would need to be warned, and that responsibility seemed to fall squarely on my shoulders, no matter how crazy it made me sound at first.

And in the second case, well, I certainly wasn't going to

jeopardize my spot in the cushy, padded cell where I clearly belonged by changing my story too much.

That's why I went quietly, if not quite as quietly as Aleman and her partner (Easton, I read backwards in the rearview mirror) might have liked.

We didn't leave right away. After watching the cops in the distance for the better part of an hour, spreading yellow tape around and conducting endless conversations with my troop and crew mates, when the backup cars and the coroner's van showed up and they were finally free to come acknowledge my existence again, I guess I was a bit of a chatterbox. Mom always said I was an attention junkie. Maybe she had a point.

"You can tell by the eyes," I explained calmly, but seriously, as the car wound carefully down the hillside. "Also by the fact that he had just died in front of me. Are you getting all this down?"

Aleman never took her eyes off the road. Easton had his notebook out, but his pen hadn't moved in a while.

They had both slipped into the sullen, offended sort of silence people get from watching pre-civil rights film strips, things reprehensible enough to be beneath arguing with. That's what they thought of me.

"Hey!" I kicked the grate protecting them from people in my position. "*I'm* the one who lost my almost-boyfriend today!"

It was dangerous thinking about that enough to say it. There was an excellent chance that I would slip back into incoherence without Norman there to help pull me back, but I could tell that nothing I said would be heard anyway until I could prove I wasn't a complete sociopath.

"You didn't know him!" I shouted, letting that strangled sound grab my voice a little again. "You didn't have to see him die, not even once! I did! You won't miss him, but I will! Will you just *talk* to me for a second?"

During the silence, I wished my hands were free to blow my nose.

Easton sighed, pulled a card out of his pocket, circled something on it, and pushed it through the grating until it landed on the floor of the car.

I flattened it out with my shoe and looked down at it. Circled on a pre-printed Miranda Rights waiver was "the right to remain silent."

"Very funny," I said.

Maybe it's just me, but when I used to think of the words "Police Station," I always kind of pictured something out of *The Andy Griffith Show*. My parents' house was set into the side of the valley, big and private and peaceful, but not far from LA. I knew that I effectively lived in metropolitan So. Cal., yet somehow I'd still been expecting something quaint and small town-y.

I could tell that wouldn't be the case after one glance at the high concrete walls and heavy, wrought-iron gate. The most welcoming touches were a pair of surgically-sculpted hedges around the entrance and a news van parked outside, a reporter with her station's logo on her microphone already waiting on the sidewalk. I heard a few details of my story in her introduction to her camera man.

I didn't know who had gotten the word out, and I didn't care.

Of course, a pretty, well-off, goodie-goodie teenager, beaten to death by a less-pretty but equally well-off and formerly goodie-goodie teenager now claiming to have seen a zombie was sure to catch the interest of at least a few reporters. They'd present me as a nutcase whether I was or not, but at least the Z word would be on the airwaves. If it made the difference between a hug and a headshot in the impulses of the next person to see the dear departed sit up and reach out, it might be life-saving.

I was about to say it loudly enough for her mic to catch, even with Easton between us, shooing her away, when her hand shot to her earpiece, and without so much as a thank you or goodbye, she was gone in pursuit of some greater, breaking news.

I let myself be ushered through the door of the station, leaving her outside, along with all other comforting signs.

There was a key-coded door before the fingerprint machine, and then Aleman had to flick her ID card past a sensor to open the cell in the back—the drunk tank, I guess they call it. Just touching the bed in the corner made my skin crawl, and I wished I was wearing more clothes. I didn't have much for her to take and put in those safekeeping bags—no jewelry, no extraneous gadgets, just a wallet, a keychain, and a cell phone.

The next words spoken directly to me, Easton's, might have had a hint of pity beneath them. I'm not sure.

"Do you want to tell your parents, or should I?"

My parents were among those staying at the little resort near the campground, further down the mountains, close but not too close, enjoying their own, less rustic vacation. I certainly wasn't looking forward to the task of talking to them, although looking back, there's nothing I'd rather do. I wish I could hear Mom yelling at me in her scary attorney voice for not calling her the instant I knew I was in trouble, Dad berating the first officers who would listen to him for not making sure that I was warm enough.

At the time, the only thing that made me dial the number myself was the fear that Easton wouldn't tell it right, that he'd leave out the Z word. If I had the responsibility to warn anyone of what I now knew to be possible, my family had to top that list.

I thought of a million different ways to explain myself while Dad's cell phone rang. I couldn't remember any of them when I heard the answer *my* calls never received.

"Please leave a message after the tone."

CHAPTER THREE

SPECIAL ACCOMMODATIONS

This is where I could describe what spending the night at the police station is like. I could go on and on about how you lie down and close your eyes, but you don't sleep. I could go into exactly how long you stare at the softly discolored blanket before wrapping it around the goose bumps on your shoulders, or how, once you've washed off as much of the blood as you can with your clothes on, there's nothing left to do other than worry.

Honestly, all of that was boring enough the first time around.

Trust me, it's not like I was worrying about anything important. It was stupid stuff: what juvie would really be like, how long it would be before my friends' parents let them speak to me again, being kicked out of school and Venturers, being disqualified from the vote before I qualified in the first place, how everyone from my parents to my cousins to my children's children would be completely screwed if they ever wanted to run for president.

I didn't worry about whether I'd ever have to look Mark's little sister in the eye again. I certainly didn't worry about the fate of the world. Yes, there were zombies, I had that information, and it would have been unforgivable not to share it; but it was just like having information important to cancer research. It might save some lives, but in the grand scheme, not much would change either way. Not much ever did. People did their best for worthy causes, we had to, but it was only ever just enough to keep the world as mediocre as always. If all my efforts fell flat, things would be no worse than they had been before my discovery, and if I succeeded beyond my wildest dreams, a new threat would arise before anyone could decide how to celebrate.

I knew that night that the dead could rise, maybe they always had under freak circumstances, creating and encouraging the zombie stories I knew so well. It hadn't ever occurred to me that they'd start making a habit of it. They couldn't because the world as I knew it was something that was always there the next morning when whatever else I was worried about had blown over.

Just like my parents.

That's why I didn't worry about their sudden unreachability either. At least, not the first night.

So let's skip ahead to when something happens outside of my limited imagination.

"Cassie, isn't it?"

It was eleven in the morning when a cop I didn't recognize asked me this, three hours after they'd brought me the drive-through breakfast biscuit and too early for lunch, so I sat up instantly to listen, scared and relieved at the same time, expecting real news.

"Come on," he said. "We're moving you to the family room."

"Why?" I asked. "Is my family here?"

"No."

"When are they coming?" I demanded. I knew it wasn't his fault if they still weren't answering, but I wasn't going to miss the rare opportunity to demand information from someone.

"No idea," he said. "But it's about to get a little crowded in here for you."

Aleman and Easton were among the four officers corralling a group of three men, all late college age, all built like horses, all looking scared out of their minds. One of them kept trying to push his way back to the door. I thought at first that they'd just been celebrating spring break too loudly and were freaked out about getting caught. Then the skittish one turned again, and I saw at least as much blood on his hands as I'd had to scrub off my own.

I didn't argue with the move any further.

The family room smelled a little less like liquor than the drunk tank, and just as much like bodily fluids. The naptime cot wasn't designed for someone of even my meager height and weight. At least the baby powder smell made it easier to avoid imagining the swarms of microbes it was probably crawling with.

There were two wide, sunny windows with bars on the outside, not that they were necessary. I gave up trying to figure out the child locks to let in some air after the first fifteen minutes anyway.

The ancient black and white TV in the corner could pick up three stations with some fiddling, allowing me the choice of a Korean soap opera, a small claims court, or a guy in a bright green rabbit suit singing about the importance of oral hygiene.

Halfway through the February issue of *Highlights* from 1992, I began to debate whether the room change qualified as an upgrade.

The little window in the door didn't let me see as much of the hall outside as the barred cell front had, but it was a twist of the corridor closer to the front desk, more frequently trafficked, so I was able to overhear snippets of conversation.

It took me an embarrassingly long time to notice this advantage.

It's a funny thing. Worries and unfamiliar surroundings can make it almost impossible to sleep through the night, but they don't do anything to stop you from dozing off in the middle of the next day, or having really intense dreams when you do, so the historic day I spent listening to the world end sounded not so much like a bang or a whimper as like this:

"This old man, he played one, he played knickknack on my thumb . . . ."

"*One* person left standing. Mark? Mark!"

"Nan dangsin-eul salang haeyo. Nan eonjena dangsin-eul salang haess-eoyo!"

". . .never seen so many domestic disturbances in one day . . . disturbances of the peace . . . in broad daylight."

". . . not sayin' he did it on purpose, but them bills ain't gonna pay themselves."

"Just let me talk to her, Greg. She seems to be the start of all of this. She has to know something."

"Even *we're* not allowed to question her without representation."

"But I'm not one of you!"

"Run it without comments, Jan."

"You can't keep pretending the situation is normal!"

"Mark? Mark!"

". . . can't just hold her here like this much longer."

"The parents aren't picking up, and the child advocate's having some sort of family crisis. What do you suggest?"

"Dangsin mom-i jjogaejineun geoya!"

". . . gotta be some new drug, right?"

"Mark? Mark!"

Around the time the sunlight from the window turned that golden, late afternoon color, the channel with the court shows and the occasional sound bite of local news cut out into a technical difficulties screen, relieving me of the still image of Mark's yearbook photo and his mother's quote, "When will he be laid to rest?"

I flicked groggily back to the Korean channel, which was playing a breaking news broadcast of a riot in Seoul, and suddenly, I was wide awake. Even through the fuzzy, copter-borne camera, I recognized the same thoughtless, deliberate way of moving that Mark had demonstrated for me in those critical few seconds after his first death. The picture was even more degraded in the zoomed attempts at close-ups, the features indiscernible, but there was no question what those people were doing to each other.

There was definite biting going on.

That's when I finally realized what you already know, unless you found this book lying in a ditch, missing the back cover and most of the first two chapters, after escaping from a particularly strict isolationist cult compound on the moon.

My world didn't just contain zombies, it was overrun with them.

"Gina?"

That was Aleman's voice, answering her phone. This time I listened to every word.

"News? What? No, don't tell me you've lost another one! You're serious? No, of course, someone will be right out."

"Gina Clark again?" Easton asked her, and I recognized the name of the local hospital when she verified it. "Another vanishing terminal case or another rampaging junkie?"

Aleman paused long enough to make it clear that she was serious.

"First one, then the other."

For the first time, I checked that my door was, in fact, locked from the outside.

"They're not junkies!" I called out, pounding on the glass out of pure optimism that someone would take notice. No one did.

I turned my attention back to the old TV, searching for any more information it could give me.

The news channel never returned, and the children's channel continued with its regularly scheduled programming. Maybe they weren't set up to change it, or maybe they thought they'd get better ratings keeping the kids calm while parents watched the other channels in other rooms.

The Korean channel didn't translate much into English, but at least the images were useful. More useful than test patterns, anyway. The riots in Korea itself were inter-spliced with similar scenes against different skylines. I recognized New York, London, Tokyo, Dubai, and what I think was Moscow.

I tuned out the eerie familiarity of the different flavors of the scenes and focused on the unfamiliar constants. That mechanical determination of movement was one of them. That low, animal throat scream was another, like they needed to make noise but couldn't be bothered to open their airways properly.

I paid special attention to the few kills I could identify in the background of the recycling shots. Almost everything was zombie on human, not the other way around, except for one old Japanese lady driving her cane through one of their eyes. It supported my best theory, but it wasn't proof.

That sound.

I was getting a little hazy again from too many hours staring at the grainy screen, and from the time of day and the darkness. I had been conscious for fewer than ten straight hours, but it was well past midnight, I wasn't exactly well rested, and I hadn't bothered to go looking for the light switch when the sun had set. For a second or so I thought something funny had happened to the volume, or to my ears.

When I heard it again, I scrambled off the cot so fast that its frame finally buckled.

It was coming from the hallway outside.

". . . never stopped fighting from the moment we arrived. Nurse said he couldn't even lift his own spoon yesterday. Hasn't said a single word."

I could barely make out Aleman's voice through the continuing, echoing, throat screams.

"You think he somehow got his hands on this new PCP?" a separate, authoritative voice asked.

"No." I must have been pretty desperate for a friendly voice because even Easton's was comforting. "I mean, yes, he's like the ones we encountered on the streets, but it's *not* PCP. It's like nothing I've ever seen before. The eyes . . . they respond almost normally, but they don't look like they should."

From my tiny window, I watched them drag the thrashing,

moaning cadaver along the hall, and I could hear in his voice that Easton knew the look in its eyes as well as I did, but hadn't been able to understand it yet.

My sympathy for him was cut short by the beep of his keycard, reminding me what he naturally planned to do with the thing.

"Stop!" I yelled. As usual, no one listened. The inhuman shrieking coming from the space between me and the officers this time wasn't helping. "Don't let it near them! Check its pulse, its *pulse!*"

Just out of sight, around the corner, I heard the cell click shut again.

Unlike me, I guess the dozen guys who'd accumulated inside it over the course of the day were supposed to be big enough to take care of themselves.

For anyone wondering how a small, coddled, fifteen-year-old girl (with no more remarkable tools or talents than an encyclopedic recollection of every *Mythbusters* episode ever aired) managed to survive to tell a story that involves almost no one else managing to do the same, this is an excellent example of one of those times when it's actually been really useful to be me.

I listened to the screams, both living and undead. I heard when each distinct voice in the first category went silent, and when it returned as part of the second. I listened to the false confidence of the orders to "settle down in there," thinly veiling the confusion of the officers who could see the unusual brawl I was almost glad I couldn't.

Easton's voice was coming from just in front of the cell at the same time the keycard reader beeped.

"Don't open that door!" I shouted uselessly.

The zombies poured out into the empty hallways of the

station. The calls that night had been more demanding than any emergency response organization was ever meant to handle, so there weren't a lot of other cops standing by. The three who were trying to subdue the zombies made a tactical retreat in my direction, far enough that I could see the flash of a taser gun in one of their hands and observe its effect. Not that it was much to observe.

"Stop where you are!" Aleman commanded and then drew her gun. The force of the two bullets passing through its chest took the first zombie off its feet. For a few seconds.

"Go for the head!" I yelled.

Easton did, and the first zombie went down. The other twelve didn't seem to mind stepping on it to overtake the trio of cops.

Easton caught my eye through the little window while one of them bit off his ear. He didn't nod, didn't waste the time to tell me I had been right, just held up the ring of keys with the card hanging from it, and threw it underhand at the gap beneath my door.

CHAPTER FOUR

THE LEGEND OF SUPRBAT

A childproof, soft-edged, weaponless room, a writhing hallway full of zombies, an almost-as-hostile world waiting just out of reach, and there, at my feet, a glimmer of hope. Freedom. It's one of those defining moments that you remember whenever you're trying to remind yourself what you're made of.

There was never going to be a better time to make a break for it. I seriously doubted that the zombies would leave while I was alive so nearby, and with nothing to fight them with, my best chance for getting past them would be to do it while they were occupied with the cops.

You know, occupied eating them.

So why did I stay crouched behind that door, listening until there were no more sounds of human protest, nothing but the precious, finite soundtrack of the ripping and cracking of flesh and bone, winding ever closer to its last note?

Had my nerve failed me, the loss of all that was normal and familiar finally sunk in, the twin guns of cynicism and good, old-fashioned denial finally expended their last rounds? Had the secret substance of my character at last been called out into the light to be measured and fallen short?

No, it's just really, really difficult to pull a well-stocked keychain through the gap under your average door.

The key card had slid under first, pretty easily, lucky for me, but the ring and most of the real keys, including the one that would unlock the family room door, were still stuck on the other side of it.

I pulled, hard but carefully, afraid the plastic would rip before I made any progress. After jerking the card back and forth a few times with negligible results, I dragged the ruined cot over to the door and jammed the bent part of the frame into the gap, trying to pry it a little wider. It sort of worked. After some pretty horrifying creaking sounds, which I guess don't even bear mentioning next to the sounds that were coming from outside, I was finally able to get my fingers around a metal part of the keychain. I thought it might snap before I could get hold of anything more useful, but after a few moments of yanking, readjusting my hands and the bracing of my legs, and yanking again, the lumpy tangle of steel came free, along with a sizable hunk of splinters.

After that much effort to get them, it was actually pretty easy not to think twice about using those keys.

The zombies outside were still mostly distracted, their throaty noises replaced by chewing and something close to the sound of taking apart pieces of fried chicken, so that's what I pretended they were doing as I pushed past them. I pictured the crispy, golden, deliciously not-human limbs, the salt and grease and clear, well-cooked juices, and discovered probably the worst possible time *ever* to realize just how hungry you are.

One of them reached for my ankle, and I kicked out, breaking its nose, not that it seemed to notice. It gave me time, at least, to run down the hall to the confiscated goods room where I'd watched the college guys get their stuff sorted, fumble it open, and shut myself inside. I didn't stop there because I couldn't have made it to the door by the front desk in time. I could have. I stopped there to look for my cell phone, and I didn't stop for my phone because I'm that hopelessly addicted to Angry Birds. I did it because I wanted to contact someone, anyone I knew, and I don't actually know any phone numbers by heart other than the three (home, Mom's cell, Dad's cell) that the cops had already tried a hundred times.

Make all the jokes you want about the curses of technology. Go on, really, I can take it, because I've *seen* how society crumbled, and it wasn't because of the failing attention span of first-world youth.

My phone wasn't there. One of the cops probably had it in a desk drawer somewhere, but when I turned on the light in the little, utility-sized room I almost forgot what I'd been looking for. The phone would have been nice. It could have been pretty useful for the next couple of days. The things that *were* in there, however, promised to come in handy for a much bigger chunk of my new life.

I took a few luxurious seconds to examine the array of blunt and bladed weapons.

Claw hammer. Too short.

Chainsaw. Too unwieldy.

Katana. Too flashy. Whoever it had been confiscated from had probably ordered it from a collector's catalog, and they hadn't even bothered to have it sharpened.

Baseball bat.

Perfect.

It was old but perfectly intact, and the weight of the wood felt divine in my hands. The brand name had been scraped off, and burned into the side of it, probably with a magnifying glass, were the words, "Suprbat ~~2000~~ ~~2001~~ 2002."

I don't know what "Suprbat" was used for in 2002 that got it confiscated. I don't know if its previous owner is still out there somewhere, knocking off mailboxes and zombie heads alike, or if he gave up crime, stayed in school, won the national spelling bee, and then got bitten on the way to work one day. Wherever he is, I'd like to thank him for making a special appearance on the ever-expanding list of people who've saved my life. In fact, he's probably in the lead for sheer volume.

There wasn't much else there that could do anything but slow me down. There were a couple of phones, but the batteries were shot, and like I said, who would I call anyway without my own contacts folder?

I did grab a couple of the many, many Swiss Army knives and Zippo lighters, some road flares, and a large, grey knapsack. The flesh-eating bunny printed on the side probably wouldn't be funny for much longer, but the fireworks inside, including bottle rockets and some long garlands of firecrackers, had the potential to be pretty useful.

For the purpose of getting through that corridor again, to the relative safety of the front desk, I only ended up needing Suprbat to push one body out of my way long enough to make a run for it and get that bulletproof door behind me. My reasons for not making sure that door latched afterward are definitely on the list of things so stupid they'd have no place in history if I were to sink so far as to change it.

The cool, half-true reason is that with the fresh, comforting, new-toy sturdiness of Suprbat in my hands, and that nice, narrow, Thermopylae-esque doorway at my disposal, who could blame me for wanting to hang around for a few practice swings before making my escape?

The whole truth is that I needed to make sure that I could.

Yes, I was, for all intents and purposes, the first zombie slayer. I'd already won that title. I'd done it before. But that first time had been so sudden, so impulsive, and as sure as I was that the memory was real, the best adjectives I could attach to it by that time were "blurry" and "uncomfortable," sort of like my first time riding a real rollercoaster, or my first kiss when Kyle Alderson from algebra study group had stuck his tongue so far down my throat that I thought I might puke on him.

In fact, "blurry" and "uncomfortable" ended up fitting a whole lot of the firsts in my life, now that I think about it, even the best ones.

The point is that, even though it was real, it was also so far removed from reality that I simply couldn't wrap my head around re-creating it.

In order to do that, well, I just had to *do* it.

That's the real reason I kicked the door back open, took a step backward, and shouted, "Batter up!" though, to be honest, I don't actually know what that means.

It turned out for the best, anyway. They didn't overwhelm me, and who knows? If I'd had to feel the exact resonance of the crack of wood and bone for the first time outside where they could surprise or surround me, without having the chance to teach myself to minimize that reflexive closing of the eyes, the results could have been disastrous.

As it was, after I finished bludgeoning what had been left of Aleman's head when she reanimated, I was able, finally, to step out into the cold, faint light of the slowly rising sun, armed not only with Suprbat and the rest of my loot but with a heavy, completely unwarranted, but very, very helpful dose of confidence.

The windows of the family room had only overlooked a piece of dry, scrub-covered hillside, so this was the first look I got at the apocalyptic vista below. I couldn't possibly do it justice in description, so I won't.

I was a bit more concerned anyway with figuring out which one of the dozen-odd identical squad cars parked outside fit either one of Easton's car-shaped keys, without turning my back to any one side for too long at a time. I was alone for the present, but I could hear rustling and shrieks at an undetermined distance.

It turned out to be the very last car, tucked away in one corner of the lot. Isn't it always? I locked the door behind me, fastened my seatbelt, took a moment to savor the protective casing of steel around me, then several more to figure out that the way I was leaning on the steering wheel was stopping the key from turning, and then, okay, okay, I'll do my best to explain the state the valley was in because it sort of affects this next part.

The day's first light made it possible to see the few small columns of smoke rising from the houses that were burning unchecked, without interfering with the starkly perfect outlines of the patchwork power outages.

It reminded me a little of the mornings after bad earthquakes or storms, with one important difference. All of those mornings had been the calm after when the damage is assessed and rebuilding begins.

This was what you would get if you took one of those mornings, shrank it down, and sprinkled it with monster insect larvae. The whole valley still wriggled, not with normal, productive human activity, but with continuing disaster.

From the mountain police station's height, I couldn't see every detail of the walls and windows and gardens that had been torn apart in the single-minded attempts to reach the live people barricaded beyond. I *could* see the movement of the bodies that were doing the tearing. It was that same determined, methodical destruction from the broadcasts, heedless of the rule that said bad things were supposed to be gone when the sun came out.

The police presence was still visible, too, but it was sort of like a spider web in the path of a garden spigot, impressive only in its optimistic persistence. The little clusters of blue lights stood out against the sea of red because, oh yeah, here's the important part: The streets were completely, bumper-to-bumper, Super Bowl stacked parking lot *packed*.

I've been late for school more than once because just one traffic light was out, or one road was blocked with accident debris, or someone was getting busted on too public a sidewalk, begging everyone to slow down to stare.

All of those things were happening fifty times over at once in the valley that morning, and that's why, even though the car's aging GPS might theoretically have been able to lead me home, I turned back onto the road leading back up the mountain, back in the direction of the campgrounds and resort.

Well, "turn" is actually an excessively graceful word for what I did. It doesn't quite conjure up the grinding sound of the few seconds between finding the reverse and noticing the parking break, or the screeching flash of sparks when the bumper clipped a metal gate on the way out, but the end result was mostly the same.

My chosen route wasn't completely abandoned, but most of the other cars I passed were headed down instead of up, or pulled over to the sides, either with their hoods open or with their occupants simply staring at the bleak scene below. I passed them with the siren on, trying to look taller, wishing I'd taken a uniform shirt to cover my stained, grey tank top, but no one looked at me closely enough for it to matter. A sight that might have raised eyebrows on any other day was just part of the chaotic background noise now, a minute scrap of help already claimed by someone else.

Really, considering the fact that this was:

1. My first time driving alone
2. My first time driving practically at night
3. My first time driving mountain roads
4. My first time driving during a state of emergency
5. My first time driving on roads full of human-sized walking obstacles that don't try to stay out of your way, and
6. My first time driving, ever,

I think I did a pretty good job.

In a way, my lack of conditioning actually seemed to be an advantage. I'm pretty sure most of the other people out driving had figured out what the zombies were, but some old, irrevocably instilled instinct made it really hard to run them down. One guy coming down the other lane in front of me swerved so hard to avoid one that he drove headlong into the face of the mountain. I didn't mind accelerating when it ran out in front of me and ripped off one of my windshield wipers, but I couldn't help muttering under my breath as I did so, "Seventeen."

Seventeen murders, if people wouldn't admit that these things weren't alive in the first place, or just one instance of manslaughter if they would, I counted off in my head, plus escaping police custody, grand theft auto, driving without a license, oh, and plain old grand theft if you counted Suprbat and the rest of the stuff on the passenger seat. And I was pretty sure that precisely not a single one of those things would end up mattering.

One way or another, life was definitely never going to be the same.

But like I always do when annoyingly big, smothering thoughts like that one start creeping into my head, I looked extra hard at the moment right in front of me, and I was getting all ready to pat myself on the back for finding the resort safely, with all four tires intact and two hubcaps still in place, angled neatly between the white lines and everything, when I gave the brake an extra tap, only it turned out not to be the brake, and the world disappeared into darkness and stars as the airbag claimed the space I'd been sitting in.

CHAPTER FIVE

WE'RE ALL GOING TO DIE

I came around pretty quickly, I think. The level and color of the light outside hadn't changed much. By then, I kind of liked the idea of unconsciousness. I knew, without really thinking about it, that I was going to have to do something dangerous and difficult when I came out of it.

I could tell by the screams. And the hammering.

The sound of the crash must have drawn a lot of attention because sure enough, when I blinked and coughed the gunpowder-y residue off my face and sat up straight enough to see over the puffy, white, well-meaning cushion that had knocked me out, at least ten or twelve zombies, probably all that had been within earshot, were gathered around the car, screaming, hammering, and searching for any possible weakness in my protection. They were finding it, too. The passenger window was already webbed with cracks.

There was no strong strategic position this time, not like the police station's front office. The moment a door or window opened, they would be on top of me. I'd never have the chance to get on my feet.

I reached instead for the gear shift. The engine was still running, still trying to idle its way further into the low concrete wall I had mashed it into at the edge of the lot.

Reverse came easily this time, but movement didn't. The front bumper dragged along the asphalt, and something in the car's inner workings—the gears? The axles?—fought me for every inch I pushed it with a very broken scraping noise, and I knew that, in the long run, it was going to win.

I backed up far enough to turn the wheels in the direction of the welcome building's front door and stomped on the gas, on purpose this time, thinking that maybe I could get close enough to safety and far enough ahead of the horde at the same time to run across the gap, but the car's new top speed hardly made them break walking stride to keep up with me. Something in the metal allowed a moment's give, and with an extra, desperate engine rev, I rammed the building's front wall, pinning the quickest zombie against it, snapping its back. Its lungs were too crushed to continue screaming, but its mouth kept snarling just the same, its arms flailing forward to reach for me.

If I'd broken its arms, too, I probably would have shifted gears and tried the same thing again, and again, until I'd taken out as many of them as that poor car could handle before they broke through. But the flail of that arm caught the dawning light just right, or just wrong, just the way it had to, anyway, to reflect the distinctive red-green alexandrite color of its wedding ring.

I hadn't recognized her with the bite on her face, or the dirt and gashes on her clothes, which were always perfect, even on vacation. I hadn't wanted to.

"Mom?"

Even then, I knew it was a stupid question. She couldn't answer it, plus I knew the answer in advance. Yes and no. Mostly no.

As little good as the sight of her was doing me, I couldn't help looking around for the one that would make it twice as bad.

In the rare moments completely away from work, they were never apart. If one of them had risen within shouting distance of the lot, so had the other.

I spotted my dad by the silly deerstalker hat he always wore on days off. He was the one right behind me, for the few seconds that any of them were right behind me, before they all piled onto the hood with the collective focus of a latchkey kid who's just realized which end the can of Spaghetti-Os opens from.

The windshield had cracked by then, too.

I haven't forgotten my whole truth promise, really, but it's not like you need a decoder ring to figure out why I couldn't quite get my head around a brilliant new escape plan at that particular moment. If you want to toss on some tight jeans and black eyeliner and describe the moments I spent in that driver's seat, petulantly beating up on the airbag, waiting for the hands to reach inside and get me, wondering if the first ones would be the same hands that had tucked me into bed and put Band-Aids on my scraped knees not too many years ago, be my guest. You'll probably do a fine job of it.

But if you're more interested in the second time that morning that I had the daylights knocked out of me by something really, really heavy, keep reading.

The overhang on that wall of the welcome building was a concrete slab, artfully trimmed with hardwood, so when it fell, if the airbag hadn't already deployed, it soon would have. The fractured windshield shattered inward as its frame ceased to exist. The roof caved in against my head, which already hurt a lot.

At least this time it only sent me loopy for a couple of seconds, not enough to stop me from realizing that I'd probably survived the impact thanks to the cushioning of all the zombies on my hood, zombies that also wouldn't be able to give chase in the immediate future.

The door wouldn't open.

Here's where I'd make a joke about the engineering standards of some former country or other, only I didn't actually take the time to check the car's brand name while I was grabbing Suprbat, slinging the evil bunny bag over my shoulder, and wriggling out through where the driver's side window had been.

"Eighteen!" I shouted as I clobbered the recovering zombie on the very left, which had only had its right shoulder and the right side of its jaw crumpled by the overhang.

I wasn't counting the ones under the slab, because I hadn't meant to bring it down, and I couldn't be sure how many of them were down for good.

I saw the next one out of the corner of my eye, a blur of color. My brain put together the costume of that clown who was always making balloon animals in the kiddie section of the arcade as I was already swinging around to meet it. It raised an arm at the last moment with a self-preservation instinct I'd never seen from one of them before. I didn't dwell on it.

"Nineteen!"

"Ouch!" it answered.

Then I stopped.

Zombies didn't use consonants, certainly not in that familiar, freshly broken voice that had never dropped quite as deep as its owner would have liked.

"Norman?" I gasped.

"Yes!" he matched my tone, reminding me that this was apparently my morning for stupid questions, then grabbed my free hand and pulled.

"Why are you dressed like that?"

"Why aren't you *running?*"

Two more of them had wriggled free of the rubble, and the throat screams were beginning to rise again as they started after us with that dogged speedwalk they used, so I let Norman lead me at a sprint around the side of the building.

There was one in our way in a net hanging from a tree. Norman batted it aside automatically, drawing my attention to the heavy wrench in his other hand.

"Did *you* drop the roof on them?" I asked.

"Yeah, lucky it only had two bolts left to take out."

"How the hell did you know to set that up?"

"I didn't," he panted, stopping to tap on one of the back windows in rapid Morse code. M-E-L-L-O-N. "The bolts make good checker pieces."

An industrial A-frame ladder hit the ground next to us with a thud, and Norman pushed me onto it, turning to keep an eye on our pursuers' progress.

I climbed onto the roof, or what there was of it around a sizeable hole in the chosen section, in as little time as I could, but by the time Norman had room to join me, one of the zombies had reached the base of the ladder, and he had to lean back over to swing at it with the wrench. He missed the first time, and it made its way up a few rungs, twisting its limbs awkwardly between them, like it had absolutely no knowledge of how a ladder was meant to be used but was determined to figure it out.

The second swing bloodied the side of its head. I joined in with the longer range of Suprbat, and after a few nervous seconds, we knocked it loose for long enough to drag the ladder up after us. Norman gave me the "after you" gesture, and I lowered myself carefully through the hole. The fall was broken by a strategically placed pool table. I had just a few seconds to absorb which room I was in, as well as who had been there to hoist the ladder out of it in the first place, before Norman landed and made the bruises on my head throb with a hug that would have taken me off my feet if I'd bothered to find them yet.

"You made it!" he said. "I'm so sorry. I swear I didn't think you were a total basket case for more than a few minutes. An hour tops."

"Either you're lying," I choke-laughed through his grip, "or *you're* the basket case."

He laughed, too, not because I was at the top of my comedic game, but out of pure, obvious relief, and let go to allow Hector to hug me, too. Hector was there, he was alive, Norman was alive, and I was alive, and for a moment, those facts were enough to make me glow.

Hector retrieved one duffle bag from a pile in the corner and handed it to me. "We saved it when it looked like no one was going to come pick it up," he explained.

I unzipped it and held it to my chest for a moment. I'd never thought beef jerky and clean socks could look so much like heaven.

"What happened to you?" he asked, looking me over. I could practically hear his brain filing my condition under "shaken but unharmed."

"You guys first," I said, shoving a handful of jerky in my mouth. It wasn't quite fried chicken, but it was food, and I didn't feel like diverting the efforts of my jaw from it for long enough to explain. "What happened here?"

"Mountain View Rest Home happened," Norman answered, piling the pool balls into the triangular rack.

"Where everyone who's anyone goes to die?" I continued for him. Our tagline for the old folks' home next to Whitetail Village is one of those things you just have to say whenever it comes up.

"Yeah," said Norman, "well, one of them did die. Around the time you were getting carted off, we're guessing. And from there it was like head lice."

"They made it up to the campground from there?" I asked.

He made a "pshaw" sound as he chalked his cue. "Nah, but after Kim waited 'a reasonable length of time' for as many of the parents to come for pickup as possible, the Kent clan piled us all in the vans and tried to bring us down here."

"Kim?" I repeated, re-scanning the room, as if she could somehow have hidden from me the first time around. It was still just the three of us.

"Yeah," he continued, lining up the break and following through with a loud *crack*. "But when some confused-looking old geezer with blood on his smock ran out into the road, arms waving, guess what she did?"

I groaned. "She was a good scout about it."

"She was a good scout about it," Norman agreed. "Stopped her van with Kim's-Son-the-Eagle-Scout stuck behind it in the other one."

Kim's-Son-the-Eagle-Scout. You have to say his name all in one piece like that, or just "The Eagle Scout" for short, or people pretend not to know who you're talking about.

With a leap a cricket could have envied, Norman was on

the table, treading lightly between the pool balls. He cocked his head at an angle that suggested a cape billowing from his shoulders and, in his best Kim Kent voice, which was also his best Superman voice, said, "Citizen! I couldn't help noticing that you appear to be in distress! How may I assist you today?"

Hector had his face in his hands. I wasn't sure if he was stifling a laugh or a grimace. Either way, I was pretty sure I was doing the same.

Norman mimed being caught in the neck by something and rolled backward onto the floor, gasping and gurgling.

"*You* didn't want me to get out to help her," Hector interrupted, only half accusing.

"Well, I was right, wasn't I?" Norman dropped character on a dime, rolled back to his feet, and began lining up his next shot. He ignored the considerable distance most of the balls had travelled from where Newtonian physics had originally left them. "The old guy almost took you down all by himself."

Crack.

The orange striped ball disappeared into the far corner pocket, and Norman looked briefly up at me. "He's lucky he got back to the van at all when Kim got back up."

Hector smacked him on the back of the head, making him cry out "Do-over!" when the cue ball skidded off in entirely the wrong direction.

"You mean *you're* lucky," Hector corrected. "At least I can *drive* the van."

Norman was old enough to get a driver's license, barely, but his father had owned a motor scooter dealership, so he'd been raised mostly riding those instead. He'd been able to handle one solo (and illegally) for years. He had even less experience with actual cars than I did. Hector had passed his driving test on schedule last year, but even the small dimensions of his parents' Lexus were still a challenge for him to maneuver.

"That's the spirit," said Norman. "You can do anything you put your mind t—Crap."

He scratched and limboed under the table to the pocket he had hit.

"Any idea what happened?" I asked. "How it started, I mean?"

"Nope, still taking all bets!" said Norman, arbitrarily repositioning the cue ball. "My money's on aliens, but satanic curses and chem warfare are very popular, too."

"That's a no," Hector translated unnecessarily. That left one more very important, but even scarier, question.

"So, who else?" I prompted.

"Oh, right." Norman dropped his cue and threw open the lobby door. "Good morning, Castaways! Say hello to your surprise teammate!"

He stepped aside with a flourish to frame me in the doorway for the benefit of all of two people who were inside.

Kim's-Son-the-Eagle-Scout was kneeling in the corner, still in his immaculate uniform as if this were all some advanced exercise, surrounded by medical supplies arranged for cataloguing. His little sister, Claire, fourteen going on ten (forever convinced that because her brother was "successful," she would be, too), was helping him with a bland expression, which melted into excessive enthusiasm when she saw us enter.

I had always tolerated her because she had convinced her mother to help form our Venturer's Crew even though Claire didn't actually like camping or anything else Venturing involved other than being in the same place her brother got all his attention.

"Glad you could make it," The Eagle Scout said.

"How did you escape?" Claire squealed like a kid begging for a bedtime story, and suddenly I didn't feel much like bragging, whether my mouth was full or not.

"It's the drunk tank," I said, "not Alcatraz."

"Where?" Claire asked blankly.

I let the silence hang for a moment, wishing for a cricket-filled night. I had to settle for the cries of frustrated zombies. At least it wasn't hard to come up with a change of subject.

"Take two: Why are you dressed as a clown?"

Norman turned his theatrically painted face down to look at the bright motley of purple, green, and orange like he'd forgotten it. "Oh, this."

The Eagle Scout scoffed with disapproval. Claire looked pleased with the prospect of a conversation she'd already heard at least once before. It gave her a much-needed head start toward understanding it.

"Well, you know how whenever there are zombies, there's always at least one dressed as a clown?"

"I guess," I agreed.

"Well, the poor bastard wearing this had his brain scooped clean out before he ever got to be one of them. So I'm just making sure that when I die, and then un-die, at least I'll be filling the quota."

"You're not going to die!" I shocked myself as much as anyone with how loudly I shouted this at him, grabbing his hands and pushing back his violet sleeves, searching for hidden bite marks or anything else that might coincide with his logic. I'd only just gotten him back, the biggest piece of life as I'd known it that it looked like I might get to keep, and he was *not* about to be taken away again. I wouldn't allow it.

He didn't fight me off, but he was laughing at me. The familiarity of the sound would have been comforting in any other context.

"We're all going to die, Cass," he said, finally. I couldn't decide whether to laugh along or punch him when I caught his meaning. "Sooner or later, older or younger, by zombie or heart disease or falling space junk, and there's no way to tell when, especially lately, so best to be ready all the time, right?"

I leaned against the doorway, all nonchalance, pretending that I hadn't just committed the mortal sin of implying that I cared about something in front of what might have been, for all I knew, everyone alive in the entire world, no less. This time the substitute crickets were for me. "Right," I said, "of course."

"But in the meantime"—Norman tossed the pool cue from one hand to the other and then offered it to me—"I believe it's your turn."

"Norm," Hector cautioned slowly, looking me over again out of the corner of his eye, like he thought I wouldn't notice. He'd put it together, all the important details of what had happened to me that morning, especially in the parking lot. "It's been a long day. Maybe a bath, a nap-"

"I'll nap when I'm dead," I said, grabbing the cue. Then I listened to the howls outside for a moment. "Or not." I shrugged. "Whichever way it works these days."

I didn't ask either of them—as we argued over whether "eight ball, corner pocket" means any corner pocket, or if you have to pick just one—about their mornings two days earlier, how much they resembled the one I'd just had. I didn't ask what, exactly, they'd found in Whitetail Village right next to Mountain View, other than the ladder and sledgehammer they'd fashioned their secure entrance with.

Don't get me wrong, we were good friends, and among the three of us, we could talk about anything, including caring-too-much stuff, but we were *best* friends because we could also *not* talk about anything, like that time I tried wearing a strapless dress with tape that wasn't quite sticky enough, or like that conservatory rejection letter that had made Hector resign himself to following in his family's psychiatric footsteps.

Sometimes that was a lot more special.

CHAPTER SIX

ALL IN FAVOR, SAY "BRAINS."

"Should we maybe go in there and help?" I asked after our second hour in the arcade. Norman was beating me at that two-player racing game, but only with five games out of nine. The power was on, for the time being, and he had pried open the coin compartments on most of the games so we could keep playing. Hector watched from behind, waiting to challenge the winner.

I had sort of assumed that whenever they had finished with whatever project they were currently working on, the Kents would relax enough to join in, and by then, I might be up to the task of not talking about things with them as well. I was certain after those two hours that I was right, that I could have handled it, but they hadn't so much as checked in with us.

"Help with what?" asked Norman.

"I don't know. Whatever they're working on."

He snorted and fed the quarters back through the slot.

"He's already scoured this whole building for any bit of help he could possibly need, and everything he's found, he's sorted, re-sorted, cleaned, sterilized, alphabetized, and sorted again at least three times by now."

I took a moment to break my personal record for staying

on the virtual road before asking, "Well, then, maybe we could *invite* him . . ."

Hector cleared his throat. Too tactful as always to use his dad's psychotherapy terms word-for-word to bring up things like coping styles, he just said, "He's happier where he is."

Agreeable as the current division of activities was with everyone, however, it came to an end around then anyway. It wasn't The Eagle Scout who made first contact. Claire came to deliver the latest news with nervous good cheer.

"Rory's talking again," she said. "And she's calling a meeting."

"Rory's here?" I dropped my hands from the miniature plastic steering wheel and twisted around to look at Norman, peripherally watching my own car fly off a cliff and through a tree on his screen. "Why didn't you tell me?"

Rory wasn't close with Norman and Hector—the most contact she usually had with either of them was deflecting Norman's endlessly hopeful attempts at flirting—so the day probably wouldn't have gone much differently if I'd known, me with them, her with the others. But she was my friend, and she was a living human we knew by name. Those were in short enough supply that it seemed blatantly unfair of them to have kept one a secret. Even if she would only have been off with Lis, doing Rory-and-Lis-ish things-

Lis.

No one had mentioned Lis.

"We . . ." Norman started to explain with exaggerated sheepishness.

"We weren't sure she was really *here*, here," Hector finished for him in his calm, factual voice, as Rory appeared in the doorway

to check on Claire's progress. I got up to hug her as well, but she put out a hand and I stopped, not wanting to do anything that would make her stop being *there* again.

"What your friend means," Rory corrected, "is that Daddy never taught him the difference between catatonia and *distraction.* But it's okay, because I'm not distracted anymore."

She held up her phone in its glittering fuchsia case, exactly the same shade as her nail polish, to indicate that it had somehow un-distracted her, but that we would have to follow her back into the lobby to find out how.

We did.

"Has anyone else been able to get a signal yet?" Rory asked as soon as she had everyone gathered around her.

"Not since eleven thirty, two days ago," The Eagle Scout rattled off promptly. He'd never been good at letting anyone else lead a meeting (even with Kim, it had been difficult for him), but at least he usually dealt with it by cooperating a little too completely and loudly rather than not at all. "The network seems to be over-trafficked, but at least that means there are other survivors. Did you?" he asked earnestly.

"Not enough to call out," said Rory, "but with some concentration," —she glared at Hector, who had probably tried to ease her out of what would have looked like a dangerously compulsive behavior loop— "enough to receive a text that's been backed up since then."

She turned her phone around to show us the time stamps, Lis's name, and a few words.

At Doc Defoe's, C U Monday.

"Oh," I said. Claire made a similar sound of recognition and sympathy when the screen turned in her direction, but probably only because she had guessed that some unnamed sad thing had happened.

Defoe was Lis's therapist. She had been attending sessions for a few years, her "checkups," as she called them, routine care for acute anxiety.

She was sixteen. You can do the math on how acute her anxiety could get sometimes.

"She ran off when she saw . . . the first body," Rory said carefully, trying to block out anything that might damage her composure. "She told me she just needed air, or I would have gone with her instead of wasting my time babysitting Cassie's stupid, psychotic ass."

Okay, she didn't actually say that last part, but the look she gave me was clear enough.

"Instead, she freaked out, took the car, and ditched me."

"Rory." I let the seriousness in for a moment. It wasn't quite as hard when it was about someone else. "I'm so sorry."

"Why?" she chirped with determined, defiant good cheer. "This proves where she went *and* that she made it there safely. All we have to do now is go and pick her up!"

I was starting to get used to our cricket substitute.

"Uh . . . huh. Good luck with that."

This was a pretty taxing exhibition of The Eagle Scout's talent for humor. Simple, basic, but acceptable. If you think he was being completely unreasonable, well, I don't really have to explain his reasoning, because when Rory pushed the issue, he did that pretty well for himself.

"Pretty much all the human bodies that existed on Earth two days ago, the ones that were annoying when all they usually did was make places crowded, are now actually, actively trying to kill us and everything else that moves, and your plan is to go *into* Manhattan?"

Yeah, Rory and Lis's parents were divorced, so they were *very* frequent fliers. As in every-other-weekend frequent. The apartment they shared part-time with their father, stepmother, and half-brother, and the hospital Defoe practiced out of were both in New York City.

Once more, out of consideration for the future lunar cult escapees in the audience, New York and Hollywood are about 2,788 miles apart. Lis had made it onto what was probably one of the last planes to leave LAX before latte steamers and pencil pushers everywhere gave up and went home to lock themselves in their basements, or started ripping out their coworkers' jugulars, whichever they'd fantasized about more often. But for us, that meant 2,788 miles of *road,* covered, by that time, with riot wreckage, potentially as many as three hundred million zombies, and approximately zero gas station attendants.

That's how cricket-worthy it was.

"I'm going to find her," Rory said firmly.

"Good luck with that," The Eagle Scout repeated in exactly the same tone. Maybe his humor wasn't improving after all.

"I . . ." She faltered, just barely. "I probably can't do it alone, but I'll try if I have to."

"Good luck with that."

To The Eagle Scout's credit, the joke would have been on the verge of becoming funny again that time if it hadn't been so sad.

"There's a blue Prius in the parking lot," I spoke up after a few moments. "I know where the keys are."

I didn't want to go digging under that slab for Mom's purse, but I knew it was the least I could do.

This wasn't quite what Rory had been hoping for, but she nodded her dignified thanks.

"Anything else?" she asked.

Substitute crickets.

I knew what I wanted to say, but I wasn't really on a roll in the not-making-a-fool-of-myself arena, so I also wanted to keep saying nothing for a while. Like I said before, I'm a listener. People tell me things, I do my best to understand, and that makes them want to tell me more things, and after a while, some of them, like Norman and Hector, start asking me what I think, and then they start listening back, but if I start off by saying things, not a lot of people take me seriously. Even with Rory and Lis's honorary best-friendship, I was still basically one of the freaks, so that was just how it worked.

But like a freak, I said it anyway.

"Wait. Pretty much everyone we know is dead, the six of us somehow managed to wind up together and safe, and . . . you guys really want to ignore that? We don't even know when we'll *see* other living people again, and there's no way for us to contact each other again once we split up." I nodded at Rory's phone. "Wherever we decide to go, or stay, wouldn't it sort of make sense for us to stick together, at least until we know a little more about what's going to happen long-term?"

Substitute crickets.

"I think it's a good idea," Hector said simply. Like I said, he wasn't close with Rory, and he had never really *liked* the Kent family, but he'd always had more patience for them than most people did. Actually, Hector had more patience for most people than most people did.

Claire looked utterly anguished by the question. I knew she would have loved to have as many people around as possible, it meant a wider rotation of people's patience to feed off of, but wherever her brother went, she would follow.

"We're going to have to move around anyway, right? You said it yourself, we're safe enough, but the stuff won't last forever." She picked up a battery from one of the carefully arranged piles, "and we'll all do better if we pool everything than if we argue over who gets to take what, right?"

The Eagle Scout took several seconds to straighten the pile to exactly the angle it had had before. "That much is true," he agreed stiffly, making Claire almost faint with relief.

"Of course we'll stay together!" she gushed all over the rest of us, as if she'd ever had a vote.

"But," he followed up after her, "I was talking about an actual *survival* pact. Staying organized, staying civilized, keeping each other alive. I do think, with so few of us left, it is our responsibility to preserve what we can. We could be the difference between the end of humanity and the dawning of another age, maybe a better age, but it's not going to do any good if not everyone is on board."

I'm the leader, do what I say or else. We all knew the translation. We all pretended not to.

"Sure," I said. "That's exactly what we're talking about."

"Good," said The Eagle Scout. "Norman!"

Norman was standing on the front desk behind him and had spent most of The Eagle Scout's attempt at motivational speaking holding the nearest flag up behind him, fluttering it a little for emphasis now and then. This might have worked better with an actual star-spangled banner, but at least the Whitetail Golf League crest had most of the right colors on it.

A sudden snap from The Eagle Scout would have made anyone who wasn't expecting it drop whatever they were doing. His voice was that commanding. But years of being "led" by it had given us all a certain level of immunity, so Norman didn't budge.

"Norman?" Rory tried instead. She had always claimed to be annoyed by the effect she had on him, but I noticed that this never stopped her from exploiting it. She asked more quietly than The Eagle Scout, entreatingly, if he would please play things straight just long enough to get the matter at hand taken care of.

She could have sung off-key in Latin and the effect would have been the same. Her spare scrap of attention alone made him drop the flag, and The Eagle Scout jumped on the opportunity.

"What about you?" he asked.

"Well, that depends," said Norman. He climbed off the desk and went over to lean on Rory's shoulder. His posture radiated confidence, but I didn't need to be able to see through the makeup to know that he was blushing. He always was when he talked to her. "On who's asking."

Her answer was always the same, as predictable as the color of his face. Only the level of venom sometimes varied. That day it was maxed out.

"Not unless you were the last man on earth."

Norman mimed looking at a watch, even though I couldn't remember the last time I'd seen someone actually wear one.

"I think I can wait that long," he said, "but no promises. Until then, sure, yeah, the more the merrier."

She decided not to spend any longer arguing with him. "Fine," she said. "Thank you, everyone, and this is all very nice, solidarity among the last remaining humans and all, but just to be clear, we're talking about my *sister* here, not just someone I took shelter in the same hotel with."

She didn't look at me then, and I'll admit it, as catty and manipulative as it was, it hurt. I'd known Rory and Lis since before we needed deodorant. We'd made cootie-catchers, and rated the cutest boys in the second grade, and gotten grounded for trying to cut each other's hair with pinking shears because we'd somehow believed that if all *three* of us could look alike, all three of us would somehow count as sisters.

We hadn't looked alike, of course.

Lis isn't short for Alissa, by the way, or Melissa, or Elisabeth. It's short for Borealis, because apparently everyone who gives birth to twins is cosmically obligated to immediately grow a cruel sense of humor. Guess what Rory's short for.

Yup, Aurora and Borealis, kind of like peanut butter and jelly, not a whole lot of room for improvement there.

I'd always been a few steps outside, looking in, and I knew we'd drifted a bit further than that since I'd started hanging out with Norman and Hector, since I'd realized how much I liked never feeling like I was less than completely one of them.

And I knew that if I hadn't shot Mark, we all would have found out about the zombies some other way, at some slightly later time, and Lis would have had no reason to freak out and run all the way across the country before then. She and Rory would have been together.

But I didn't want all of that to reduce me to the level of someone Rory had taken shelter in the same hotel with.

"Everyone who wants to help me is welcome," Rory continued calmly, "but I *am* going, as far as it takes, with or without anyone else."

"Okay," Hector, started, and I knew he was trying to patch together everything that had been said to make it sound like we were all on the same side. "Okay, so—"

"So." The Eagle Scout stood up and took the floor, the way he'd been bred and raised to do. "We, Troop 146," he said, "and Cassie."

"Of Venturer Crew 23," I pointed out. I could have thrown Claire a mention, too, but she was more of an appendage than a member.

"Yes. We, as a group, are being offered the *option,*" he pronounced the word carefully, "of tagging along on Rory's rescue mission. We may have better survival odds if we take a different direction, but it seems only fair to put it to a vote. She's not participating in the *group* decision, so her vote won't be counted. Majority rules."

Norman cleared his throat theatrically. "Those in favor, say—"

"By a show of hands," The Eagle Scout contradicted. "All in favor?"

His own hands stayed at his sides. Despite her visible distress, so did Claire's.

Hector and I both raised ours. Rory wouldn't look my way.

"Norman?"

Norman hadn't raised his hand, but that seemed to be because, by then, it was busy feeding coins into the pinball machine by the door, the one positioned to beckon kids in the direction of the arcade while their parents were busy checking in.

"Do you even remember the question?"

If The Eagle Scout had kept his mouth shut, he might actually have won the vote, but I'll give him his due credit, that wouldn't have been in the true spirit of the Boy Scout handbook.

At that moment, the overhead lights flickered once, twice, and then died. The pinball machine gave a sad, shutting down noise, the insides clicking and settling into place.

Norman stared at it for a moment, his painted smile offset by that heartbreaking expression you see on children standing over dropped ice cream cones. Then he shook it off and waved an arm in the air.

"Road trip!" he whooped.

The Eagle Scout almost pretended to hide his sigh. "The hands have it," he announced.

Wait, did I say waiting for the cops with the first dead zombie was the most surreal experience of my life? Hmm, watching the six people in that room all agree on something, all at once, without Kim there to make us, that's a good contender, too. I'll let you know if I make up my mind.

"But" —he cut Rory off before she could reclaim her meeting— "there's no excuse for us not to be smart about it, and everyone's going to have to contribute."

"Says the guy who's already stamped his name all over pretty much everything we have," Rory pointed out. "We actually get the sharing thing, believe it or not."

"*Someone* has to keep us organized," he said. "And I'm not talking about granola bars, anyway. I'm talking about information."

"Oh, okay, you think I'm not capable of handling supplies

intelligently, and now you thing I'm *lying* to you? You know what? Maybe you should keep your dumbass minions! All the talk would just slow me down anyway!"

"I never said anything about lying." He had this amazing way of shouting without actually shouting. I often wondered if Kim had taught him the technique, or if it was hereditary. Either way, as mad as Rory was, the sound cut across her without making the debate feel like a full-on, reality-show-worthy bitch fight. "I just mean that we need to swap notes a little. We need a strategy."

Rory sighed and put a hand to the bridge of her nose. "We're surrounded by mindless, senseless murder machines. What more is there to know?" At least her tone suggested that she was ready to be reasonable. Actually, at the time, the words seemed perfectly reasonable to me, too.

The Eagle Scout clearly disagreed, so it was probably best for everyone that Hector was the one who answered.

"Well, there's how to kill them, for a start."

"Get them in the head," I said automatically. It hadn't occurred to me that this needed any discussion.

"No way!" said Claire. "That actually works?"

"Yeah." I had that awkward moment when you realize that people are actually listening to you, and suddenly everything you say feels at least twenty percent dumber. I took a careful recap of my memories, every time I'd seen them go down and stay down, the mortal injuries I'd seen them keep walking around with. "Yeah," I repeated, "You just have to do a good job. It takes a little more . . . oomph than on a live person."

Hector was nodding. "Good, yes, that fits with what everyone else has seen, too?"

There were a few nods, mostly what people call "silent assent."

"We should also know how not to become one of them," Hector continued calmly.

"That's easy, too," said Rory. "Don't let them bite you."

"Is that all?" Hector prompted.

One dip into my own thoughts was more than enough for me for one meeting. I wanted someone else to say it. Norman and Hector had figured it out, too, based on the old folks' home, but I knew Hector wouldn't do more of the talking than he had to, in case it made Rory or The Eagle Scout see him as one more leader wannabe to worry about, and Norman was still doing his best not to pay attention at all, so that left me.

"I don't think so. I mean, they definitely bite people, and a lot of the ones I've seen look bitten, but . . ." I didn't want to say his name. Why did *I* have to say his name? "Mark wasn't bitten by anything."

Rory was looking at me like she was going to shout "Blasphemer!" and start piling kindling around a stake, but shutting up then would have been a waste.

"And he didn't bite anyone, not successfully. I'm pretty sure the only way not to become one of them . . . is to not die."

"Great," said Rory. "So we buckle up, drink bottled water, and be careful with the explosives and sharp objects. It's not like we were planning on dying anyway."

"Wait," said Claire. "I'm confused. Why do they bite, then?"

"Same reason they do everything else that kills people," her brother said like it was even more obvious than head-cracking. "Bites are a great way to cause infection. Do you know how dangerous a bite is even from a healthy, living person? Or weren't any of you paying attention in First Aid? And these are rotting, decomposing corpses."

"Yeah," Hector agreed. "That makes sense." I could feel him trying to placate The Eagle Scout, make his ideas seem acknowledged. It only half worked.

"Great," said The Eagle Scout. "Thanks."

"Hey," said Rory. "You were the one who wanted to trade info."

"I know, I know. We've just got a few more important issues on the agenda than *why* it's a good idea not to go out there and stick our hands in their mouths."

"Like?"

"Like does anyone actually know how to get to New York from here?"

CHAPTER SEVEN

FIFTY POINTS FOR THE ONE IN THE FLANNEL

Lucky for us, most hotels, including Whitetail Village, have a decent assortment of guidebooks on hand, if only for the immediately surrounding area. It was also lucky that we'd all taken an orienteering class the previous summer, so the maps were a little closer to our mental grasp than they probably would have been otherwise.

It wasn't a Google-Maps-quality direct route, but after a few hours, The Eagle Scout was able to draw out a plan as far as Salt Lake City. Rory insisted to him repeatedly that we were sure to find more maps by then, and eventually I guess her point was too airtight for him to argue with anymore. With some cajoling, he backed away enough to let her lead Claire in packing up the supplies for transport while he wrote out his own directions step-by-step, and we all argued over the smaller details, like cars and drivers and weapons.

I offered up Mom's Prius again, setting Norman off on his T.V. commercial car dealer impression, extolling its economical hybrid technology (and surprisingly roomy interior). There was no pretending it was roomy enough for all of us, but I liked the idea of taking at least two cars, so we'd be less likely to end up completely stranded, and (whole truth, remember?) so I might end up spending less time sitting next to the Kent kids.

Rory and The Eagle Scout actually banded together to shoot me down on that one, though, on the grounds that we only had three fully qualified drivers, the two of them and Hector, and we'd be able to stop less often if we didn't have to have two people driving at once. I pointed out that we weren't exactly going to get busted for driving unlicensed anymore, but given the condition of the cop car I'd showed up in, I couldn't blame them for their wariness.

So it was decided: we'd all pile into Kim's minivan—which was in slightly better condition that the hand-me-down version she'd given The Eagle Scout—like this was just one unbelievably long Scout expedition.

The Eagle Scout got dibs on the one crowbar we were able to find. That was okay because he was the only one who might be able to get in more than a few swings with it without giving himself a debilitating case of tennis elbow anyway. Well, Hector could have, but he hadn't let the steering wheel lock from Kim's van out of his sight since we'd been at Whitetail.

Norman kept his wrench and, as hard as even *I* tried to talk him out of it, that foam-covered mallet from the Whack-a-Mole game.

I could have joined the others carrying handfuls of pool cues and golf clubs, even Claire was swinging a sparkly purple kiddie putter and giggling, but I stuck with Suprbat. It had served me well enough so far, and it still felt more sturdy and reliable in my hands than any of the other options.

With all of that settled, The Eagle Scout ordered us all very forcefully to bed, so we could "leave when we're rested and focused."

That part I didn't understand at all. I don't think anyone actually slept before dawn, not Norman, Hector, or me, in the first room we could break into with two beds and a decent couch, not Rory in whatever deluxe suite she ended up staking her claim to, probably not even the Kents in their sleeping bags, surrounded by the stuff, as if the zombies might try to stealth their way in by night and take it, and by the time any of us *were* in danger of becoming reasonably rested, The Eagle Scout was making the rounds again to wake us.

"Bet that's why he's so crazy about 'resting.'" Norman proposed the theory as he retouched his face paint where it had smeared overnight and I brushed my teeth with bottled water in front of one of the newly bone-dry taps "Gives him a chance to show off his lame-ass superpower."

"Morning personhood is a superpower?"

"Sure, as long as you make sure everyone else is in bed by nine, it's almost as useful as being Hawkeye."

Theorizing about anything is more fun when you disagree, but with the sunlight still stuck at that cold, grey, almost-rising shade, I couldn't come up with a good counterargument for that one.

Once everyone was up and dressed and together, though, with all the bags gathered around us—well, remember what I said about the awesome power of unjustifiable confidence? I guess it's contagious.

The minivan was parked at the far end of the lot, maybe a hundred-foot run. There weren't too many zombies out there, at least not that we could see from the windows. If nothing else, our attempt at sleeping through the night had probably shaken the interest of a fair number. There were a few, pacing aimlessly around the lot and the green, vocalizing periodically from the backs of their throats. If there were more hiding nearby, the sound of us would draw them fast.

Funny, what with the whole rec center lock-in drama we had going on inside, I'd almost forgotten they were real.

"Just had to find legal parking?" I couldn't help asking Hector as we all surveyed the task ahead.

"Hard habit to break," he said.

It was a rush, somewhere between the ecstasy of Christmas morning and the illness of the morning of final exams, when The Eagle Scout gave the countdown, took his sister's hand, threw open the formerly off-limits front door, and led the charge.

They saw us, heard us, sensed us, whatever it is they prefer to do given multiple options, and the throat screams began for real. Just like I'd been afraid they would, more of them came out of the more thickly wooded areas to investigate the sound. That weird, overly efficient walk was more than they needed to gain on us, weighed down with all of our luggage. At least walking at us seemed to be about as complex a plan as they could come up with. They didn't even correct their paths to aim for where we were going to be, instead of where we were, as any gamer will tell you means the difference between a player and a player's grandmother logged into his account by mistake.

Still, most of them didn't need an understanding of four-dimensional spatial relations to get to us before we got to the van. I had to hand it to The Eagle Scout, he was handy with that crowbar. He knocked down the first three in as many swings, and they didn't get up again. This gave me time, between the necessary swings of Suprbat, to wonder if the ones left standing were made more or less dangerous by the fact that they did absolutely nothing to avoid the same fate.

More, I think. Sure, we left almost a dozen of them finished on the asphalt. All six of us did eventually make it behind the closed sliding side door of the van after The Eagle Scout finally fumbled out the right key. That one that managed to get its fingers in Rory's hair and keep them there for three swings of a sand wedge and one from the wrench . . . a working brain in its head wouldn't have let it anywhere near her.

Hector climbed in last and slammed the door with a jolt like the "pencils down" timer on a good day when it brings with it the "that wasn't so bad" tingle.

"Who's awesome?!" Norman cried.

"We're awesome!" Hector and I echoed, and so did Claire a beat later. I almost thought for a moment that The Eagle Scout might join in, even if it was just in a condescending, "team building" sort of way. He was smiling, at least, which was rare enough. Even Rory looked happy just to be moving.

The Eagle Scout had planned ahead, you could always trust him to do that, and he got us out of the mountains as far as possible from downtown anywhere, onto the emptiest, least claustrophobic roads he could. A lot of lanes were still blocked, but there was technically no traffic. There were hardly any signs left of real human life at all, just the occasional flicker of a battery light or fire inside one of the trashed buildings that I hoped meant someone was trying to read or cook.

The further we got from the relative isolation we'd started from, the thicker the zombies were, and so was the obvious destruction. Even on side streets, there was always at least a small crowd of them, and after a lot of twisting and turning and doubling back through that mess, there was a very boxed-in feeling, almost enough that I might have had the urge to hyperventilate a little if Claire hadn't already been doing that enough for all of us put together.

"Your brother's a very good driver," Hector noted to her in a way that I know was meant to be very comforting.

"Yeah," Norman agreed. "Betcha most of the ones he squashes'll be in jeans. You want to go for pajamas or business clothes?"

The next one to run out in front of us was in a lacy floral nightgown, making Claire squeak, "Pajamas."

"Damn, in the lead already," I said. "Business clothes for me."

"Dun, dun, dun," Norman started to sing, "Another one bites the—One for me!" he exclaimed. "Another one bites the—Oh, yeah! Look at those rhinestones fly!"

The Eagle Scout maintained his obligatory expression of disapproval and stubbornly refused to swerve for the sake of anyone's count, but he didn't try to stop us either, probably because that would make Claire stop laughing which would make it only a matter of time before she would burst into full-blown tears.

We managed to avoid that, thank God, but we lost count somewhere in Apple Valley when we fell into arguing over what those flannel pants that are printed to look like jeans count as, and given enough time, exhaustion always trumps adrenaline anyway, so the mood was already less than chipper when The Eagle Scout pulled into a gas station.

"I don't think we're safe here," Rory said as if the rest of us couldn't hear the undead screams not too far behind us. "We're too close to—"

"This is as far from anywhere as we can get without stopping somewhere," The Eagle Scout pointed to the glowing warning light on the gas gauge. "Hector, Norman, I'll fill the tank and the cans while you two stand guard, and Claire can work on fitting everything in the van so we'll all be able to get back in it fast." Somehow, it didn't surprise me that the Kentmobile came pre-equipped with spare gas cans. He turned to Rory and me. "You two, get to the minimart, close the door behind you, and grab whatever you can until we pull around to pick you up. Mainly, we need protein and water, lots of water, and extra gas cans if there are any left. Everyone ready?"

"Hey!" said Rory. "Why do *we* do the shopping? Do you *know* how to get gas from a gas station when the power's out?"

"No," said The Eagle Scout, "and if you'd asked me that before we'd started, I would have told you, but now I can either figure it out when we get out there, or we can all give up and sit right here for the rest of our lives."

Rory stormed out to the minimart without waiting for me.

On a more idealistic day, I would have stayed and taken over for her, calling The Eagle Scout on his obvious, undisguised bullshit of not wanting *me* watching his back with my unrivaled non-vehicle-assisted kill count. But this time there was something else I had to do, and my hunting-free, gathering-only assignment was going to make it a lot easier. Not that it had any chance of actually being *easy*.

It was the part of having friends that I liked least, the part when you have to second guess whether or not you have them at all. It's still just a form of listening, but listening is hardest when you have to listen to the blame that falls on you. It wasn't like anything I could do or say could be worse than doing nothing. At least, that's what I always told myself in such situations.

When I caught up with her, Rory was leaning against the counter, her head resting on her hands, her fingers smearing the scratcher lotto ticket display.

"It's not too late to tell us all to go back and jump in the water hazard," I said from the doorway. "I wouldn't recommend it, but it's not too late."

She didn't lift her head, and I didn't move to an angle that would have let me know for sure whether or not she was crying. "That's okay," she said. "I wouldn't know the first thing about how to loot gasoline either."

I nodded, even though she wasn't looking at me. "Yeah, we're kind of going to need him. Doesn't mean you have to *like* him."

She snorted. Her sinuses definitely sounded wet. I braced myself before getting to the point.

"Or me," I said.

Rory took a breath, stood up straight, but didn't turn around. "We haven't talked much lately," she said. "I mean, *really* talked."

I wondered for a moment whether we had anything left to *really* talk about, or if we had run out when I'd moved from horseback riding with the Girl Scouts to camping with the Boy Scouts and realized that there was more to boys than the relative dreaminess quotient of their eyes. I wondered when I'd stopped putting in the effort to listen to all the stupid, pointless shit *she* said, and whether I still could like I did whenever Norman went on his endless tangents about the growing, art-crushing influence of CGI, or if my concentration would fail like it did with the jocks. I wondered if she still *really* talked to Lis, and what they talked about.

But all I said was, "I know."

"If you'd stayed and talked with us instead of running off to play guns with them, she'd still be here."

"I know," I repeated. "Do you hate me?"

Ask a straight question, sometimes you get a straight answer. Sometimes. Like, three times out of five.

"No," said Rory.

Call me a sucker, but I believed her. I know we'd drifted, but I was pretty sure I still knew her well enough to trust my instinct on that.

"So, what do you want me to do?" I asked.

She put up a hand like she was nursing a headache, like she always did when she needed to wipe her eyes, and finally, she looked at me, her face as fresh as a Lysol-drenched living room, like when one of our mothers was expecting guests. If you'd only had a snapshot of her face at that moment, you'd never have guessed that wet sinus sound a few seconds earlier.

"Help me find her," she said simply. "And don't ask me to be completely fair or reasonable before then."

Two for two, when it came to simple answers. Not bad, given three out of five odds.

"Deal," I said.

Finally, she let me hug her, awkwardly and only for a few seconds, but she did. And maybe I should have been thinking about how exactly I was going to maximize the odds of successfully keeping my promise, but all I was thinking about was how, eventually, I was going to have to get used to Rory not smelling like Rory because there was going to be nobody manufacturing vanilla body spray anymore.

I let go when the door opened loudly behind us.

"Yes, perfect!" Norman exclaimed, and I looked up, wondering if he'd thought of some vital tool we didn't know we were looking for. After a year and a half, nine years if you count just knowing him without hanging out on purpose, you'd think I'd have known better.

He tore a scrap of wax paper from under the cold, idle hot dog heater and wrapped it around the pocket comb in his hand. Norman never carried a pocket comb, but I didn't waste a question on that. He put the comb in his mouth and blew.

New York, New York, the fourth note squeaked and went sharp.

"Wait, I've got this," he shushed me as if I were just waiting to criticize his kazoo skills.

New York, New York—

He stopped short on the second try to give himself time to run into the stockroom, out of sight, just as The Eagle Scout tripped over himself running in after him. It was around then that I remembered who it was I knew who *did* carry a pocket comb.

"Norman, I swear . . ." The Eagle Scout recovered enough to reroute his momentum into the stockroom after him, his voice getting muffled as he slammed the door and stomped up a set of stairs. "If you break a single tine."

I doubled over laughing. With Lis still freshly missing, I didn't want to be too loud about it, so I did that silent, diaphragm laugh, the bottling-up laugh that sometimes distills itself and becomes several times as funny as it started out. This was one of those times.

Rory marched over to the glass front door to check that it was locked.

"Honestly, Cassie," she said, "I don't know how you live with that."

It didn't sound like she was attacking me, it sounded like she was making an attempt at *really* talking, so I made an attempt at *really* listening, and *really* answering.

I took a deep breath to stop the laughter and refill my lungs, which had that amazing refreshed feeling you can only get from successfully stretching out a stiff muscle.

"Honestly, Rory," I said, "I don't know how you live without it."

CHAPTER EIGHT

"MELLON" MIGHT NOT CUT IT THIS TIME

So much for a quick, easy in-and-out supply run.

The screamers we'd been hearing through fences and hedges had broken onto the parking lot by the time we'd filled the first bag, and even after Hector had circled in the van a couple times to distract and crush as many as possible, The Eagle Scout, Rory, Norman, and I had to fight all the way from door to door.

Maybe it was stupid to stop for the newspaper from the stand outside, but if it had been *your* face on it, next to the face of *your* dead crush, and the words, "FIRST OF MANY?" in big, all caps news header print, would you have been able to leave it alone?

I've got to admit, even though I'd always been well taken care of, nice school district, all the extracurriculars I'd wanted, updated phone and computer and all that, there was a giddy little thrill to just *taking* that newspaper, not to mention about a month's supply of Twinkies, Power Bars, Slim Jims, and Smartwater, without owing anyone anything for it.

I could get used to that.

Not being able to buy a nice hot serving of nachos to go with them, Google the anonymous snippet of song lyrics repeating maddeningly in my head, or walk across an outdoor parking lot without having to fight for my life on the other hand . . . that was going to take some more adjusting to.

The space around Rory in the back row was quickly filled in by Claire and her personal bags, and The Eagle Scout claimed the middle one right away, dragging Norman in beside him, so he could keep lecturing him while navigating at the same time, so I settled for shotgun, next to Hector in his less than entertaining "don't talk to me, I'm trying not to crash and die" mode. If I'd had something better to drink than Smartwater, I could have amused myself by taking shots for every time I felt him graze those bumpy reflector things that separate the lanes.

Yeah, I had the newspaper, and being as far as I was from Rory spared me the trouble of keeping the picture hidden as I read it, but it was only worth a couple minutes.

Since these were the last papers ever printed, they stayed on the rack for a lot longer than their recommended shelf life. In fact, as I write this, most of them are still there, some of them still readable. But if you're reading this far enough in the future that they've all disintegrated too far for you to know what I'm talking about, here's the gist:

Boy meets girl, boy becomes zombie somehow, girl kills boy, girl goes into police custody, zombies start popping up elsewhere, this reporter believes girl might have had something of value to tell us, police uncooperative, girl not available for comment, blah, blah, blah. All the stuff I already knew, the stuff you already know, even if you've never read anything other than this book in your life.

I've seen similar articles in a lot of different publications since then, all pretty much the same, mostly true, completely useless.

There was never any explanation for what actually happened to us. There probably never will be.

And that's about all I could read anyway before getting really, really carsick, leaning against the glass and waiting for something to help pass the time that didn't require taking my eyes off the road scrolling by beneath us. And waiting.

And waiting.

There's one thing about the U.S that you can't learn just by growing up in it, or going to school in it, or watching too much *Cops:* It's *big*. I mean, really, really *big*.

Okay, yes, that was in the textbooks. I did learn how to arrange most of the states on a blank map as a kid, and I'm sure at some point I jotted down the figure of how many miles it is from coast to coast, and maybe how many feet there are to a mile, though I don't remember that one exactly, but at some point, having all the pieces doesn't mean your brain can actually fit them together. It's like trying to do a five-thousand-piece jigsaw puzzle on a fold-up card table with a lazy Suzan in the middle of it. You can see the scale-model picture on the box, and you can make little parts of the real thing, but it's not the same as seeing it all.

You can know how many copies of your coffee table can lie end to end between your front door and the Great Divide, but it's not the same as watching it go by, and by, and by, imagining what it would be like to *walk* across that space, what it would be like just to be dropped in the middle, how completely trapped you could be without any walls, or fences, how insignificant all the movement you could manage would be against the pure vastness of the continent.

On the plus side, zombies can't drive, so once we'd gone a few days' walk from what had been, until recently, civilization, we stopped seeing them as well.

I'd thought it was a pity at first that The Eagle Scout was able to arrange such a good detour around Vegas. I'd always wanted to go there, and there would be no one to kick us out of the casinos now, not that we could play the slots or anything, but at least we could *see* them, maybe stop for lunch around a blackjack table or something, but the smell of the wandering corpses we started seeing around the same time the Vegas skyline came into view kind of turned me off the idea. I don't know if I'd just lost my acclimation to it as soon as we'd gotten away from L.A, or if the sun-baking of the ones in the desert made them that much worse, but I was glad when we got back out of range, far enough to give our legs a real stretch at the Utah Welcome Center, secure in the knowledge that even if every zombie in the world suddenly began running straight at us, we'd be long gone before they could catch up.

The Eagle Scout didn't really take advantage of this for his own legs, as long as they were, and as obvious as it was that they were fast asleep when he tried to step outside. One beeline to the rack of maps and guidebooks, and he was curled right back up on the uncomfortable thin-carpet-over-concrete gift shop floor.

One thing about the desert, other than the terrifying size of it and the extra-crispy decomposition style of the zombies, there are not a lot of good places to use the bathroom.

I don't mean the distance between rest stops, which sort of goes along with the mind-boggling-size thing. No, by the time we got out there, rest stops were only good for looting purposes, and decently sized bushes had become much more important for casual use.

Well, for about half of us they were important.

I've spent a lot of time around guys, not just since I really started to notice the cute ones, but when I was little because they were what most of my parents' friends happened to have. I've been accused plenty of times of wanting to be one. Actually, that one's come up almost as often as "slut."

Here's the truth: I like them, I click with them, and yes, I paid enough attention in history class to know how pissed off to be at the unfair advantage they'd have if we were all spontaneously teleported to another randomly determined place and time, but in my own world, this was the first time I really, truly envied them.

When the toilets stopped flushing.

After the first few stops, they hardly bothered looking for anything resembling bushes anymore. It was just a turn, a zip, easy as that. It made me gag a little the first couple times, but after that . . . envy. Just envy. No looking for a safe way into the natural blind of a prickly pear thicket, no fiddling with paper, no dirty looks for having to use bottled water on their hands.

I'd never really been into the whole "let's all go to the bathroom together" girl thing before, even when it just meant adjacent stalls and bra-adjusting in the same mirror. It was on the road where I started to understand it, where I got the idea that maybe it was a tradition that predated indoor plumbing.

Rory and Claire started taking turns holding a sheet up in front of each other, and I only lasted a few stops before I had to give in and join their rotation.

They were a lot more talkative than the prickly pear, particularly Claire, but at least they caused fewer splinters.

The convenience store section of the Utah Welcome Center was sparser than that first gas station, but at least it was untouched, and its fridges had doors, so the sandwiches and yogurt inside were still edible.

I don't care how many times I've said I could live on nothing but Hostess cupcakes. I was wrong. The charm wears off by the end of lunch time, and by the time we got to those sandwiches, they counted as an early dinner.

I'm not sure if it was meant to be a reassurance or a demand when Rory and The Eagle Scout gathered us back into the van before any of our spines had truly unknotted, and he told her he was sure we'd get around Denver by bedtime.

I don't mean it as a compliment or anything, but I think that was the first instance I witnessed of The Eagle Scout being wrong.

He took the front seat this time for navigational purposes. From the backbench, it was easy to ignore their bickering, and I passed a few hours in whispered conversation with Hector, who had the middle row all to himself.

I don't remember what all we talked about, it couldn't have been anything that required too much movement or other animation, not with Norman and Claire passed out with their heads on my left knee and right shoulder respectively, and I'm pretty sure nominations for the best ever movie villain quote of all time took up a good third of it. I do remember that we were debating the merits of dream analysis, and I was just saying, quite honestly, that I would be drifting into something for us to analyze in the imminent future, when The Eagle Scout's voice forced me to sit up.

"Guys," he said, "we might have a problem up here."

The sky was bright orange by that time, and so was its reflection in the spring remnants of the Rockies' snowdrifts, leaving us just long enough to find a good sturdy building on the outskirts of the vacation developments to barricade into for the night. It was a gorgeous sunset, really, the kind, I was only just realizing in my almost-dream state of mind, that we usually only got in California after a major brushfire.

Brushfire plus snowdrifts. Not a classic combination.

I felt the dusting of ash in my airway right before the first zombie hit the window since Vegas.

I wish to revoke the title of "extra crispy" from the zombies of the desert. The ones in the Rockies took that title firmly with the streaks of soot and fire-blackened skin they left on the glass. I jerked fully awake with another painfully vivid flashback to the joys of pre-apocalyptic, mass produced fried chicken, but with the aging, rest stop grade turkey and Swiss kneading sluggishly in my stomach at the time, at least this one had the decency to make me slightly sick.

"Don't tell me," I said. "Denver's on fire?"

"Glenwood Springs," said Rory with so little immediate reaction that there was sure to be a really big delayed one building up. "We're not even in Carbondale yet. But yeah, probably."

"So?" I didn't mean it to sound callous, really, I didn't, but it wasn't like I could be expected to be *surprised* by that sort of revelation anymore. "We weren't going into the city anyway, were we? Can't we just drive past it?"

"That's the problem," said Rory, and she jerked me forward by the collar so I could see, making Norman and Claire knock heads behind me.

The zombies were thicker than I expected, because their exodus from the cities ahead was funneled through one of the paved passes through the Rockies. I saw a few of them stumble off the edges right in front of me, some of them clear into oblivion, but most of them had at least enough instinctive sense to shamble on down the road in our direction. That alone would have been mildly alarming.

The real problem was that the same thing had happened to the people of Colorado while they were *alive*, and when live people on the run start to burn, or just burn out, they usually don't just disappear off the edges of cliffs or collapse into small, squishy speed bumps.

They leave cars behind.

It had taken a few tries to find a viable way out of L.A county, but the web of side streets through the suburbs there is so thick, the space to the east so flat and empty, there was always a way around the wrecks. The road out of (and, consequently, *into*) populated Colorado was stacked solid with ruined or abandoned cars, completely and inarguably impassable.

By the time I'd processed that fact and woken Norman and Claire thoroughly enough to pass it along, Rory and The Eagle Scout had already moved on, very loudly, to whose fault it was.

"Okay," Rory was saying, "*your* first route didn't pan out, we'll just back up to one that cuts across into a less populated area."

"This *is* the one that cuts across into the less populated area," The Eagle Scout snapped. "That's why it's Glenwood Springs we're smelling instead of Denver. This was the best shot we had at crossing the Rockies directly, like *you* wanted."

I don't remember whose idea it was. I'm not covering for either of them, I honestly don't, and I didn't bother trying to figure it out then. I just waited for the part of the argument where they stopped talking about anything relating to getting across the Rockies and started focusing on how we were going to get around them.

"New York is to the *north*," Rory was saying, "*way* to the north. I don't care how long it takes us to get past them that way, we'd have to be closer when we do than if we have to go get ourselves abducted and probed down to fricken' New Mexico."

"Aliens?" The Eagle Scout rolled his eyes. "Really? You want to work our travel plans around your fear of *aliens?*"

"We're mowing down flesh-eating zombies *as we speak*, and you haven't even stopped to think about aliens? And I don't even care if there aren't any aliens, it's still frickin' New Mexico! It would need a bath and an exorcism to be a state!"

"You're thinking of New Jersey," Norman mumbled, rolling over and brushing stray flakes of theatrical makeup off my jeans.

"It's the fastest way, I swear." The Eagle Scout shoved the map in front of her face, stuck again in that limbo he had between comforting and berating. "Look, unless you're suggesting that we double all the way back to Cedar Mountain, there's only one road north from here, and parts of it don't even have a name. There's no guarantee we'd be able to steal more gas by the time we'd need it, and it cuts through pure rock until at least Casper. No alternate routes, absolutely no off-roading potential. If there's anything, *anything* blocking it—snow, stalled cars, fallen UFOs—anything at all that we can't move with our bare hands, which there almost certainly will be, we'll be praying to make it back down to New Mexico before we freeze to death. Can Lis gamble that much time?"

Brutal but to the point. That's The Eagle Scout in a nutshell.

It would be twenty-five miles back the way we had come before we would be able to start moving forward again, even in a roundabout way, and we only made it a little more than half of that before The Eagle Scout called a temporary surrender to the fading sunlight and directed us to the lookout post at the edge of a small, vacant campground.

We were past most of the traffic, dead and undead, but he still insisted that we all barricade inside, out of sight, to avoid ending up on the receiving end of a siege by morning. One room, concrete floor, six of us, five sleeping bags, and in case you're getting any creepy ideas about how we handled that little problem, I let Claire crawl into mine, nestled between Hector's and Norman's.

Oh, and before you get all smug about how you would have thought far enough ahead to bring extra comforters from Whitetail, we *did* think that far, we just didn't notice until the sun went down that they were barely thick enough to be worth accessorizing a real sleeping bag with.

Not exactly comfortable, but very non-creepy, and we did survive even though it was exactly the sort of scenario we'd always joked was a few levels above our scouting level of hardiness and expertise.

I even slept with Claire's shared warmth almost making up for her snoring, though I don't remember quite drifting into anything analysis-worthy after all. I would never have told Rory so, but the only realization I came to that night was that I would be very, very happy to take a detour through the UFO state if it meant being warm again for a while.

CHAPTER NINE

NOTHING. NOTHING EVERYWHERE, AND NOT A—WHAT THE HELL IS THAT THING?

I'm going to save us all a bit of time and curiosity whenever pit stops come up, since, by the nature of this story, there are quite a few of them.

Whenever you stop to wonder, yes, Norman was still wearing that awful costume, and no, that really wasn't that unusual.

He'd had manias like it that had burned out sooner, like the time he'd tried to change his dominant hand and given up when he kept dropping his toothbrush. On the other hand, there was that time he'd carried a D20 in his pocket for almost a year and rolled it to predict the advisability of everything he did—and I mean *everything*—from eating a corn dog at lunch to whether or not he should sign up for the Argentinean Exchange Program if Rory refused to accompany him to the Spring Formal (thankfully the D20 declined almost as vehemently as Rory did).

Based on the fact that the only clothes he'd kept in his duffle since Whitetail were the balloon artist's collection of spare costumes, this looked like it was going to be the second kind of habit. I didn't mention it after his first explanation, and after five or six reiterations, the others gave up, too. And really, was it that much weirder an affectation than the uniform The Eagle Scout still put on every morning with the bandana adjusted just so?

The only thing about it that had me a little worried was how I couldn't give Claire a hard time for how long *her* makeup ritual delayed us in the mornings when Norman's was actually a few seconds longer.

I timed them.

The Eagle Scout took the first driving shift, the one that took us back to Grand Junction, where we took the turn to the south we had passed up the first time around. That's the best evidence I have that the whole Rockies detour was probably his fault, the way he took it so firmly upon himself to fix it as well and as quickly as it could be fixed.

Or maybe it was just because he liked to do as much of the driving as he could rationalize anyway. He did prefer it, which admittedly made it a pretty lame form of apology, but that in no way meant that it couldn't be his idea of one.

After that, the nothing around us was a little more scenic than the day before, but even pine forests and snowcapped outcroppings start to run together after a few hours, so much that they almost make you want to join in Claire's endless list-making game. I could think of plenty of types of sandwiches she'd forgotten to include in her "different types of sandwiches" list.

Norman filled in a few of them (BLT, egg in a nest, McRib), but when she switched to "different versions of Barbie," he just started making stuff up. He managed to pass off "Whale Flenser Barbie" as an obscure Sea World cross promotion, and I think he got as far as "Ghostbuster Barbie" before Claire caught on, and "Gynecologist Barbie" before The Eagle Scout punched him hard enough on the arm to make him stop.

"Would it *kill* you to be serious now and then?" I asked him even though I was laughing myself, and to be honest, I was mostly just trying to score a few cheap points with The Eagle Scout since we all seemed to be falling dangerously far behind on that front.

Norman looked at me like he was about to make the deepest confession of his life and said, "You know something, Cassie? I think it just might."

He held my gaze for just a few seconds too long before breaking off laughing again, and when he did, I had to laugh extra hard with him to shake off the momentary too-serious feeling.

It was one of those "be careful what you wish for" moments.

I was glad for the ready gas cans and heavy steering wheel lock and all, but there were times when I would have killed to have a working stereo in that van instead.

On the other hand, having one would also have given us one more thing to argue about. In fact, for the past year, music had been the one thing that could put even *Hector* in a confrontational mood.

Yeah, that's one of those things we were supportively not talking about.

Anyway, without one, we argued about New Mexico.

"I didn't expect it to be so . . . wooded."

That's all I said, honestly. I didn't mean for it to set anything off. The air had been getting nice and warm and thick again as we headed south, closer to the texture I was used to, and I was actually feeling pretty good when I got to take my jacket off during a stop in the nice, dry, blind-spot-filled pine woods.

The trees hadn't faded back into flat desert like I'd expected but had followed us all the way into the habitable climate.

Considering that the nearest city that showed up on our map went by the unprepossessing name of "Farmington," the scenery was surprisingly close to what might be called breathtaking.

"Are you sure we're out of Colorado?" Rory asked when I pointed it out.

"We saw the welcome sign," The Eagle Scout reminded her.

"Need a break from that?" Norman asked, offering to take the wrinkled map. What he meant was, "Need a break from that?" no more, no less. She'd been glued to it for about two hundred and fifty miles, long enough to make anyone lose focus after a sleepless night. But I could easily have told him how Rory would hear it.

As much as I usually loved the way Norman could say all the things I never would, this wasn't the first or the last time I kind of wished he could run them all by me first.

"I can handle it!" Rory snapped. "We all took orienteering together, remember?"

"Yeah," said Norman, "we did. I finished the orange course, too."

"Oh, right," said Rory. "It's 'helping old people across the street' that you failed, right?"

"He wasn't just *old,* he was *dead,*" Norman defended himself on this point for about the hundredth time, and I could tell by the way he laughed at her that she was starting to get to him.

Of course, she couldn't tell.

"You are *so* out of Scouts."

"We're all out of Scouts," Hector cut in blankly. "There is no more Scouts. There's just us and what it taught us."

He held out a slightly melted Snickers bar.

"Like what low blood sugar can do to a person's judgment."

On second thought, maybe we should all have run our thoughts by Hector before trying to communicate them. I'm sure I couldn't have pulled off getting the chocolate into Rory's hand and the map into Norman's with as little ugliness as he did.

"Okay," said The Eagle Scout because, of course, every slight change in arrangements required his approval, "but if you even *think* about telling me to make a left turn in Albuquerque, I swear I'm leaving you there."

I'm not sure Norman could have resisted, given a good opening, so it's probably best that we veered north again and skirted Albuquerque by a wide margin.

The trees eventually did give way to jagged orange rocks, which struck the compromise of making it possible to tell that space was actually going by without acting as a reminder of the previous day, and that had a certain calming effect on everyone for a while.

But then we got into Oklahoma. A new state, a new argument.

We kept mostly a straight course along our side of the northern border, but we did have to dip across it once or twice, and after his great restraint in New Mexico when Norman found himself briefly in Kansas and then not in Kansas anymore . . . well, I guess I've already given that punch line away.

The state of the uninspired but aptly named musical, Oklahoma (yeah, Norman had a field day with *that,* too) was mostly flat again. At least a lot of it was covered by farmland, nicer to look at than emptiness, and potentially more useful.

That was what caused the first dispute of some substance, a field of sugar snap peas, the first crop that looked ripe.

Claire was the first to suggest that we stop to gather some, which came as close to turning me against the idea as anything could, but The Eagle Scout's retort that we hadn't come this far to die of E. Coli made me realize quickly just how delicious sugar snap peas sounded right about then.

"We can't just eat out of wrappers forever," I put in.

"Actually, we could," said The Eagle Scout. "There's plenty left in the world for how many people are probably left to use it."

"I'm not talking about running out."

"It's a needless risk," he said. "We'd be out in the open dodging them for something we don't even have enough water to wash properly."

"Dodging *what?*" Claire asked.

Oh, yeah, the zombies. I probably should have mentioned that they'd started showing up again. Not many, just one or two here and there, and not in great condition, most of them were at least missing sizeable pieces, but the shelter of the massive distances wasn't perfect anymore. They'd had too much time to spread. We were still more than three days' walk from anywhere for a live person, but without having to worry about *staying* alive, the dead ones had been able to make much better time.

Still, there were none to be seen at that moment, just miles and miles of sugar snap peas, unwashed or not.

"Uh, I've actually been thinking about that," Hector began tentatively. "Now that they've had some time to clear out, it might not be a bad idea to see if we can get close to an actual city. You know, somewhere with a real supermarket, water by the gallon, soap, some more blankets, full-sized toothpaste—"

"Yay!" Claire cheered approvingly.

"Maybe even a working phone or radio." He directed this at The Eagle Scout, making the miracle of causing him to look thoughtful seem almost easy. "At the very least, there's sure to be somewhere to clean what we pick."

The Eagle Scout pulled over, the steering wheel jerking a little with the ruts in the side of the road that he hadn't quite slowed enough to handle yet. It's really hard to judge speed when you can't judge distance. When we did reach a stop, he looked thoughtfully at the map and then at the piece of junk where a stereo should have been for a few moments more. Half of us were already outside by the time he actually said, "Okay, we wash in Tulsa."

I would have been part of that half if I hadn't been boxed in by Rory, who disembarked with the same "it's a necessary evil" sigh and reluctant pace she used on stops of every kind. Norman muttered something about "not in Kansas" and "red poppy field" but then ran out past her anyway.

Of course, the fact that there would be water in Tulsa didn't actually mean the non-obsessive-compulsives among us were actually going to wait for it.

I'd never really noticed how much I loved sugar snap peas until that day. In fact, I'm pretty sure I'd complained that their name was a lie, applied to something about as far from confectionary as you could get, but in that field with a perfectly temperate wind rising almost to the howling point and lifting the sweat-matted hair clean off my neck, I took it back.

They actually were sweet.

Before Rory could gather even a handful, Norman landed a cartwheel in front of her, did that "nothing up my sleeves" magician's flourish, and then presented her with a full bouquet of the little green pods out of thin air.

I didn't like it.

That was normal. It was just some sort of overactive protective instinct that always irked me about his crush, I was sure—a feeling that if she didn't understand him, then she shouldn't get his attention. I also had the gut feeling that interfering between them could easily get really painful somehow, so I looked the other way as she bypassed his bundle to gather her own, and I took my annoyance out on The Eagle Scout instead.

"Really, you've *never* snuck a bite of something from the produce section before washing it? Ever?"

I munched on one of the pods after asking, savoring each refreshing crunch.

"Really," he said.

"It's not like they're imported from somewhere where you can't drink the water," I coaxed between bites. "They're not even organic."

"Great," he said, dropping another untasted handful into one of our emptied snack shopping bags and then holding it to the side to make sure Claire did the same. "So instead of hepatitis, you'll all get the latest, undiscovered variant of DDT poisoning."

"Mmm." I swallowed another sweet, crunchy mouthful without difficulty. "Mutate-a-licious."

No one can say I didn't try, or that I didn't get a kick out of doing so, but he never did give in.

What you *can* say (and I frequently did, with great

amusement, over the course of the next day or so) is that he and Claire, the only two people who didn't eat the peas fresh off the vine, were also the only two whose health was even slightly damaged by them.

Claire's cheeks started to redden a little alarmingly with sunburn after less than an hour. The Eagle Scout sent her back to the van (empty-handed so she wouldn't be tempted to taunt fate with the rest of us), and when he tried to carry their shared haul back by himself, he tripped over a stick or something so spectacularly that his official Boy Scout slacks (not required, but marketed to the true Scouting purists) had a bloody tear on one leg when he got there. He collapsed onto the backseat to make first use of one of the first aid kits underneath it.

Even with the directions not being given from directly over his shoulder by the map keeper himself, somehow Hector didn't have much trouble following one of the very few roads in northern Oklahoma down in the direction of Tulsa.

The wind only continued to rise as the day went on until I could feel it actually pushing on the broad side of the van, like it was trying to steer us off the road, and I saw a couple of actual tumbleweeds pass us by up ahead. They weren't on the list of things I was expecting to be surprised by, if it's possible to have such a list, but they caught me off guard just like the true size of the desert did. They're one of those things you see so often in movies and never in real life that you start to think of them as a myth, or at least a thing of the past—like covered wagons and buffalo herds, something you can only really hope to see an imitation of in a nostalgic novelty tourist trap.

Oh, there's one other thing on that same list that we ran into that day, but not until the golf courses and neat, matching beige houses at the north end of Tulsa started to fill in on both sides of us, and the anticipation of resupplying in a place intended for comfort started to sink in.

"Hot chocolate," Claire was saying. "Wherever we go, I hope they have hot chocolate."

"There was hot chocolate at the last rest stop," I said.

"Yeah, but not the good kind with the cow jumping over the moon on the box."

I thought about pointing out that we probably wouldn't have hot anything, but then again, maybe we would. If we kept driving for as long as the light lasted, like we had the day before, if cities in the flat states weren't out of the question anymore, we might end up spending that night gathered around a nice, big, brick fireplace for all I knew.

"I'm okay anywhere as long as . . ."

I couldn't hear the end of Rory's sentence over the rush of the wind outside, but it didn't seem important enough to worry about. I didn't even think much of the sound of Hector cursing under his breath as he tried to keep a steady course between the more frequent zombies and that whole sail effect the van was having. He usually cursed under his breath as he drove, but it was nothing serious, practically an unconscious tic. He never really lost his cool.

So it was when he let loose a string of expletives so loud that even Claire could hear them from the backseat, over both the weather and the sound of her own voice, that I looked up and saw the clouds dipping down in front of us in that unearthly, storybook funnel shape.

CHAPTER TEN

PIGLET THE PYGMY MARMOSET

"Oh, holy shit."

That was all I could think of to say.

Claire went from hot chocolate daydreams to full water works in less than ten seconds.

"No, no, dammit, no!" Rory moaned, slamming her head against the window like this was just one more infuriating roadblock between us and New York.

"What do I do?" Hector asked, reasonable as always even in the absence of reasonable answers of his own. "Eagle Scout!" he barked. "What do I do?"

The Eagle Scout tore his eyes away from the window.

"We need to get below ground level," he said. "You drive and find us somewhere we can do that before we have to ditch the van."

Hector nodded and continued along the road, eyes scanning, a little faster than before. It doesn't sound that difficult, or at least it didn't to me, but that's probably because I'm not from Oklahoma. Being in a city meant there were buildings rising out of the flatness, but there wasn't a single underground tunnel or parking structure, nothing that looked like it might actually cut into that massive slab of earth.

I should have been helping look, but I just kept watching that column of air. I watched it brush the ground, just beyond the edge of what I could see of one of those tidy housing developments, whipping more dirt up into itself, and I was still watching when it barely touched the edge of one of the houses and most of the roof peeled up like it had been shingled with playing cards. I watched the human-shaped figures that had been pacing around that end of the city (all of them already dead, I hope) lift off of the ground and scatter against the houses' walls like a flock of pigeons that all have either inner ear infections or massive depression.

Debris started to hammer against the side of the van along with the air itself, flecks of wood and gravel and plastic, and what you can only pretend isn't bone until you're unfortunate enough to see a full rotted hand among it somewhere.

"I don't see anything!" Hector yelled over it all without taking his eyes off the road, and I made myself scan the cultivated greenery on my side, hoping for a bridge over a canal or a skate park half pipe, anything that might be strong enough to act as some sort of windbreak.

"Up there, keep going!" the Eagle Scout pointed.

I couldn't tell what he was pointing at because right about then, my window cracked a little with the impact of a high-heeled boot with the shin bone sticking out of it, so it was taking a lot more of my attention than usual to continue looking cool.

Hector kept going until The Eagle Scout directed him into a parking lot, across a walkway, and onto a wooden bridge over a pond that definitely wasn't intended for public vehicle traffic access.

"Everyone grab the weapon and bag closest to them!" The

Eagle Scout shouted, and without a single muttered joke or argument, we did it, threw the doors open, and followed him over the side of the bridge, onto the grass pond bank, up through a bed of decorative shrubs, and over a chain link fence. Norman boosted me over it first, and while I waited for him to follow with my jacket pulled up over half of my face to block out the dust and fragments, I peaked enough to see a ticket booth with a big poster of a sea lion next to it.

There was a ditch in front of us, not much, just the track for a kid's train ride. The sturdy concrete walkway we were on crossed straight over it, forming a pretty sizeable tunnel, and one end of it was already boarded and tarped over.

I always thought that whole walking-against-the-wind routine that mimes do was ridiculous, even when Norman did it (okay, especially when Norman did it), but walking across that little bit of outdoor space was harder than crossing the same distance in a California parking lot crawling with zombies. I really did lean against the wind like mimes do, just to cut through what should have been thin air, and I honestly thought I might not get as far as the tunnel's mouth without losing my grip on the ground and wafting away. When I *did* get there, sheltered only slightly by the dip in the ground, I wasn't thinking far enough ahead to understand why The Eagle Scout was holding out his hand to stop us from going inside just yet.

"Cassie!"

I'll never know how The Eagle Scout could keep his voice that loud without losing it.

"CASSIE!"

Okay, it took me a moment to recognize the sound of my own

name in all that other noise, but I did get around to shouting back, "What?!"

"Do you still have those firecrackers?!"

Of course I did. The evil bunny bag was the natural one I had grabbed along with Suprbat when we abandoned the van. I handed over a garland and spread my jacket out like wings to divert enough wind from the fuse to let him light it after a few tries.

I still didn't understand—not until he threw the firecrackers as far into the tunnel as he could—how ready I'd been to run blindly into a dark corner without even thinking to swing Suprbat ahead of me along the way.

The series of bangs and flashes mostly just added to the general noise and confusion, I was even sure for a moment that I did hear something screaming in the dark, but after a few seconds had passed and nothing speed walked or crawled out in search of the source of the disturbance, The Eagle Scout dropped his hand and shepherded us into the relative stillness inside.

The sun was only halfway down from midday. There were hours left of daily travel time being lost, but between the deep shade of the tunnel and the dust the tornado had covered the sky with outside, we couldn't even see each other's faces. It was like a third night, only as well as not being able to sleep or see, we also couldn't talk. There was no point to trying to be heard over the howling, which was even louder at the entrance to the tunnel than it had been outside, like someone was blowing across the end of a giant bottle.

I think it was Rory's elbow in my left side. There was still a distinct fragrance of vanilla around her. I know it was Norman on my right, and I know I beat him fifty-two times against forty-seven at thumb wars while we waited for it to be possible to do anything else. I have absolutely no idea how long that actually took. The tornado must have been coming toward us because the wind got even louder before it got softer, and sometimes even the cave of the half-boarded tunnel didn't stop it from feeling like it was trying to crush my eardrums or suck the air right out of my lungs. Just like distance, air is one of those things that's really hard to imagine being immensely powerful until you feel it for yourself.

It was even darker than it had been when we arrived, either because of the time or the thickness of the particles still hanging over us, I wasn't sure which, when someone tried again to communicate over the fading roar.

Someone whose voice I didn't know.

"Welcome to Tulsa Zoo and Living Museum," he said. "Y'all sure do know how to make an entrance."

I wish I could say I didn't scream. At least I can say that I wasn't the only one who did.

The Eagle Scout flicked his Zippo on in record time, illuminating the very back of the tunnel and the extra figure sitting between the train tracks there.

He was about seventeen or eighteen, holding my burnt out firecrackers in one hand and a tiny, shivering ball of fur with a tail in the other, and the first thought that entered my head when I saw him (whole truth, remember?) was that he and Rory could have gorgeous babies together.

Yeah, even while he was squinting against the sudden light, you could tell he was hot. He had that perfectly tanned skin, that balance as delicate as perfectly toasted bread, just enough to let you know he can take the sun without making him look all leathery, or clashing with baby blue eyes and the exact shade of naturally blond hair that peroxide can almost imitate, but not quite.

"Sorry!" I was the first to say it on everyone's behalf. It was my firecracker, after all. "We didn't see you!"

"I could tell," he said, holding the fluffy thing closer to his chest, trying to calm it.

"We can go find another spot," Claire suggested timidly. I could actually feel the heat of her blushing in the enclosed space, and for a moment it surprised me, not because the guy wasn't perfectly blush-worthy, just because I guess I'd sort of assumed she still believed in cooties.

"No offence," he said, "but no one with an ounce of sense is setting foot outside for another hour, at least." When he smiled, even the flame of the lighter was enough to confirm that he had really, really nice teeth.

That was all the invitation any of us needed.

"Thank you." The Eagle Scout lit a road flare as a gesture of settling in. Then he tripped over me to get close enough to play ambassador and introduce everyone, very precisely and thoroughly, like he was scoring major reelection points by demonstrating the ability to remember strings of syllables as long as "Hector Zane," "Aurora Hart," and "Norman Kaminsky."

Most of us ended up correcting him anyway. Even my mother doesn't call me Cassandra.

Didn't call me Cassandra.

No one bothered to correct him on his own name, as much

as he probably would have liked us to. "Eagle Scout" is the sort of name you can embrace when it's assigned to you, but you're not allowed to admit it, and even he understood that much. It'd be like calling yourself "Dragon Slayer."

Well, almost that bad.

He did keep the flare held nice and high when he reached out his hand, though, showcasing the rank on his shirt, and by the way the other guy's eyes raked over it, you could tell he knew what it meant. He repositioned the animal clinging to his own khaki shirt so the Tulsa Zoo emblem and Volunteer tag could catch the light, too.

"Caleb Summers," he answered on his turn.

They both did that sort of half-smiling nod while they shook hands, like they could hide the fact that they were both trying to decide who was in charge of that tiny little cave even though all anyone could do in it was sit and wait anyway. The Eagle Scout was actually sweating a little. I couldn't understand why at the time. It wasn't *that* big a deal.

When they had finished squeezing the life out of each other's fingers, Caleb returned both hands affectionately to the little ball of fur. "And this here is Piglet, 'cause she's scared of everyone and everything, so don't mind her. She's a pygmy marmoset," he added automatically, probably the same way he had introduced her to regular classes and crowds of tourists not too long ago.

His accent was the texture of melting milk chocolate, which was surprisingly pleasant, considering how much melting milk chocolate I'd already been forced to eat over the past couple days, that accent that says, very sweetly and politely, "I dare you to wonder if I'm as dumb as I am pretty."

It could have gone either way. Personally, I was betting that he wasn't, which already put him a notch or two above some people I knew.

"What's a marmoset?" Claire asked, for example.

I would have mocked anyone else mercilessly for this, of course, but it was actually a pretty reasonable question coming from someone who, on a breakfast run during one of Lis's vegetarian phases, had brought her a cheese omelet but gotten it "without the yolks, just in case she'd gone full vegan."

Yeah, that actually happened. Come to think of it, I'm surprised that she seemed to know what "pygmy" meant.

Luckily, Caleb didn't need to know about the omelet to be nice about it. In fact, he looked really happy to have a new visitor to ask him questions.

"They're a category of monkey," he told her, "a few closely related genera, actually, from South America. Pygmy marmosets like Piglet are the smallest true monkeys in the world."

Can I lay odds on an IQ or what?

"How old is she?" I asked. Sue me. It's what I do when I see someone itching to talk about what they love, or to talk about *anything* to avoid thinking about what's actually going on. And no, it doesn't hurt when that someone is a hot guy.

"Two." Piglet had stopped shaking, so he held her out for Claire and me to pet. She made a clicking, twittering sound, like a nervous version of a purr.

Piglet, I mean, not Claire, although the sounds she made over Caleb weren't that far off.

"That's fully grown for a pygmy marmoset, though," he said.

Piglet was barely the size of a tennis ball and, I had to admit, completely, heartstring-tuggingly adorable.

"They mate for life," Caleb went on, "and they're threatened in the wild, or at least they were, while people were cutting it down. The zoo was already arranging some trades, trying to get her a partner, but I guess that's not going to happen now."

He didn't have to say any more about that, I could see it in the way he was holding her, relief that she wouldn't end up being the one traded away from him, guilt over not wholeheartedly wanting what was best for her. I felt the same way about every single person who had been cut off from the past we never mentioned and stuck with me in my present instead.

"With everything isolated like this, I guess that's not going to happen for a lot of us," he said.

It was a corny line, especially the way he made that super intense eye contact with Rory, Claire, and me all in sequence as he said it, the kind of line you can only pull off in a gooey Hershey bar voice. Since he happened to have a gooey Hershey bar voice, he could. I smiled at him and enjoyed that prickly out-of-time feeling, The Chase, realizing that I'd missed it with all the life and death stuff going on.

"Does she like sugar snap peas?" Norman asked. I didn't mind him cutting in. It was better than waiting for The Eagle Scout to do it.

"They're gumophores, mostly, Pagliacci," said Caleb. He lifted an uncertain eyebrow at Norman's costume.

"Don't ask," said Rory, and she and The Eagle Scout shared a rare, joint eye roll.

Caleb nodded and seemed to file Norman diplomatically in a "miscellaneous" folder in his head, somewhere separate from the spectrum that includes the levels "Eagle Scout" and "Zoo Volunteer."

"But you can give it a try," he went on. "They'll go for insects and fruit when they can find them, and she's probably hungry enough to try anything right about now."

The guilt again, this time without the relief.

Norman held out one of the pods. Piglet looked at it uncertainly for a moment, then snatched it eagerly with her tiny hands and began to nibble.

"So, west coast, am I right?" Caleb asked.

"California," said The Eagle Scout, still compelled to be the voice of the group, but he said it more like it was a task than his calling this time with his head against the side of the tunnel and his eyes half closed, like he was too tired to open them further than he had to, to avoid accidently hitting anyone with the flare. There was still a shimmer of sweat on his face.

That was all he said.

"So, given the state of things," Caleb prompted politely, "why?"

The Eagle Scout said nothing, so after a few seconds, I started to tell the story myself. I'm not sure how I put it, exactly. I was too lost in marveling at the novelty of The Eagle Scout passing the mic, so I skipped as quickly as I could to the part at the end where you say, "So what about you?"

By the way Caleb sighed, I guessed it was even harder to cut the Unspeakable Past out of his story than ours.

"Just taking care of the animals, like always," he said. "There's enough stores and storm cellars around to make supply runs for most things for a while, if we're careful, maybe enough to last until the danger rots away. We're sure gonna hold out at long as we can."

"We?" three or four of us asked at once, including The Eagle

Scout, who opened his eyes and sat up straight long enough to wait for an answer. Something about the way he'd said it made it sound like he wasn't just talking about himself and a pygmy marmoset.

"Yeah!" Caleb sat up straighter too, realizing that he'd forgotten to tell us. "I was stuck at the wrong end of the place when the twister touched down. The others'll be hunkered down in the elephant shelter. We can join them and get a little more comfortable as soon as it's safe."

Again, I expected The Eagle Scout to answer for us, but he didn't seem to find it of pressing-enough importance. Rory looked a little alarmed by this, too, so as much as a little R&R appealed to me, with a little of The Chase on the side, I tossed her my own support instead.

"I don't know. . . ." I said.

"It's gonna be darker out there than it is in here before we can even check how much of the road is clear," Caleb reasoned. "And trust me, they're all just aching to see some new faces."

"Just for a night," Rory verified hesitantly, "while we get our stuff back together, if we wouldn't be imposing."

"Yes, thank you," The Eagle Scout agreed shortly.

I'd been expecting him to fight a little harder to escape immediately back to nowhere where his leadership was universally assumed, but he had been known to be reasonable before, even when it didn't suit him, so it didn't strike me as too unusual. He responded normally enough when Norman remembered the switch in his sleeve that made his bow tie light up, and we all pretended not to be able to see the occasional brief flashes of neon green until The Eagle Scout finally deduced, by the corresponding timing of Piglet's chittering, that he wasn't imagining them.

I didn't mind the excuse to retreat further into Caleb's corner to avoid being crushed when The Eagle Scout clambered past me again to pin Norman, face first, to the awkwardly curved wall and rip the double A batteries out of his battery pack "to conserve what was left of them."

When Caleb finally declared it safe to go outside, those were the first two to take advantage of it, sprinting across the littered concrete paths, Norman with The Eagle Scout's pickpocketed Zippo, trying to keep it out of reach until he could negotiate a trade for the batteries.

The rest of us hung back with Caleb, partly watching, partly listening to him point out the best-kept enclosures visible by the last of the sunlight, listing off the animals that still lived there and promising to introduce us to them properly when it was time to bring them out of their shelters in the morning.

"I love the animals, don't get me wrong," he said, opening a gate that Norman and The Eagle Scout had already vaulted and doing that gentlemanly almost-bow to tell the rest of us to go ahead of him, "but I sure am glad to see some new human beings myself. Even if," he caught up to walk between Rory and me, glanced at the guys up ahead and then back at the two of us, and lowered his voice, "now, don't take offence, even if your boyfriends *are* kinda complete lunatics."

I didn't take offence, but I did say, "Hey, not *complete* lunatics."

"And *not* our boyfriends," Rory added, very emphatically, looking at The Eagle Scout and shuddering. Hector stifled a snort of laughter behind us.

"Oh, yeah, not that either," I agreed extra fast, realizing by the way Caleb was smiling that Rory's answer was the info he was looking for.

"Really?" He paused a moment for thought. "Glad to hear it."

Oh, the things you can get away with saying when you say them in an exotic way.

CHAPTER ELEVEN

THINK OF IT AS A REC CENTER LOCK-IN

Day 1

Zombie specimen was in poor condition, not ambulatory, at least five days of decomposition evident. Bite to extremity of living subject is shallow, no damage to arteries or tendons. Immediately cleaned and treated with iodine. Close observation to follow.

No, that journal entry isn't mine. More on that later. Promise.

It's a pity we couldn't have gone straight to the elephant shelter when the tornado hit because it really was the perfect place to hide from one—a huge room of smooth, solid concrete set below the ground behind the elephant paddock to keep it cool.

The rest of Caleb's group of survivors had outfitted it in advance with plenty of food and bedding, even some spare clothes, if only of souvenir-shop quality.

As promised, they did welcome us with open arms, at least, when the woman's arms were finished hugging Caleb and violently ruffling his hair while she lectured him for letting her worry all day. She was even shorter than I am, about the right age to be his mother, and definitely on the over-tanned side of the toast balance.

Caleb introduced us, passing along Rory's advice of "don't ask" when he got to Norman. The woman stopped him when he got to me.

"You're Cassie Fremont, aren't you?"

My sparkling celebrity response was something along the lines of, "Um, yeah?"

She handed me a local paper with that same pair of yearbook photos of Mark and me, and essentially the same article as the one I already had, in slightly different words.

"Small world and getting smaller," she said. "Nice to meet you."

"Alison," Caleb introduced her, "my mentor."

"Damn right." She hugged him roughly to her side once more. "They always saved the best shadows for me. Of course, that's mostly 'cause I've been looking after these animals since twenty years before he could tie his shoes."

"That's Mr. Garret," he continued.

The man sitting in the corner, surrounded by about fifteen kids—a second or third grade class, by the look of them—greeted us with a friendly wave, gesturing to the open book he was reading to them to excuse his not standing up. He was about Alison's age with rimless glasses and the grey beginnings of a beard. Even sitting down, you could tell he had never outgrown his tall-and-gawky phase.

"And that's Tink."

When Caleb had told us we were headed to the elephant shelter, it hadn't occurred to me that there would still be an actual elephant in it.

Tink was small as far as elephants went. She was the Indian

kind and probably pretty young, kind of killing the hackneyed irony of giving her a name short for Tinkerbelle, but she was still an elephant, standing and rocking back and forth in her own little stall of the cave, like a huge dog waiting to play. After the first shock, I couldn't resist the true awesomeness of the chance to see her so close up, and most of us enjoyed an evening of feeding her more of the sugar snap peas, watching the end of her trunk wrap around each one like a gloved hand.

Mr. Garret encouraged his class in naming as many animals with different prehensile appendages as they could. A lot of the novelty must have worn off on them many nights ago already because after a while they seemed more interested in a gift shop board game about penguins than the feeding.

Alison and Caleb just looked happy to see Tink get a good meal.

"She's the only one we were able to keep," Alison explained once all the children and, incidentally, The Eagle Scout, were asleep. He had passed out on the floor even earlier than their bedtime, like chasing Norman across the park had completely drained the life out of him.

"She was the smallest. We've been able to get by on mostly cultivated foliage for her so far, but I'm not sure how long we'll be able to hold out."

I tried not to think too hard about that. In fact, I kind of wished I'd been asleep by then, too, but even then, I didn't want to *go* to sleep. It was too nice being around living things, being around people I hadn't met before, being reminded that there *were* still people I hadn't met before.

The sooner I fell asleep, the sooner I would wake to my part in the task of examining what was left of the van and the road beneath it (assuming we could even *find* the van and that it wasn't up some tree two counties away), arranging, as always, to put as much distance as we could behind us, between us and the shelter of the night before, and that was fine. It was for the best. I just wasn't quite ready for it yet.

When Alison and Mr. Garret had dimmed the lanterns and gone to sleep themselves, the rest of us dragged our sleeping bags into a circle so we could keep talking a while longer. Caleb dropped his not-so-randomly beside Rory's, and Claire did the same on his other side. I ended up right across from him, so I could see his face properly.

I asked all the right questions to help him talk, what the zoo had been like before, how he'd started there, the rarest animal he'd ever seen, what animal was making that deep, booming sound in the distance, and I was the last one awake listening, almost too fascinated to bother keeping track of his fading awareness of Rory's proximity and the unfair way her features stayed perfect and delicate even while she was asleep.

I don't know what time it was when he drifted off and I closed my eyes to do the same, but I was there almost immediately.

I knew in the back of my head that I'd still be tired when The Eagle Scout came to wake me, that I'd feel his hand on my shoulder, or hear his voice not being lowered, or see the lights suddenly brighten uncomfortably at any moment. I forced myself not to brace for it, just like I'd trained myself not to listen for the alarm clock before school. It's the only way to make real use of whatever time you do have left, so I pulled the sleeping bag over my head, curled up against the side of it that was pressed against Norman's, and slept as if nothing would ever disturb me.

And slept, and slept.

And nothing did.

I thought something felt weird when I realized that I was awake and not tired anymore. I figured it was one of the tricks the cycles of your brain play, and if I tried again, I'd end up wondering how I'd thought I could get by without the extra sleep I'd get, so I rolled over, trying not to let the outside of the sleeping bag move, in case it made someone watching me say, "Oh, good, you're awake!"

No one did, and I still wasn't tired.

I let myself pull back the flap enough to check the level of the light, and then that had me sitting up pretty fast.

The lanterns were off, the door to the elephant paddock was open instead, and by the glare coming off the desertscape outside, it had to be close to noon.

"Why didn't anyone wake me?"

I wasn't sure exactly who I was asking. Norman was still beside me, awake, but only for about as long as I had been, based on the bleariness of his eyes. The other sleeping bags had been put away. I could hear the kids playing tag or something outside, and Mr. Garret was probably supervising. I couldn't see Caleb anywhere, just Alison leaning over and looking at something on one side and Rory sitting off to the other, folding clothes really slowly, like she was doing it just to have something to do and was afraid of running out.

"There wasn't really a point," Hector answered. He'd been sitting so still behind Alison that I hadn't seen him. There was a black box with a silver latch open at his feet, and I started trying to guess what was inside it.

"Why aren't we packed up yet?"

I looked over at Rory. She just kept folding clothes and looking strained but resigned to her task. What on earth could stop *Rory* from being in a hurry?

"The Eagle Scout isn't feeling up to it," said Hector.

I craned my neck a little to see for sure what, well, *whom* Alison was leaning over, but I had already figured it out. He was sweating worse than the day before.

Alison reached out and Hector handed her a bottle of something out of the box. It was a medical kit of some sort, obviously a lot more extensive that what we'd picked up in Whitetail.

"What's wrong with him?" Norman asked before I could. He looked unusually worried.

"Nothing," said The Eagle Scout when he'd swallowed whatever pills she gave him. He would have been better off not saying anything. I could hear his frustration with how weak his own voice sounded. "Too much sun. My fault. I'll . . . I just need to rest a little. Sorry."

"You *do* need to rest," Alison agreed, "that's for sure. But a little sunshine doesn't turn you into a space heater. Looks more like a nasty flu to me. He's not going anywhere until this fever breaks, not in this heat."

"Yeah, I'm working on that," The Eagle Scout mumbled, lying back on a gift shop cushion with brightly colored flamingos on it.

"Okay, and we'll be ready to go when he is, right?" I asked.

"Yes," said Rory.

I think it would have been a while before she brought up the practical subject herself, but she looked glad that I did.

"The van is upside-down, and so are most of the other cars in the area, since the tornado went right over us, but most of the zoo vehicles survived. Alison said we could take the large mammal transport, and it looks pretty zombie-proof even though it gas-guzzles like a bitch and probably can't break the speed limit if it tries. We've transferred most of the supplies that are worth saving already."

So that wasn't so bad. It sucked for The Eagle Scout, of course, and for Rory, and for Lis stuck waiting alone in New York. That's how I always imagined her, just sitting in some tower, watching for us out the window. And it sucked to think about how easily we could be tied down and shorthanded with no notice by a couple of random acts of nature, but of all the places we'd seen so far to be stranded, this was easily my favorite. There was some definite guilty happiness for me when Caleb, Claire, and Piglet came bounding through the door of the shelter to ask who wanted to come along to help with feeding time.

I volunteered right away, of course, almost as fast as the kids who came crowding in after him, guessing what time it was. Rory and Hector both hesitated, but Alison practically kicked them out. She insisted that she could take care of things herself, so we left her with The Eagle Scout, and the rest of us followed Caleb outside.

The zoo looked, well, like a tornado had hit it with splinters of trees, signs, and kiosk roofing everywhere, but most of the underlying structures were remarkably intact. I guess anything designed to withstand a Cape buffalo stampede can handle a little wind. By then, the air had gone painfully still and, as Alison had pointed out, blazing hot.

Even with her day old sunburn getting steadily worse, none of this seemed to bother Claire at all.

"We've been hunting all morning!" she told me proudly. "You won't believe it when you see how much we caught!"

"Hunting?" I asked. As hard as I usually tried not to encourage her, I had to know. It just didn't seem like something you did with a guy in a zoo volunteer shirt.

Luckily for me, she didn't insist on explaining out loud. I got the picture when we reached one of those things that look like a golf cart that the employees use in places like zoos. There was a trailer attached behind it, and it was piled higher than I could reach with dead zombies.

Completely dead, I mean.

"It's not all from today," Caleb said right away, like we were going to accuse him of cheating. "But it's a better haul than ever. Claire sure can handle a modified tranq rifle."

I was automatically ready to show him that I could handle any projectile weapon at least ten times as well as Claire could even though I knew he was probably only saying it to keep her smiling. It worked, and she needed it, given the circumstances.

She was still glowing in the background a little when she had to get serious and ask, "Is he feeling better yet?"

"Depends," I said. "Better than what?"

"He'll be just fine," Caleb told her, and I tried to gauge by his inflection how many times he'd said it before. Six or seven at least. "Alison's the best large animal vet in the state. Hell, she might be the best doctor alive today, period. Worst that'll happen to him with her around is that he won't get to say he's handfed a lion."

That took Claire's mind off things and, I'll admit, mine, too. He first offered Rory the key to the cart, citing the fact that he and Claire had had all morning with it, but she declined, and Claire eagerly took the helm. That was fine by me. It left both Caleb and me in the group walking alongside, and it came down pretty quickly to just us and Rory actually talking. Mr. Garret's class crowded around him, Norman found the exhibits we bypassed without due attention more interesting than Caleb's narration of his favorites (not that I could blame him—the tiebreaker between the two delights was strictly hormonal for me), and Hector kept a tactful distance. You know the kind of distance. It was the kind that always reminds me of the way people watch the rest of a poker round after they've already folded.

That's how hot Caleb was, so hot that even Rory could feel it. I can't emphasize that point enough. I mean, Rory was so pretty herself, and popular, back when we had people to be popular with, that her flirting style usually defaulted to the old standard "I'm above caring too much what you think of me" aloofness; I knew her, maybe not as well as I once had, but well enough to catch the way her eyes kept gravitating back to him before being consciously dragged away, the way the pitch of her voice rose about a semitone when she answered him.

It's not that she stopped caring for a moment about getting back on the road and closer to Lis, that much was obvious, but for as long as we were stuck there by circumstances beyond her control, Caleb's presence definitely had a calming effect on her. "Calming" is a strange word for The Chase, considering the adrenaline involved, but it's true. The way it narrows your brain, gives every passing moment that out-of-time significance, doesn't leave much room to worry about the future.

There are days, like that one, when this effect can be an incredible relief.

Not to knock Caleb or the fun of the time I got to spend with him, but sometimes I think that relief is the real reason I didn't just fold like Hector and leave him to Rory and Claire.

Oh well, whatever the reason, I didn't.

"And this big kitty is Aslan," Caleb introduced us.

I probably don't need to describe what kind of big kitty he was talking about.

"What was Aslan's scientific name again?" Mr. Garret prompted his class with the kind of enthusiasm that almost made me nostalgic for elementary school.

"Panthera leo!" they chanted back to him.

There was no college or even middle school left for those kids to prep for, no paid jobs as vets or zookeepers or biology professors, but they looked so happy just to know, like how you always think you'll feel if you get "accidentally" locked in at some really cool field trip destination, forced to spend a little longer without having to go home. It must have been even harder for them than the rest of us at first, blocking out the Unspeakable Past, but Mr. Garret was doing a hell of a job helping them with that. I hope he's still alive.

"Who wants to give him a snack?" Caleb called out. He even glanced over at Norman, but Norman was amusing himself with his balance beam act along the railing of the cheetah enclosure. A year earlier, that might have made me nervous, but I'd learned over time to trust his almost superhuman coordination.

All the kids raised their hands like they had at all the slightly less intimidating exhibits we'd hit already, but I'm sure Caleb had already settled on picking someone a little taller and stronger for this one, for safety's sake.

"Someone who hasn't taken a turn yet." He offered a fairly fresh severed arm to Rory. "Just remember, give it a good, strong, underhand toss with a nice high arc for distance."

Rory smiled weakly at him, but when she looked at the arm,

something shifted. She mumbled something about how grateful she was for the tour, but that she really should be working on packing up.

"I thought that was all settled," Caleb tried to encourage her. She wouldn't listen. She just mumbled a little more and then insisted on turning straight back to double check everything.

Whole truth? I was sorry for her, and a little giddily victorious. It might have been different if it had just been because of Lis, but it wasn't the first time I'd seen this happen. A window would open for her to jump from just admiring to connecting, and she'd turn it down. Or maybe she couldn't see it past the little momentary details like severed arms. Either way, it was the reason that, even though she could catch more eyes than I could, that was *all* she could ever seem to do.

I hadn't kept the secret from her. I'd tried to explain it a hundred times, and if we'd been dealing with a guy she'd had dibs on, I'd have been rooting for her to do things right with all my heart, but we'd met Caleb at the same time, noticed him at the same time. He was fair game and, forgive me, I liked winning.

So when he offered me the arm, I took it even though the thought of stepping over the gate to throw it from the best vantage point made me a little weak-kneed, too. Aslan was closer than you were allowed to get to the lions in LA or San Diego, and my brain had never really processed how huge and powerful they were. I could actually see his eyes, big and otherworldly-intelligent, like he was sizing up the twice dead human hand and the live one, mine, holding it at the wrist, and not seeing much of a difference.

It was stalling as much as flirting when I looked at Caleb a while longer, tapping into my fascination with him to make conversation.

"This stuff doesn't make them sick?" I asked, holding up the arm.

"We were afraid it might, at first," Caleb admitted. "But when it came down to giving them this or nothing, we had to try it out, and turned out most of them like it just fine. Humans have pretty pitiful immune systems compared with your average carnivore."

Mr. Garret launched into a quiz behind us on the pH and temperature requirements for botulism cultures, and I wished I'd had an elementary school teacher who'd covered things like that. I guessed that in the pre-zombie classroom, he probably hadn't.

I couldn't think of any more questions just then, so I jumped the safety rail with all the grace and dexterity I had in me, and to my absolute delight, Caleb followed me to demonstrate that throwing technique he had been describing to Rory. I could have gone along with my plan of just showing off my perfectly competent throwing arm, but it was more fun to let him move Piglet from his chest to his shoulder, step in close behind me, and guide my arm in that wonderfully transparent, cornball excuse to touch someone.

His skin was as warm as the toast it reminded me of, he leaned just a little closer than he needed to, just enough to assure me that it definitely wasn't just a throwing lesson, and the nerves from being so close to the edge of Aslan's territory amplified everything, like someone had turned up the contrast of the picture I was in but cropped out the edges. No zombies, no Lis, no Unspeakable Past, no Norman rattling the chain link he was walking on as if he were *trying* to make as much noise as possible. Just me, and Caleb, and Aslan, and The Chase, oh, and a severed limb that for some reason wasn't a total mood breaker, right up until that moment in my backswing when I heard the unthinkable happen.

Norman lost his balance and slipped down the wrong side of the fence and the hill below into the cheetah exhibit.

CHAPTER TWELVE

KOMODO DRAGON THEORY

Caleb who?

Oh, you mean that guy who was yelling in the background for me to come back? The one I had the annoying task of elbowing away from me on top of having to cross a hedge, two fences, and thirty horizontal feet worth of tornado debris to get to the top of the drop off my best friend had just disappeared over? That guy?

Yeah, I remember him now, fondly, even. At that moment, though, I couldn't have told you his name.

"Norman!"

That name echoed back to me in my own voice off the contours of the exhibit below. "Answer me!"

"Sure," Norman called back, "what was the question?"

I watched him get to his feet at the bottom of the drop off. By the way he moved, he was probably pretty bruised up, but nothing was broken. I shouldn't have been surprised; his reflexes were as sharp as his balance usually was, and years of deliberate pratfalls had taught him how to roll with any impact, but having seen what a bump on the head can do to a healthy but unlucky guy, it was still a relief.

The fall was only half the problem, though.

I knew the posture of that cheetah from way too many

sick days watching Animal Planet. Seriously, the semester I went through mono, the airtime on that channel that wasn't devoted to the Irwin family was made up almost entirely of images exactly like the one in front of me.

The cat's eyes were fixed on Norman from behind the authentic tall grass at the other end of the enclosure, one of its front paws lifted in mid step, the other three flat on the ground, its shoulders and hips raised high above its lowered spine, ready bolt into its signature sprint.

My eyes automatically circled the rim of the exhibit, driven by a combination of stark terror and something else, something that thankfully brought every detail of the walls into vivid detail, searching for a way up or down.

I didn't have anything resembling a rope, wasn't even wearing a belt, not that I would have had one long enough to do any good. Other than the door into the back area on the far side, there was just a retractable ladder a few yards to my left.

"Follow me slowly!" I called down, and Norman mirrored my progress with careful steps as I shimmied along the edge to it. A padlock prevented it from extending.

"The key!" I shouted over my shoulder, rattling the metal, hoping it would make it clear sooner what I was talking about, or maybe even throw off the cheetah's concentration.

It didn't.

"Cassie, come back!" that ridiculous directive was the answer I got while it inched closer to him, rising a little further out of its crouch.

"Caleb! Do you have the key?!"

Okay, so I *could* remember his name when it was important again.

"Cassie, it's okay!"

This was even more ridiculous, of course. It very clearly was *not* okay. It was too late.

The cheetah broke out of its stalking stance and into as pounding a run as the length of the enclosure would allow. Norman was fast for a person, but his instinctive little dodge to the side couldn't scratch the surface of the ground the cat covered. In one unstoppable pounce, it had him flat on his back.

And started licking his face.

Did I have you going there?

Sorry, couldn't resist. Not after how completely and undeniably it had *me* going at the time.

"Pussywillows used to be a showcat," Caleb told me. Even though I can't blame him now, I really wanted to slug the laughter out of his voice then. I couldn't quite tell whether I wanted that more than I wanted to laugh myself. "Even the zoo used to bring her out for special demonstrations now and then. Gotta respect the old instincts like they tell you, of course, she's got them, loves hunting down moving zombies for some reason, but she *adores* living people. Never even seen her snarl at one as long as I've known her."

Pussywillows was leaping around Norman like a housecat by then. "Frolicking" is probably the most accurate term, always circling back onto his chest to lick his cheek again.

"That's nice," said Norman, in a high, shaky voice that barely projected up to us, "but she's still got a tongue like an industrial wood sander that . . . um, is really starting to hurt now."

Caleb led the way down a set of stone steps and around to the back entrance, though not quite as quickly as I would have liked him to. Pussywillows released Norman instantly at the sight of Caleb and jumped up on him in greeting.

She was nowhere near the size of Aslan, of course, but still intimidating up close, and the weight of her tested the stability of even Caleb's practiced stance.

"That's my girl," he cooed, handing Piglet off to Claire for safekeeping, and scratching Pussywillows under the chin. The echo chamber of the enclosure filled with deep, resonant purring.

I ran past them to where Norman was lying in the grass and helped him to his feet.

Then I shoved him back off of them, hard.

"I *told* you something like that would happen eventually, didn't I?" I shouted.

"Yes," he said meekly, sitting back up and putting a hand carefully to the red patch where Pussywillows had stripped off a patch of his makeup and a layer of skin underneath. "Yes, you did."

I had said something like that, sometime long before, even though I'd since stopped believing it myself.

"It could have been worse!" I added, "Much worse!" as if someone were trying to argue otherwise.

"Yes, it could," he acquiesced, and even though he wasn't arguing, there was something in the very back of his voice, some kind of happy satisfaction, that I didn't understand or like.

I helped him up again, punching him once more in the ribs before supporting him across the exhibit toward the others.

He could have walked on his own well enough, but like the punch, it gave me a pretext for getting close enough to feel him, healthy and alive, while I was still too pissed off to let him hug me.

Hector gave me a look when we rejoined the group, one I didn't quite like either. It was the infuriating one he always used when he'd just figured out a riddle or called a twist ending before I did and had started counting the seconds until I caught up.

Caleb was sweet about it. His look was as friendly as ever, if a little annoyingly amused, but I'd blown my moment, and I knew it. I spent the walk back between Norman and Hector, folded, watching Claire claim her winnings.

It was okay. It wasn't that big a surprise, really, when I thought about it. She fell perfectly in the middle of his obvious love for girls, kids, and animals. Her fascination with him was deeper and stronger than mine, fueled as it was by a vast chasm of childlike ignorance, and he seemed to be okay with that.

It was cute, almost inspirational, watching them and Mr. Garret take an animated lead, tending the animals, entertaining the class and, though Norman and I hadn't quite finished shoving each other between paces and arguing about exactly how high an edge he *was* allowed to balance on from that point onward when we circled back to the elephant shelter around dinner time, I was feeling pretty okay about the world. Okay enough that the looks on Rory's and Alison's faces when they saw us enter, flat and solemn as AP testing proctors, hit me a lot harder than was necessary to warrant the term "buzzkill."

Claire got the worst of it. She'd been soaring a lot higher, and the instantaneous, bricklike way she came down almost made me want to cry. Almost as bad was the way Mr. Garret read the room, turned on his heel, and led the little kids back out again.

"He's not better, is he?" Claire asked.

Day 2

Continued iodine treatment proving ineffective. Bite showing clear visual evidence of infection. Rubbing alcohol and antibiotic ointment also having no discernable effect. Infection appears to have spread beyond the initial injury site, subject currently exhibiting a fever of 40.16 Celsius, an increase of 2.2 degrees since detection the night of day 1. Courses of aspirin and veterinary amoxicillin administered starting this morning, also having negligible effect.

Catching on? Yeah, so was Alison. By the time we got there, she had made him roll up his pant leg and show her what was under the bandages. I don't know whether he had consciously written off trying to keep it hidden from the rest of us, or if he was done making conscious decisions altogether for the time being. He had his head pressed back hard into that flamingo pillow, and he was gibbering softly with delirium.

"No," Alison said simply, "he's not."

"Why?" asked Claire. Her voice was getting choked, and it was only a matter of time before the tears would start for real. "What's wrong?"

"He's been bitten," she said, straightforward as that, no useless softening.

"That's . . ." I had no anecdotal proof of my own, but a lifetime of abstract zombie scholarship gave those words a certain fatalistic impact for me. "That's really bad, isn't it?"

"It *shouldn't* be," she said, cleaning her thermometer with a frustrated, compulsive motion, like it was some long-cherished talisman that had suddenly and inexplicably failed. "I mean, human saliva is dirty as hell, and it can't be any better on a rotting corpse, but the bite was treated immediately. I couldn't have done a better job on it myself."

I heard her irritation with having had half the details kept from her clash with a grudging sort of respect.

"Now and then you get a really tenacious virus like rabies spreading this way, but it's not acting like a virus, especially not the way it showed up in dead things all over the world at once with no possible network of infection. And none of the animals are affected by consuming it, no matter how fresh, not even close relatives like chimps, so—"

"So what is it?" Hector asked.

Alison took a moment, like she was afraid that what she wanted to say might make her sound crazy but then remembered that we weren't scientists, just a bunch of geeky high school kids. "The closest phenomenon I've studied would have to be Komodo dragon bites."

"Those giant poisonous lizards?" Claire asked.

"Venomous," Norman, Hector, and I corrected her automatically in deadpan unison. She still didn't understand the difference even though Mr. Garret had explained it at least twice that same day: poisonous is bad if you bite it, venomous is bad if it bites *you.*

"Not venomous either, exactly," Alison corrected us all. "They don't secrete venom. Their bites kill with a unique bacterial culture found in their saliva. This seems to be something similar, but a bacterial infection should respond to antibiotics, and they don't even seem to be slowing it down."

"So what *is* it then?" I repeated for Hector. "Virus or bacteria? Some crazy mutation of one? A parasite? *Magic?*"

Alison put the thermometer away. "What is it that's been killing him since the moment his skin broke with absolutely no discernible origin or weaknesses?" she asked. "Or what is it making corpses stand up and walk without consistent breath, without circulation, without any viable metabolic function? If I had to guess, I'd say it's in the air. Something not in any textbook, that's infused the entire atmosphere of the planet. From the inside or the outside, I don't know. And that's only a guess. Believe me, no one wishes more than I do that we had someone left to ask who might know, but until we can get scientific research back to the level it was at a week ago, and then about twenty years into the future in the specific direction of discovering that answer, yeah, I'm willing to fill in the blank with 'magic' for now."

Mr. Garret never did bring his class back that night. I'm betting he had them singing campfire songs or something in one of the other buildings, making the occasion of not sitting around watching a tough, ambitious, seventeen-year-old boy die a slow, inexorable death into some special treat of a change of pace.

The rest of us weren't so lucky.

Caleb tried to coax Claire away from The Eagle Scout's side for a while, for her sake more than anybody else's, I know, but when Alison had nothing left to do that Claire could distract her from, she convinced him to leave them together.

The Eagle Scout slipped in and out of lucidity a few times, sometimes sitting up unsteadily, meeting our eyes and calling us by the right names, sometimes crying out to Alison as if she were Kim, saying that she had to sign his early admission application *today*, or he'd miss the deadline, sometimes just muttering, "I'm sorry," over and over again.

Claire ignored the phases and told him stories of our day with a forced smile all evening, as if he were listening—how she had been *this* close to a sea lion, how she had hugged Pussywillows, the friendly cheetah who hated zombies but loved people, how Caleb was teaching her to shoot and drive and tell the difference between animals that had looked the same to her before.

Alison sat close all night, watching, the bottle of aspirin in one hand and a large-carnivore's-kitchen-sized cleaver in the other.

No one had to ask what she expected to need it for.

Caleb, Rory, Hector, Norman and I laid out the sleeping bags as they had been the night before, but we didn't gather in them to talk. We didn't talk at all, or do anything else to get ready for sleep, unless you count Norman washing and repainting his face to fix the smears Pussywillows had left.

Rory looked a little disapprovingly at the paints, like this wasn't the moment for bright colors. I couldn't argue with Norman. If anything, the occasion only made me understand his point better—that you couldn't discount *any* moment, no matter what was happening in it. Maybe it had always been true, but more so then than ever before. No more cell phones. No more 911. No more ERs or FDA or AAA or dentists. Even if we never saw another zombie, we could get lost in the desert, or another tornado, or any one of us could catch pneumonia or dysentery or some other dark-aged, easily treatable disease and drop dead. We wouldn't always be lucky enough for things to happen a day's drive from one of the last doctors standing.

Add in zombies and there were things that could happen,

lying in wait in tangles of sugar snap peas, so bad that even that kind of luck wouldn't be enough.

No moment was meaningless, no moment was safe, no moment was a bad time to be ready.

I spent that night trying to rest, first sitting up against the wall of the shelter, then, when my neck got tired, lying next to it with my head on Norman's chest, listening to each beat of his heart. I never expected the next one with the full, unquestioning confidence I once had. I guess, eventually, I must have fallen asleep because when The Eagle Scout passed by, resting a pocket-sized, spiral-bound notebook on my folded hands, I thought at first it was a dream.

I thought that for long enough that, by the time I could force my eyes open to really look at it, he was long out of sight.

Day 3

Early morning. The fever has not abated. The subject's moments, my moments, of clarity, are getting shorter and shorter, so I'll make this quick.

I'm sorry I lied. I'm sorry I didn't warn anyone about what I really tripped over in that field. I swear that if we had not found such a secure environment in which to do it, I would not have allowed my condition to progress this far. I only wanted to make the greatest possible use of this opportunity, such as it is.

I'll confess, I was also afraid. I know enough about the knowledge base of at least half of my companions to guess at the kind of conclusion that might have been jumped to if I had told the truth immediately. I wanted to find out if I could beat it first.

As it turns out, the conclusion would have been entirely accurate, and I can't. All I can do is record as much about the effects of a zombie bite as possible. The Kent Case Study and Komodo Dragon Theory of Dr. Alison Teach may not be the only research conducted so far on the subject, but it is all that I can be sure exists, so I have asked her to record it in as much detail as possible in the last section of this notebook. The material's key takeaways are as follows:

1. The bite of a zombie serves no obvious purpose other than the one it shares with all other observed zombie behaviors, that is, the spreading of death at all costs and by any means.

2. The bite of a zombie is, at this time, under even the most ideal of circumstances, un-survivable.

It's not much, but I want you to have it, Cassie. You because you're the only person I can be sure will listen, understand, and be listened to, not only one or two of the above. You because I know you care uncompromisingly about truth and knowledge, no matter how small or depressing or bizarre. I've known that since the moment you stood in front of my mother and the police and told them, without proof or credibility, that you'd killed the first zombie. Keep it safe, and good luck.

Sincerely,
Peter Kent

That was when I really knew. When I read the name Peter Kent, and my brain didn't autocorrect it like it always had, that's when I knew he was gone.

"Peter?" I whispered out loud.

Alison was awake, but she was the only one. Claire was curled up beside her on Peter's empty bed. Alison put the cleaver to her lips to shush me and whispered back, "Pussywillows."

I picked up Suprbat from its place beside me, mostly just for comfort, and ran outside. There was just enough light rising up from the eastern horizon to let me find my way back to Pussywillows' den. She loved humans. She never would have hurt Peter, the real Peter. I know she sat with him to the end.

But by the time I got there, the end was long past, and she was crouched over a few remnants of a bloody Boy Scout uniform.

CHAPTER THIRTEEN

LMNoE

I really wished that Rory's compulsions had left a few clothes for *me* to fold, something brainless but necessary to do. Once everyone was awake, which happened within the hour, our exit was quick and efficient. No details to resolve, no arguments. We had stayed because Peter needed us to, and now that he didn't anymore, it was time to go.

Alison and Mr. Garret fussed over us like parents sending their first child off to college, asking if we had enough blankets, enough batteries, enough food, and I ended up having to put my foot down about how much they could reasonably offer us. They still had a second grade class to take care of, after all, and since we were headed directly out of their salvaging territory, it would serve everyone best if we made our own supply run after a couple hundred miles.

It was the kind of thing I never would have needed to think about, much less insist upon, before.

I know they were uneasy about us leaving at all, them being the only real adults around, but with the possibility of reuniting any family in New York, they really couldn't justify trying to stop us.

More than that, there was also some vague, unspoken point we'd all passed—I'm not sure when, maybe all the way back at the end of the Unspeakable Past, or maybe when we'd picked up our first blunt objects knowing we'd need them to stay alive, or maybe just when we'd agreed on a plan, no matter how harebrained, and done our very best to see it through—when we'd simply stopped being anyone's responsibility.

There wasn't even any friction when Claire announced that she wasn't coming with us, her hand in Caleb's and an apology slipped between almost every pair of syllables. If there had been a polite way, I might have suggested it myself. I couldn't think of a better place for her than with him, the animals, the children, and the real adults. Certainly not fighting for her life and passage into Manhattan with the rest of us, swinging that sparkly purple golf club of hers. They could show her the patience we couldn't afford. I bet she's happy there today, living as close to a normal life as is possible anymore. So, no, her decision didn't surprise me.

What did surprise me was how achingly I missed her.

I only took enough time to give her an abbreviated goodbye hug, leaving the rest for Rory to assure her earnestly that she didn't blame her a bit, that she was overjoyed to hear that she had already found what she needed, even if she couldn't say the same herself, and that she was so, so sorry about her brother, that we all were. But as soon as we had maneuvered that great, hulking large animal transport onto the highway, I missed her endless, inane babble—its soothing lack of vital, life-changing importance, and the way it somehow wore her out until she would collapse against my side, radiating un-rationed warmth like we were the best of friends and nothing could ever possibly go wrong in the world.

I guess after you've shared a sleeping bag with someone, it must be naturally difficult to process the idea that you're probably never going to see them again, but it was more than that. It was the fact that if there was one thing we were short of on the road out of Tulsa, one thing we desperately needed, it was a bit of that absence of vital, life-changing importance.

The transport had more than enough room in the back of it for our supplies, but it was a lot slower than the Kent's van, and there wasn't much elbowroom for the four of us jammed into the cabin. We communicated mostly about how to convert the colors and squiggles of our maps into actual movement of the transport across the earth, which, without Peter, turned out to be an intensive four-person job.

Rory slipped once into thinking back in dangerous directions, noting, "I gave him such a hard time about so many stupid things," but Hector stopped her.

"Name one person who didn't," he said.

If I'd thought a cop car was the very least likely vehicle for my driver's ed to take place in, a large animal transport must have carved out at least a few more notches at the bottom of that list.

Short a third driver, Rory and Hector started coaching Norman and me at it in turns. It wasn't nearly as easy as it looked, staying in one lane, slowing down and speeding up at just the right rate, angling around the stalled cars and other occasional obstacles without scraping the sides. It didn't help that none of us had even been inside a truck that large, much less in the driver's seat, but the mostly empty and straight roads of farmland and national parks made it about as easy as it could have been, and probably safer than letting any of us take a full half-day shift with eyes as red-rimmed as all of ours were.

At least that giant fuel tank started off full. I was dreading the moment when one of us would have to rediscover the art of siphoning.

We got in and out of a supermarket just beyond Springdale without fanfare even though it was more real food than we'd seen in days. We were all afraid that if we hung around too long, we'd meet another band of elementary school kids who needed those apples, loaves of bread, and jars of peanut butter more than we did, another group of people who, whether they meant to or not, would make a more notable mark on our lives in less than the space of three days than people who'd had years of Unspeakable Past in which to try.

We couldn't take any more marks on us just then. I could hardly take walking past that display of Claire's brand of hot chocolate with the cow jumping over the moon.

I was glad to be back on the road less than ten minutes later.

One thing I really, really hate about road maps, other than how impossible they are to re-fold correctly, is the stuff they don't show. Or don't label. Or show in pale colors and label once in some out of the way corner as an afterthought, like no one's really that interested. I don't mean the little (if obviously important) details like whether or not a street is one way only, and which way. The mapmakers had no reason to expect that information would ever stop being important. I'm talking about the stuff that shows up magnified and stamped with huge letters on bigger maps that aren't distracted by things like traffic circles and turnpikes. Big stuff.

We *did* manage to figure out what that thing was at the edge of Arkansas before we could actually see it out of the windshield. It was a stroke of pure luck that Norman remembered. That washed-out bluish section that didn't represent Indian Reservation or National Forest, the part with a healthy mess of roads on our side and a healthy mess of roads on the other, but only very sparingly placed bottleneck thoroughfares going through it, stretching all the way down to the Atlantic and up to the point where we would have needed to dig up our maps of Ohio.

Oh, right, the *Mississippi River.*

We tried to navigate on the move as much as possible for the sake of time, but that discovery warranted a special roadside debate at around Huntsville.

"Well, we're obviously going to have to force our way through one of the routes on the map," Hector started. "There aren't going to be any little forgotten side streets for this. If money is spent on a bridge that big, it's going to be where people are going to use it. And there's no way we're getting across without a bridge."

Rory nodded. "But almost all of them are escape routes from major cities. They'll be like the Rockies all over again."

"Maybe not," said Hector, though he didn't sound completely sure of himself. "We're on flat ground, plenty of room for people to leave in all the other directions."

"But they wouldn't *all* go in other directions," Rory reasoned. "There's a pretty isolated crossing to the north in Missouri."

"Just one," Hector repeated, "and not another one for hundreds of miles. It's a gamble. A city might not be so bad. More traffic means more bridges means more possibilities."

It took me several moments of silence to realize that they were both waiting for *me,* the one common friend in the equation, to say something mediating about this, like that was a completely normal thing to expect.

Now, I'm not a total moron or anything. I *can* form a plan and follow it when it's just me alone (escaping from a police station, anyone?), and I can usually choose sensible people to follow when I'm not. Actually making an effort to convince other people to do things my way, at the price of taking the blame if it goes wrong, wasn't really something I did. The cost-benefit ratio had never appealed to me.

I'm not sure exactly what made me rethink my automatic response of a shrug and a "what do you think?" Maybe some leftover inspiration hanging around that notebook, newly tucked into the deepest pocket of the killer bunny bag. I like to think so. Whatever the reason, I *did* do my best, starting by really looking at that map, trying to hold its squiggles in my head, the way you can remember regular words when they're not in front of you anymore. It wasn't so hard. I hadn't been the best of us at orienteering, but I'd been competent.

The river got narrower way up to the north, with more frequent crossings, but it also split and twisted more, so the longer we waited to cross, the more likely it was that we'd have to do it more than once, or double back to the south to avoid it.

"Memphis has two bridges," I said. "Two chances for the price of one. I think we might as well give it a shot. It's about as far south as we can aim without it being really out of the way, and if it's a no go, we trace the river north and take the first chance we get. It'd just suck to miss a good one that might be so close."

Rory looked over my shoulder to check my logic and grudgingly found no problems with it. I almost hoped that Norman would contradict me and bring us to a deadlock, just to take the pressure off, but he just shrugged.

"I like Memphis," he said meekly, a comment on a decision already made rather than a vote.

No one took the map back from me, so I guided Rory, and then Norman, and then Rory again, across the rest of Arkansas—if you could call guiding telling them to stay on one highway, then another, and then a third one for a little while. That was all it took to get into the never-again-moving queue onto the southernmost bridge into Tennessee.

Yeah, it was stacked solid, just like Rory had predicted, a pretty uncanny reminder of the pass into Glenwood, except that the air was cleaner, and there weren't so many zombies around. This was partly because they'd had longer to spread and more space to spread into, like Hector had pointed out, and partly because, unlike walking up cliff faces, which is a pretty instantly discouraging endeavor, zombies don't notice how much they suck at swimming.

I almost felt like making a note of that somewhere, a section over from all the details of their bites. The mountains had funneled the things forcibly onto the road in Colorado, but the ones in Tennessee ignored the bridges, unless they happened to be right in front of them, and wandered blithely into the water toward us. There were almost none crawling back out on our side, but if you think that made them reconsider trying for a moment, you don't know zombies.

I figured that was it, I'd just go back to keeping my mouth shut before anyone had to point out how many miles I'd lost us, and let Rory and Hector go on working our way north until one of them came up with an alternative to argue about. I was pretty adamant about that, resolved that I wouldn't even comment if they decided to do something other than check the north bridge while we were right there next to it, right up until they *did* circle around to check it.

And it was wide open.

It wasn't that Rory had been wrong about what would happen

to it during the riots; it was clear that it had been jammed like the other one quite recently, but someone had since taken a bulldozer to it, cutting a clear, wide path through the twisted metal wreckage. Wheels and bumpers and hunks of sheet metal were mashed up against the railings on both sides, spilling out at the entrance. Whoever had been there before us had been going the other way.

I wanted to enjoy Rory's grateful, congratulatory squeeze of my shoulders, but all I could think about was whether Peter had always felt that astronomically lucky every time one of his plans went right.

The sky was just starting to redden by that time, closer to our last lodging than usual, thanks to the large animal transport's top speed of about seventy, but with the Mississippi already behind us and a clear shot ahead, Rory didn't fight as hard as she might have when Hector pointed out that, with how little there was to the immediate east of us, if we wanted to sleep between walls that night, we might want to start finding them pretty soon.

Norman said, "I have an idea."

Believe it or not, even Norman could kind of tell when people were really, really, exceptionally far from the right mood for jokes of varying levels of taste, and he had even less love for negotiating plans than I had, so he hadn't ventured saying much that day. He took the map insistently at that point and directed us across a short distance of side streets, short enough to avoid answering the obvious question, "Where are we going?"

I wouldn't have recognized the old-fashioned mansion myself if it hadn't been for the sign out front, but I had a classical enough education to put it together pretty fast after that.

"Graceland?"

"Home of The King," Norman confirmed. "I always hoped to see it someday. Plus, it looks like a pretty decent fortress, don't you think?"

It was, but that was because, again, someone else had been there first. After pulling up to within a few yards of the porch and beating away a few straggling zombies to get our essential bags as far as the front door, Norman had the presence of mind to try the knob before I could resort to Peter's crowbar. It was securely latched but not locked, so there was nothing to repair or jury-rig to get it locked behind us. The windows were already barricaded from the inside, there was a smell of recently burning gasoline, and the flowers laid lovingly on the living room coffee table had only just begun to lose their petals. Someone, maybe the same someone who had been at the controls of that bulldozer, had held at least a night's vigil there before moving on.

Norman took a breath, and I saw the smell register with him, too. "You guys make sure that end's secure?" he suggested, nodding further along the right side of the hallway. "Meet me back here? I want to check something."

He headed in the other direction, wrench in one hand, padded Whack-a-Mole mallet in the other.

Hector, Rory, and I made sure there was no one inside with us on our side, living or dead, hiding behind the bed or the baby grand piano or the retro fifties TV, and then went back to the living room to wait. The side Norman had claimed for himself to scout was much larger, and the thought of him alone in it made me a little nervous, but I knew that if anything had gone wrong, we would have heard screams of one kind or another.

The daylight was just getting difficult to see by when I got up, ready to go looking for him. And that was when I heard the grinding of a motor in the distance, and the overhead lights flickered once, twice, three times, and then stayed lit, with a cheerful, yellowish tint.

Norman appeared at the top of the stairs across the hallway, grinning almost as broadly as his makeup always made him seem to, and beckoned.

We followed him past a kitchen with that display of plastic fruit you see in all disused, historical kitchens' fruit bowls, a room full of plastic houseplants and thick green carpeting on every surface, down the stairs past a smaller, almost claustrophobic room with a pool table in the middle, its walls and ceiling completely covered in fabric, and into the one room of the mansion I'd actually heard about in advance. I think my mind had filed it incorrectly under "Urban Myth."

Into one wall was set a row of three separate televisions, each showing a different DVD menu screen. I'm pretty sure most of the rest of the setup was Norman's. The little table in the middle of all the blue and yellow living room set pieces was piled with DVD cases and a snack bar assortment of candy and crackerjacks.

A menu board hung from the ceiling, turned backward, with letters scrawled hurriedly across the blank side in sharpie.

LMNOE.

"None of us are having a good day," Norman started in his best announcer voice. "Hell, none of us are having a good week. No one's denying that." Then he hyped up the announcer quality to his voice in the way that always meant he was trying to say something he actually meant and hoped no one would take too much notice. "And I know I'm not always the easiest person to be around, especially at bad times. But I *do* know something about good times, and I don't think anyone can deny that we all seriously need one of those, especially if we're going to have our heads together enough to cheer Lis up properly when we find her, which is the whole idea, right?" He picked up the first few cases on the DVD stack and held them up. "Now, I don't know a lot about gas-powered generators, so I don't know how long the power will last on half a tank, and of course, all I could find in the gift shop were old Elvis movies, and I'm not saying they'll be great, but on three TVs at once and after our fair share of this"—he pushed back a pile of yellow throw pillows obscuring what looked like half the bar—"I think they'll do, considering that this might very well be the Last Movie Night On Earth."

For a moment, I was afraid this gesture would finally make me implode under the pressure of shutting out the Unspeakable Past, along with the bits of the present that seemed to belong there, and burst into tears; that's how strong a contender it was for the sweetest thing I'd ever heard in my life. I was even more afraid when Norman poured and offered the first extra-strong rum and coke to Rory, that her requisite "Not if you were the last man on earth" was going to be enough to ruin it. I waited for it through agonizing seconds of silence to find out. It didn't come.

Instead, she took the glass and knocked it back in two gulps.

"Yeah, I think I could go for a good time," she said.

Norman's confidence returned to full strength, and he poured a full round of drinks, which we all accepted without a moment's hesitation, and raised his glass.

"To The Eagle Scout," he started.

"To The Eagle Scout," we echoed.

"To Peter."

"To Claire."

"Couldn't have gotten this far without them."

I don't remember who proposed what toast after that. I know we drank "to The King," "to being alive so far," "to friendship," and "to the LMNOE," before Rory started calling it "the LMAO" and giggling whenever she tried to remember what it was really called. Norman turned on three copies of *Live a Little, Love a Little,* almost perfectly in sync, which by then, as he'd predicted, seemed like the most awesome movie in the world.

CHAPTER FOURTEEN

HEAD OVER HEELS

I'd learned how to swallow the taste of liquor and keep it down from a few of my parents' parties already, but the LMNOE was the first time I had enough of it at once to feel more of an effect than a tingle of warmth in my chest and on my skin. I'd known the theory, of course, the way it makes it difficult to balance and think things through before you blurt them out, but I guess that's another one of those things, like big empty spaces, that you can't really understand until you feel them.

Now that I know, I'll keep it in mind if I ever have a secret or any dignity worth keeping. Luckily, on that particular night, we were all due for a lot more blurting and a lot less thinking.

One of us in particular.

"I know I'm kinda crazy," Rory told us, in that lazy way that alcohol makes your tongue move, like Caleb's chocolate bar voice, but with really chewy peanut butter smeared on top. "I know, I do, but thanks for doing this with me anyway. Thanks. I haven't said that often enough, have I?"

"A little more often would be nice," Hector agreed diplomatically. Halfway into *Blue Hawaii,* I had this really brilliant theory floating around in my head about why Rory had never even mentioned the possibility of ditching us when we'd insisted on stopping for so long in Tulsa, something about a family in the hand being worth two in the bush, and how that was totally what we were, but right about then, this amazing guitar riff started resonating through the walls from upstairs, and I stopped trying to put it into words.

There was something about that tune. I recognized it, from somewhere in the past, but from a good part that hadn't had all its goodness crushed out and put forever off-limits. I strained to focus on it for a moment, and then it fit into place.

Hector had written it, back before that rejection letter, back before he had stopped playing.

Hector was playing the guitar. *Hector was playing the guitar.* And that was kind of a huge deal.

I rolled over the back of the couch and did my best to run up the stairs even though my feet never seemed to be completely under me, and the hallway seemed to have two ends to it, both of them in front of me. Norman and Rory followed, both feeling the wall for support.

Hector looked up at us for a moment with a shy but subtly confident smile and went back to concentrating. If the Tulsa Zoo large animal vet had good odds of being the greatest doctor left alive, who was to say he wasn't the greatest musician?

I don't know if it was a testament to how little he'd had to drink so far, comparatively, or how much the rest of us had had, but that music wasn't just the best I'd heard since the Unspeakable Past, it was flat out the best I'd heard. It was the kind that grabs you by the rib cage with something stronger than its volume, the kind that you can feel as intensely as real happiness or sadness, but isn't either of those things. The kind that makes you want to play it, even if you don't know where to find middle C, the kind that makes you *need* to move to it, do it, be part of it, be in it the way it's in you.

Norman was swaying, too, like I was, with something more than a chemically-induced lapse of equilibrium. If he'd been thinking more clearly, I was sure he would have made the usual move of an exaggerated bow to Rory, asking her if he could have this dance, maybe even realizing that after the way the LMNOE (and more importantly, the words "*when* we find Lis") had finally gotten through to her, translated a small sample of his true awesomeness into her language, this would almost certainly be the time she would accept. But I was glad that, in his haze, he seemed to have forgotten that she was there, so he linked his arms into their comfortable, habitual fit with mine instead.

Dancing with Norman had always been a pretty exhausting experience, even when there wasn't any arcade game footwork involved. You can't command the attention of a dance circle for long, even at a particularly lame school formal, without pulling out at least most of the stops. He could do that pretty well by himself for most of an evening. In whatever fatal moments my own date spent succumbing to heat or thirst, I had always known to be prepared for plenty of ridiculously exaggerated gyration, getting my hands however dirty the floor happened to be, and resurrecting moves that everyone still knows the names of even though they haven't been cool since the seventies.

That would have been fine for our present surroundings, actually; the floor was immaculate, and the seventies would have been forward thinking, but just a few moments after we fell in sync with each other, after just one clumsy flip that would have been more at home in the twenties, Hector for some reason insisted on skipping to the slowest part of his song, still irresistible in its movements but utterly incompatible with the Batusi or the Electric Slide.

Not to be defeated, Norman twirled me, and to even things up, I twirled him back, which made us both a little dizzy, I guess, because after that we just leaned against each other, each supporting the other's weight, drifting in an unhurried, multi-pointed turn, something like a waltz with a whole extra beat to savor in every measure. I kept thinking that I should do something impressive, attention-grabbing, exceptional—I was so content where I was, like lying in bed on a cold morning, that I kept watching the shiny wall panels go by in a loop, drifting in that circle, in that song, its notes so perfectly spaced that your heart synchronizes to it, two pulses for every beat. I know it's not only my heart that does that because I could hear Norman's, too through the shoulder where my head was resting. That feeling of extra sharpness was back, somehow coexisting with the drunken blur, making me notice every bit of what I *could* sense, like there was going to be a test on it later. I could hear his heartbeat and feel the coarse, feathery texture of his hair and smell a blend of the theatrical paint I was learning to associate with him, and that same old aerosol body spray I always had, the kind that's supposed to smell like rain or something but just smells like the ultimate generic body spray because what the hell does falling water smell like anyway?

He felt the way he had every night and every day on the road, the way he had on the morning when the Unspeakable Past ended while we waited for the cops to show up and set whatever would come next in motion; the way he had on countless days before then when we played video games in the basement or paintball in the backyard; whenever I got dumped or had embarrassing love poetry read to me in a public forum; whenever one of us did better than, or worse than, or exactly the way we expected to in class; any time a hug was cool, any time when it wasn't, and an appropriately inappropriate body slam would have to do instead.

It was a good feeling, another good thing from the past, a bit of goodness I was still allowed to acknowledge. I didn't want that song to end, fading out like my expensive anti-stress alarm clock used to fade in, forcing me out of bed.

Norman took the cue for the big finish like he always did and dipped me. I couldn't find my feet again once I'd let them go, so I gave in and sprawled flat on the deep, soft carpet.

"Sorry!" Norman exclaimed when he saw me on the ground, thinking he'd dropped me, and offered a hand to help me up. I shook my head. That was probably the best call I could have made. I'd have been more likely to pull him down, the way he was wobbling, than he would have been to pull me up.

Hector put down the guitar and called out to Rory, who was closest to the stairway, but she was on the floor, too, a bottle of sparkly vodka still in hand, eyes drooped almost shut. So Hector went downstairs to turn up the volume of the last movie on earth's music, to fill the silence left after his playing.

Norman kept moving to it and tried once more to coax me into joining. I shook my head again, motioning that I wasn't about to try to stand up. I kept staring up at the room that was still rotating gently, enjoying that same floating feeling that you get when you twist the chains of the swing set until you're so dizzy you fall down.

There was a time, before a certain Valentine's Day, when Norman would have grabbed Hector as his next dance partner without a second thought to keep the party going, but as things were then, as smashed as we all were, he only paused for the tiniest little awkward moment before picking up the guitar and tangoing it across the room with him instead.

Not that Hector seemed to mind the reprieve at all. He pried the vodka bottle from Rory's unconscious grip and stretched out next to me with it, offering a sip.

I passed. I'd hit enough-is-enough territory, but he had plenty of wiggle room left, so he gulped what looked like the equivalent of at least three more shots while we watched Rory sleep and Norman do the twist with the guitar, oblivious to us.

"So," Hector said after a few minutes, "Claire sure found herself a looker, didn't she?"

"Yeah, no kidding," I muttered in agreement.

"I mean, he was *really* something," Hector pressed.

"Uh . . ." I blanked out on a response for a while.

Norman, Hector, and I had never talked much about the breakup that had solidified our friendship. Not that any of us were unclear on the reason we were free from the usual ex's tension, the reason Norman was currently dancing alone with a guitar, the reason why, whenever the three of us shared some equivalent of a bed, I was *always* the one in the middle. It was just one of those things, like the time Hector had spent without music, like the Unspeakable Past, that had always taken better friends *not* to talk about.

If Hector was trying to cross that line, this was something serious, something that required real listening, which I wasn't sure I was chemically capable of at that moment, but I did my best.

"Yeah, he was something," I said. "A little on the slutty side, but something."

"Completely on the slutty side," Hector agreed. "Admit it, he had you hot for him."

"Sure, yeah, of course he did," I said. "And you."

He smirked a little guiltily. "I'm only human."

We watched Norman dance a little longer.

"So why didn't you stay?" he asked.

That question was a lot more confusing than whether or not Caleb Summers had been devastatingly handsome, so I blurted honestly and without thinking, "Why would I?"

"For him," Hector pushed, "to get yourself one of who knows how many completely gorgeous guys there are left on the planet. Why wouldn't you?"

"Why wouldn't *you?*" I turned it around on him.

"Completely different situation," he said, shaking his head. "*You* actually had a chance."

My head was all fuzzy, and I kept trying to figure out how much of it was the alcohol and what the other part might be.

"Claire stayed," I said vaguely.

"Yeah." Hector nodded. "They're great together. Once you stepped down so he'd notice her."

"After Rory stepped down and let him notice *me.*" I followed this train of thought.

"Yeah, Rory's probably about as girl-pretty as Caleb was boy-pretty, isn't she?"

Neither of us really had an accurate measure to confirm or deny this, but I thought he'd probably guessed about right. "I promised her I'd help her find Lis," I remembered out loud.

"Good one," said Hector. "That's a pretty good excuse."

It *was* a pretty good excuse. It was also just that—an excuse.

"I never thought about staying," I said honestly.

"I know," said Hector, taking another swig from the bottle. "Wanna know why I think that is? Even though you were head over heels for the country boy?"

"Hey, wait," I protested. "There's a big difference between being hot for someone and being head over heels."

"Exactly," he said, like a frustrated private tutor finally dragging a slow student through some long-awaited breakthrough. I guess he said it prematurely, though, because I was still trying to figure out why he was looking so meaningfully at Norman and Rory just then. "There's a *huge* difference between hot for and head over heels for. And I think the difference is even bigger when you're already head over heels for someone else."

Yeah, there was definitely something important going on, I was sure of that. I just needed to figure out what it was. Who was head over heels for what now?

"Wait . . ." I took a stab at it. "You and me." Was he coming out to me *again?* As bi this time? "You and me . . . I was pretty sure that ship had already sailed."

"Sailed and sunk," Hector confirmed, "never to see the surface again."

"So then . . . you and *Norman?*" I tried again, ready to feel a flood of instant sympathy for what it must have been like for him all this time, watching Norman get all weak-kneed over Rory, but Hector made a face that went above and beyond "he's not my type."

That was pretty much it for me and ideas. It was easier to watch the dancing.

"He knew the cat was tame, you know."

I like to think I would have had trouble finding an answer to that even if I were stone cold sober, but maybe I could have managed a little better than, "huh?"

"He was talking to Caleb before you were awake," Hector said very slowly, watching to make sure I caught every word. "He knew, before he 'slipped' that the cat wasn't going to eat him."

I was paying enough attention to hear the quotation marks, but I couldn't understand what they meant any more than why Norman would bother to hide something so stupid from me. The closest notion I could form was that it was to make me not so embarrassed by the way I'd freaked out. Even that wouldn't quite add up in my brain.

"Not you and me, not me and him," Hector summarized for me with that forced, extra-patient, I've-solved-the-riddle-and-you-haven't smile. "What other combination could I possibly be talking about?"

I tried to solve it, I really did. But the ceiling was so spinny and the floor was so soft and the music was so repetitively, rhythmically soothing. When I woke up the next morning with my eyes too achy to open, and the room thankfully darkened by the empty generator, and my arm crushed against the side someone had rolled me onto so I couldn't drown in vomit, I couldn't for the life of me remember what it was I'd passed out thinking about.

CHAPTER FIFTEEN

RIDE ON THE MAGIC PARKING SHUTTLE

"Please don't," I muttered hopelessly when I sensed Rory's outline grasping one of our battery lanterns. The barricaded windows had kept things nice and dim until then.

"Have mercy," Norman moaned from the ornate hard wood and leather chair he had ended up in a few feet away from my bit of floor, and I wondered for a moment how many luxurious, non-neck-cramp-inducing beds there were in that mansion that none of us had bothered to find.

"Come on," Rory chided in a croakier than usual morning voice. "It'll hurt me more than it hurts you."

"Not possible," Norman and I croaked back together.

"It's just like pulling off a Band-Aid," said Rory. "One, two—"

And just like pulling off a Band-Aid, she pushed the button before we could anticipate it properly. The similarity ended there.

Turning on the lights on a normal morning when your eyes are adjusted to the dark has that same get-it-over-with factor she was talking about, but the pain of that morning's light continued after the usual few seconds, refusing to be over with, ever. Even Rory moaned, dropping the lantern and doubling over with her face in her hands.

"Ugh. Manners, people," she said with as much good cheer as any of us could hope to fake. "Don't forget to thank Norman for the awesome party."

Norman replied with a gesture and a matching, blush-free verbal suggestion, both of which were banned from broadcast television back when broadcast television existed, both of which he usually reserved for Hector and me, the small audience he could be sure would only take them in the proper spirit. I wouldn't have put that bet on Rory, but it turned out to be a smart one.

"Not if you were the last man on earth," she retorted without missing a beat, and they both burst into laughter, which was stifled almost instantly for being even more painful than the light. That didn't change the fact that, for a moment, Norman and Rory had been laughing at the same time, at the same joke, and in that moment, I stopped being surrounded by my two best friends and my one other old friend. I was just surrounded by *friends.*

Hector was a little better off than the rest of us, but not by much. He'd thought far enough ahead to crawl onto one of the couches for the night, and he was the first on his feet that morning. When I saw him, he was using a beer flat to carry an armful of mismatched cans, so he wouldn't have to pry his left hand away from his forehead.

"There is no devil," he announced when he reached the top of the stairs.

This wasn't anything like the kind of thing *I* felt like saying when my eyes wouldn't stay open and I kind of wished I could close my ears, too.

"You mean, 'there is no god'?" I asked.

"Nah, he could still be around, working in mysterious ways

and all that, but if there were a devil, he could've had my soul by now just for heating up some coffee."

I made myself open the canned latte he tossed me really fast to get the high, scratchy, hissy sound over with and took a careful sip. It stayed down which already made me feel a little better, but I could imagine with painful clarity how good something steaming hot would feel.

"Two souls," I agreed.

"Three," said Norman.

Rory didn't leave us hanging. "Four."

"No, I was actually calculating you for the third," said Norman. "I prefer mine cold."

"Well, that'll come in handy if the devil does show up," said Hector, "since we all know you don't have a soul to bargain with."

"Right," Norman nodded. "I swapped it years ago for my roguish good looks."

Rory laughed that pained, shortened laugh again.

Friends.

"Come on," she said again, carrying the lantern in the direction of Norman and me even though she wasn't quite standing fully upright herself. "Help me move the bags. We are *not* taking that trailer truck into New England with us."

Norman found the employee office where they kept the spare keys to those tour group shuttle buses and pried it open easily enough. They were even labeled so we could grab the key for the nearest one, easy as that, none of that process of elimination crap like at the police station. No one really had the strength or reflexes to stand guard while we loaded it up, even at an onslaught rate of only about three zombies a minute, so Hector just backed up the transport until the shuttle was practically inside, and Norman and I climbed onto the roof of the meditation garden gazebo and set off another strand of firecrackers to keep everything in the area clawing up at us while Hector and Rory made the transfer.

In retrospect, swinging a bat might actually have been *less* painful than listening to those explosions in the open sunlight, but somehow we did manage to hold out until the shuttle circled around to pick us up.

There were flowers still on the graves of Elvis's family, the freshest ones in about the same stage of decomposition as the ones on the coffee table. As we jumped across to our escape, I wished I had something to add, too, even though there was no one left to see the gesture, certainly not the dead old guy in the ground who would probably think we were all crazy if he could hear the latest sounds we'd paid or stolen to hear. I wanted something to offer that place, though, some sort of thank you, just for the chance to be there for what was probably the last time its music played.

I didn't have fresh flowers, so I just sort of turned back and waved at no one in particular while Hector threw the shuttle into gear and gunned it back in the direction of the interstate.

This may make me a terrible person, but even with a pounding headache and queasy stomach, even though we were still conducting a wake as much as a party or an adventure, that next day's drive was one of the best of my life. I was the one who had to squint at the map and take the nerve-wracking gamble of telling Rory that we might very well be having dinner with Lis as soon as the next evening.

The shuttle bus had lots of room to stretch out in, and with no one in the mood for tears or real, serious, self-deprecation, we dared to indulge in a little more reminiscence. Most of our memories of the Kents were a step up from the kind of DJ "humor" we would have had access to while driving in another era anyway. Like the time a couple of missionaries, I forget what denomination, wandered into a cabin summer camp and asked Peter if he'd heard the word of some particular version of Christ, and Peter asked them dead seriously if they'd bought their season's supply of Boy Scout nuts.

Yeah, those are a thing, or at least they were, and yeah, there's a reason they never reached the same level of acceptance as Girl Scout cookies. Anyway, Peter left with a free Bible, and the missionaries left with two cans of honey roasted peanuts at four bucks each. You do the math.

That wasn't all the past we talked about. Nothing about other good, absent friends, nothing about cancelled plans, certainly nothing about parents, nothing *that* Unspeakable, just little things: where our scars had come from, who had the worst ID picture, what our favorite children's shows had been.

I knew almost all of everyone's answers already, of course, but it was fun listening to Norman try to convince Rory that Ms. Frizzle could kick Captain Planet's ass.

It did occur to me how much Claire would have liked to throw in her two cents on *that* one, but it was probably best that she didn't get the chance. If sharing a sleeping bag had made it as hard as it had been to say goodbye, sharing our last movie on three TVs with her might have made it downright impossible.

We made good distance, too, in spite of the hour we spent trying to figure out how to open the shuttle's gas cap to fill the tank, before having to think about the next night's shelter. We got as far as Charlottesville, Virginia, one of the increasingly frequent midsized cities peppering the forest. Those forests were gorgeous, thick, and moist and vivid, jewel-green, nothing like the pines in New Mexico or the live oaks back home. We couldn't have explored them even if we'd had the time. With the thicker cities came thicker zombies, and thicker forests are not where you want to go to fight them if you can help it. Our pit stops didn't take us more than a few feet from the road anymore. I still envied the boys for their comparative convenience, but I'd almost completely tuned out the ick factor. It had taken me less than a week.

Even though those cities were more heavily infested than the ones in the south, they actually felt safer than the wilderness. At least they had nice flat slabs of concrete and tile where you could keep your footing and see things coming, so we were skimming the outlying residential streets for likely options. By that time, we were on the subject of the fast food we were going to miss the most.

I guess it's a natural place for your mind to stray when you've spent all day dipping pretzels into a jar of peanut butter that's kind of fused itself to the shuttle's front storage compartment. Not a bad hangover or road snack by any means, but after a while, it really makes you want something fresh and warm and preferably oozing with saturated fat.

"KFC," I admitted on my turn. Yeah, I know it had developed some pretty unpleasant associations over the past few days, but that pesky fried chicken craving hadn't gone away.

"You fail at west coast living." Rory snickered.

"I know, I know."

"Anyway, catch a fresh chicken and build a fire hot enough

to boil oil, and *I* could make that crap, but nothing's ever going to taste quite the same as a Big Mac again." Her face went all wistful. I can't think of a more appropriate moment for that word, *wistful.* "There's probably no one left alive who knows what's in special sauce."

"Because it's got, like, a thousand ingredients—"

"Ninety-five," Norman corrected me.

"Fine, because it's full of crazy almost-food substances, that makes it better?"

"No," said Rory, "it's just going to make me miss it more."

It's probably another major strike against my character that this hadn't happened until we'd managed to cheer her up a little, but I was starting to remember why Rory and I had been close in the first place.

Seriously, somehow I'd let myself spend days being pushed away, *annoyed* even, by her pining for her lost sister, and then however many seconds it had taken Norman to say those simple words, "*when* we find Lis," and mean them, had been enough to brighten everything up. How messed up is that?

"Orange chicken," said Hector. "No, scratch that. In-N-Out. Hands down. Cass? You okay?"

"What? Yeah, just swallowed a pretzel wrong."

Needless to say, I hadn't swallowed a pretzel wrong, or I wouldn't bother bringing it up. I know how stupid it sounds, with everything else we talked about that day, summer camp and *The Magic School Bus* and Hector's mad guitar skills, that In-N-Out, of all things, was what flashed me back home, to California, pre-zombie California, vividly enough for one little accidental moment of missing it. Not just conversational missing it. Really, really missing it.

Lucky for me, the effect on Rory was just the opposite.

"I know where we're spending the night!" she exclaimed, grabbing the map from the seat between us. "Turn right on Millmont!"

"What am I looking for?" asked Norman.

"Your turn to drive, my turn to be mysterious."

There was no point in arguing with that, so we let her lead us right up to the back door of a burger place with that same eye-assaulting red and white tile décor. Not an In-N-Out, though, a chain I'd never seen before. Five Guys, the sign read.

"Okay," I said when we'd dropped our bags on the linoleum and barricaded the door behind us. "Still waiting for the show and tell part."

"Lis and I used to go to one of these on West Fifty-Fifth every time we visited—every time we were in New York," she finished in the only way that would let us all keep smiling about it. "It's kind of like east coast In-N-Out."

"Um . . ." I didn't want to be the one to burst her bubble, but even with the nice spirit of friendship we all had going on, I still had the oldest, deepest foundation with her, so I guessed it was sort of my responsibility. "Maybe it *was* the east coast In-N-Out, but I'm pretty sure they're closed at the moment."

The place surprisingly didn't smell too bad, but I was sure that would change if we opened any of the big, shiny, depowered meat coolers.

Rory just gave me the ultimate "Duh" expression.

"Ha ha. But there's one thing this place and In-N-Out have that the nationwide places don't." She was already in the kitchen at the end of her sentence, and after a few more seconds she was back, both arms full of fresh potatoes.

They weren't quite In-N-Out, or KFC, but combined with the real, bonfire-worthy wooden furniture that even In-N-Out couldn't boast, Rory's magic touch with aluminum foil, a full burger toppings bar, and plenty of never-rotting, all-American almost-cheese, they could have given any Big Mac a run for its money.

We all gathered our sleeping bags around the embers of the bonfire afterward, pleasantly full, all four of us, not just three, close enough that I could hear Rory mutter as we started to drift off, "Lis loved baked potatoes."

"Bet she still does," I whispered back immediately.

"Yeah."

"Hey, when we find her, we can take her to West Fifty-Fifth Street to celebrate."

"Yeah," Rory repeated. "Tomorrow night?"

It didn't seem like the time to hesitate. "Sure, tomorrow night."

It's a good thing we had that damn near perfect day to hang onto because when the sun rose over the outlines of the solid wall of zombies pressed against the glass on all sides, I started to think maybe it was time I stopped making promises like that.

CHAPTER SIXTEEN
WHO KILLED THE PIZZA BOY?

"Please tell me you've got some more of those firecrackers left," Hector said, very calmly but with none of the warmth of last night's bonfire, just loudly enough to be clear over the endless chorus of screams from outside.

I wondered when exactly we'd all become such heavy sleepers.

"A few," I said.

It wasn't that it was impossible, or even an excessive challenge to our fast-developing skill set, drawing the hoard to one side, sprinting out the other to our already strategically angled shuttle with just a few deflecting swings along the way, and slamming the door behind us.

The problem wasn't escaping from one tight corner. The problem was that there weren't any not-so-tight corners left to escape to.

Remember what I said about thicker cities and thicker zombies? Well, we were getting pretty good at making it through that kind of rough patch, but this time it wasn't a patch. This time, as impressive as all the progress we'd already made had seemed at the time, it was getting hard to argue with Peter's original assessment of why the whole plan was certifiable.

"Pretty much all the human bodies that existed on earth, the ones that were annoying when all they usually did was make places crowded, are now actually, actively trying to kill us and everything else that moves, and your plan is to go *into* Manhattan?"

There was no getting past the cities anymore. Just a few hours past Charlottesville, there was nothing *but* city, no way to tell where one ended and the next began.

I know that sounds kind of like how things are back in the valley, too, in fact, I'd never really pictured a city having actual edges until I saw the ones in the desert, but this wasn't even close to the same. Other than the fact that they don't end, except on the map, and, you know, the way they're basically made up of roads and buildings, there's *nothing* the same about California cities and New England cities.

Not for zombie surviving purposes, anyway.

There aren't any side streets, for one thing. Just streets. More of them than back home, yeah, but more cars, too, and more people, or in our case, former people. There was no way to guess from the maps where we might find passable space. We just had to keep trying, one route, then the next, then the next, and for a while I was actually considering the possibility that there was no right answer to find, like on one of those circular mazes in kid's activity books, if someone just drew an extra line across that one gap in the wall to the next inner circle. Or more like if whoever designs those mazes had just forgotten to leave the gap in the first place.

The route options got even more limited at the Delaware Bay, the way they always did around water. It felt like a small miracle that the *fifth* crossing we tried was actually passable, but we all knew there was more water to come, more miracles we'd need to get past it.

After crossing well over three thousand miles in five days, including the day we'd spent sitting in one place, guess how many we got behind us before we started to lose the light of the sixth day?

Fewer than three hundred. Well, based on the map. The odometer racked up quite a few more.

That day was harder. There's no denying that. There wasn't a lot of laughter, not even with all the easy New Jersey material just waiting to be put to use. It's hard to fault one particular state for smelling like death when the ones around it do, too. There was no getting away from the stench anymore, just like there was no getting away from the city wreckage. You do get used to it eventually, even that too-sweet, tangy-in-the-wrong-way, blood-and-compost smell, but there are the moments when the wind changes and you catch a hint of it again and try not to remember that it never left you.

I was still among friends, that feeling never wavered, but it only really showed itself in the smoother, easier way we rotated driving, directing, eating, resting, and other things. There were no pit stops, at least not if you have to slow down and open a door at the same time for it to qualify as a pit stop. That combination just wasn't worth the risk.

How did we manage that?

One word: Bucket.

Yeah, I know, it's an even less sexy word than "corpse," but given the choice between the two, it's the preferable option, even when the "bucket" in question is the even less sexy substitute of a gallon water bottle with the top cut off. At least our latest vehicle had plenty of room in the back to use it.

So far.

The big, comfy shuttle was part of the problem, and we all knew it. If we were going to finish what we'd started (and after all we'd been through, no one was willing to suggest the idea that we might not, never mind suggesting it to Rory), it was hard not to start thinking about contingency plans.

I was thinking about them every moment, but not in any way I could put into words with a straight face.

None of us knew anything about boats, and I was pretty sure the little, recreational kinds that we might be able to figure out weren't meant for the distance we still had ahead of us. I couldn't think of anything I trusted completely to cut through those streets short of a tank, and three years later, I *still* don't know how to hijack one of those.

I didn't say any of that. No one did. We just kept trying the streets, driving up on the curbs, inching a little closer, a little closer, doubling back and inching a little closer, a little closer again, like we still had a hope of making it to dinner with Lis on West Fifty-Fifth before it was time for breakfast, like I hadn't already screwed up one promise with another one just waiting to follow.

I was almost glad when Rory finally said something other than, "I think we can squeeze through there," even though she said it from the back row, the bucket row, and the thing she said was also beyond the old boundaries of television.

"What's wrong?" Norman called back from the driver's seat, nervously trying to watch the cluttered and squirming road at the same time.

"Nothing," said Rory, "just . . . Cassie, do you have anything?"

That particular inflection of "anything" is another bit of Girl Talk that *did* happen to be in my spotty, hit-or-miss mental phrasebook.

"Just one," I said, digging in my duffle bag for my solitary, emergency maxi pad. I wasn't due for a couple of weeks myself, so I hadn't wasted space on more. "Um . . . you don't?" I asked with as little judgment as possible.

Rory shook her head and looked like she felt more like slamming it against the railing in front of her with regret. "The camping trip would have been over by now. I forgot to worry about afterward."

"Don't you guys feel it coming in advance?" Norman asked, very kindly not pointing out how verbally *I* always felt it.

"I used to," said Rory, that slight constriction audible in her sinuses again, "too much. But I barely feel it at all since they put me on the pill."

I didn't say anything about that, but I was thinking three things:

1. How much further out of touch we'd fallen than I'd thought.
2. How relieved I was to know that she hadn't come by her perfect skin and extra two cup sizes without a little help.
3. How long that one emergency pad was going to last.

Rory was onto my last train of thought, at least.

"It's okay," she said. "People got by before they sold these in drug stores. I'll manage with something. We've got . . . socks, and—"

"No," said Hector. He kept his eyes forward, away from us

and the bucket row, but he spoke as easily and directly as if we had eye contact.

"I can—"

"No," he repeated. "Look at this." He nodded toward the nearest window at the constant background of straggling screamers. "If anything happens, if we need to go outside for anything, we *all* have to be completely mobile. That's not going to happen using socks, is it?"

Rory leaned her head back against the window and looked at the ceiling like *it* was doing this to her.

"No," she admitted.

"Okay. So we have to find more. Simple as that."

Of course, there were very few things that were *less* simple than that.

"That market in Oklahoma," Rory moaned, "gas station bathrooms, so many chances before now."

She said it. No one else needed to.

Instead we agreed that if we were going to leave the shuttle for anything, it was going to be somewhere secure enough to barricade into for the night.

Pharmacies are actually pretty good for that. Even in a city as innocent-sounding as Cherry Hill (it sounds more innocent if you leave out the "New Jersey" part at the end), even moving at a crawl through the wreckage, it didn't take long to find one that had the metal shutters intact over the door, already fortified against armed robbers before zombies had ever entered the picture.

Norman put on an extra burst of speed right before parking, nice and close to the wall, to give us a little extra distance from the dozen-odd zombies whose attention we had at the time.

He was on the roof of the shuttle and then the roof of the drug store before the first few started to catch up and the next wave started to trickle in from the surrounding buildings, drawn by the screams.

It's remarkable, really, how much ground one set of human bodies can cross in the time it takes another set to climb just ten vertical feet.

Right foot on bike hitching post, left hand on shuttle door railing, left foot to left hand, both hands to roof overhang, swing both feet up to one side.

Sure, having a bag or two over your shoulders doesn't help, but it still doesn't sound so hard, no worse than a good climbing oak.

With zombie-walk progress to measure it against, it feels like a slow motion replay. Half speed at best.

The funneling angle of the shuttle gave most of the zombies an extra left turn to take before they could get to us. Norman still had to intercept eight of them with the crowbar in the time it took us all to go through the climbing steps in sequence and Hector to drag Rory the last few feet by the hood of her sweatshirt. She'd never climbed a tree in her life, but at least she wasn't very heavy.

Intercept, not deflect. Those eight went down on the first swing, a hole clean into each of their skulls, and didn't get up again. We wouldn't all have made it if they had.

When he handed the crowbar over to me to break through the roof at the weak spot around the air conditioner vent, I got a flash in my head of one of those security footage shows, sure that I'd seen one of those dumbass criminals get a back full of glass trying this exact move on a liquor store.

I did it anyway, of course, but I stood back and felt for a

good support beam under my feet before I started prying up an opening. It didn't end up mattering much. We weren't over the liquor store section, just the stockroom loading dock area, right over a pallet of paper towels.

I whistled between two fingers to get the attention of anything already inside before jumping down, saving my remaining firecrackers for more dire circumstances. There was nothing there, just us and the disposable kitchen linen and the motor scooter and thermal saddlebag of some unfortunate, long gone pizza delivery boy.

The pizza box itself sat open and empty. I could still smell the pizza. I've never understood that, how finished food can still smell good after it would have gone bad if no one had eaten it.

I opened the evil bunny bag and distributed a few handfuls of those little explosive caps they sell at Halloween and Forth of July.

Used to sell at Halloween and Forth of July.

"Hey, we'll find a breakthrough tomorrow. Isn't that always how it goes?" It was Norman who said that with a hand on Rory's shoulder, so cheerfully that she actually tried to nod back.

"You take the left and work right, you take the right and work left. Rory and I will take bird's eye and watch your backs until we all meet in the middle."

I'm the one who said that. I'm the one who opened the door for us to sweep the sales floor, helped Rory climb on top of the first row of shelves for a better view, and then did the same on the last row myself, the way Peter would have done it.

We had only taken a few steps down the first aisle when that growling, throaty screaming started from somewhere closer to the middle, answering the first cap Norman dropped.

I spun around to find the source, knocking over bottles of store brand Tylenol under my feet, Suprbat ready in both hands.

"Coming at you from the front," I warned Norman, following what I could see of the thing, stumbling its way around the checkout counters. I could practically see the gagging smell wafting off of it from under its bright red hat and jacket. There were streaks of congealed blood all over it from an old, probably fatal neck wound.

Norman backed into some shelves as close as possible to a blind corner, to make it march almost past him before it could change direction, and buried the wrench in the back of its skull. For good measure, he pushed it away with the whack-a-mole mallet and kicked it onto its back, whooping as if he'd just beaten his high score.

"Think we found the pizza boy," he called.

I had to squint a little in the twilight to read its hat from my perch. He was right.

The little pops of gunpowder, both from Norman in the aisle beside me and Hector at the far end started off frequent and steady like always, then tapered off, partly from needing to ration how many caps were left, partly from the rising certainty that if there were anything around to hear us, we would have heard it already.

After a few aisles with nothing more to kill, Norman stopped at a display of cheap winter accessories to try on a pair of hideously bright gloves, and I had to remind him that we'd have the place to ourselves all night once we'd finished the safety check.

"Seriously, though, who designed these?" Norman turned his hands over in front of him to see the gloves from all angles.

They were purple with rows of shiny silver yarn. "They're not even in children's sizes!"

"*You* put them on," I pointed out.

"Duh, it's different when *I* do it."

"Yeah, a guy who can fit in women's glove sizes. That's different, alright."

"Think they'd look better on a girl?" he asked, reaching up to me.

I grabbed the ends of the fingers and pulled. One got stuck on his thumb, but I got the other one and put it in my bag. "After the sweep," I said again.

Leaving him with one glove didn't get us there any more efficiently. If it had been hard to focus on jumping between aisles already, listening to him dancing down them singing "Billie Jean" didn't make it any easier. I didn't entirely want him to stop. It was better than thinking about West Fifty-Fifth and the possibly impassable maze between it and us.

The last section where all of our paths converged was in that half-assed food section that big pharmacies always have, with the freezers full of now-melted ice cream and rows of chips and candy and soda.

No one was particularly worried by then. We'd pretty much checked everything, and Norman was doing the moonwalk along the freezers to the beat of the last few caps in his share while Rory and I flanked Hector down the last aisle when we found what had killed the pizza boy.

There was a reason we hadn't flushed it out sooner. The pizza boy, or someone before him, had put up a hell of a fight. Both of the zombie's ears had been roughly stabbed, probably made useless, but the vital parts of its brain were working, and it could sure as hell *see* Hector when he passed by the bargain display it had been shoved into. When it crawled out after him, I could see the punctures all across its chest as well as the weapon—a jaggedly broken electric toothbrush, still sticking out of its throat. It must have been lodged right in its larynx, or something else vital to vocalization because it looked like it was trying to scream, like they all do, but it only made this low, rasping sound that could hardly be heard through the noise we were all making.

Still got your eyeliner and skinny jeans handy?

Sorry. I'd like nothing better than to hand this part over, but I can't do that this time. There are details that someone else's guesswork, however impassioned and eloquent, might miss, things that I can't pretend aren't important to the whole truth.

I won't say I could have gotten there in time. Suprbat was poised in my hands, and I wouldn't have lost a single second smashing another skull myself if this one hadn't been impossibly far on Hector's other side.

What I had to do was much simpler. One crisp, clear verbal directive, "look behind you." That's all, the kind of thing Peter could do even better than he could smash skulls, the kind of thing he had done in his sleep, but I couldn't.

Maybe he knew that about me. Maybe that's why he wouldn't let me guard him at that very first gas station because he knew it, just like he knew I would safeguard his journal for the rest of my life, or until I could find some revived scientific movement solid enough to make use of it. I don't know. I sure as hell didn't know it about myself before then.

I saw the distance closing, the few seconds of my window running out, and I wanted to swing, I wanted to swing, but I had to *speak*, and all the possible phrases, "behind you," "turn around," or even just "zombie," all the words that could have done the job just fine by themselves all crowded together in my throat and came out of my mouth sounding as broken and useless and indistinct as the zombie's rasping attempt at a scream, and then the seconds were over and the teeth were in and it was my fault.

It was my fault.

Norman didn't see it, he didn't see me freeze, and he never believed me, no matter how many times I tried to tell him. He just heard Hector's scream, and the chorus of his rendition of "Billie Jean" ended in mid syllable. He came sprinting around the corner from the perpendicular aisle, both the wrench and the mallet flailing, though anyone could see it was too late.

Hector looked up at me, not angry, not judging, not pleading, not wise or calm or reasonable, just sad and scared, too sad and scared to be anything else at the same time.

I landed hard on the balls of my feet when I jumped down to help, swinging Suprbat at the back of the thing's head, but not nearly as hard as I wanted to, in case I hit Hector or Norman and his wrench instead.

"Get out of the way!" Rory shouted above me.

This part happened so fast that even in detached Chase time, it wouldn't have been possible to think. Rory didn't wait to see if we'd obey before showing us the reason, so please don't interpret it as complicity, the way I grabbed Norman by the collar and flung him down the aisle under me, away from the hundreds of pounds of soda can boxes she sent cascading down on the dead and almost-dead man with a few well-placed shoves.

Norman lay still with shock for just a few seconds before rolling me off of him so that he could stand up and look.

A few of the boxes had opened on impact, sending cans rolling in every direction, hissing as foam sprayed out of the cracks, mixing with the pool of fresh blood on the tiles, making it spread even faster than it would have on its own.

There was no other movement, no other sound.

"Did I get them?" Rory asked shakily, feeling backwards for footholds as she slid down to us.

Them, like she was aiming for them both.

Neither of us answered. We didn't have to.

"He . . . he was going to be one," she said, like we didn't understand that.

I looked at Norman, standing so still and quiet, streaks of sweat and Diet Mountain Dew cutting their way through his cartoonish, painted smile, remembering the first time I'd seen it on him. "We're all going to be one," I reminded her.

"He was going to be one *today!*"

We both nodded, and for several seconds there was silence, except for the hissing of the soda cans.

Then Norman grabbed Rory by the shoulders, slammed her against a rack of potato chips with a deafening crunch, and shook her, like he'd forgotten who she was. He shook her like she was me, or Hector, someone he touched every day, like the physical contact could offer some shadow of comfort, let off an ounce of the crushing pressure, leaving room for a glimmer of hope for things to start moving back in the direction of okay. That's not what happened.

"He's gone, and we're still here!" he shouted hoarsely in her face, the knuckles of his one bare hand white against the burgundy of her sleeve. "As long as there are enough people left to look for *your* family, *mine* can rot in hell, is that the idea?!"

Shake him back, I thought hard at Rory, *you're supposed to shake him back.*

But if thinking at someone hard were good enough, she never would have been in that situation in the first place.

Rory wasn't the shaking type. She only knew how to do much worse things. She just stood there, distant and cold, and under that, about as hurt as it was possible to be without being bitten.

"Yeah," she said, "that's pretty much it. Isn't that how it was when Peter and Claire's family needed *your* help, Boy Scout? Is this what you've got planned for an encore? You want to top things off now by hitting a girl?"

That stopped Norman in mid-shake, and I watched him remember that she hadn't been one of us, they didn't come from the same place, they had never had an understanding in the old world, and maybe no amount of vodka, fifties rock, and fighting for our lives together could really change that in this one.

I just waited and watched them trying somehow to communicate across that gap.

There was silence, and silence.

And more silence.

And then Norman laughed. And laughed, and laughed, this high, endless, hysterical peal.

"Good one, Ror!" he cackled. That really is the best word for the sound he made as he backed away from her, slapping his own knee like some demented, washed-up old prospector at the bar of a saloon (or as Caleb Summers had so delicately put it, like kind of a complete lunatic), and half-stormed, half-skipped back out into the stockroom, knocking a rack of multicolored condoms to the floor with that little padded mallet as he passed it, leaving Rory and me alone with the mess and the silence.

CHAPTER SEVENTEEN

NO, THE GUYS TOTALLY LIKE *YOU* BETTER

Norman kept me sane when the world fell apart.

There's no question about it. He gets full credit for that. Most of the time, I thought of him as an anchor point that would never be uprooted. We explored that all-but-empty world, waiting to find out if we were its new beginning or just one of its more stubborn loose ends, like a shipment of orphaned worker ants in a kid's ant farm, digging tunnels to nowhere and waiting to die because it's illegal to send queen ants through the mail.

Was illegal. I don't think anything is anymore. Not that it matters without a postal service.

During those times, his jokes, his laughter, those reminders of what it's like to be human, to be happy and alive, they were what kept me going. He gave surviving a point.

But then there were the moments like that one, when he laughed too hard; when I closed my eyes and couldn't separate the makeup from his face in my mind; when I was aware that he might be even closer to the edge than I was, even as I leaned on him for balance, and at any moment he might trip over, slap on an acid-filled boutonniere, and call it a day.

I knew that, if that happened, it would be my job to give in to my pesky weakness for the serious, to pull him back onto solid ground. But failing that, I also knew that I would let him take me with him, spraying laughing gas and dueling windmills all the way, before I would *ever* let him leave me in my right mind alone.

That was, if he ever unlocked the stockroom door.

I hammered on it for a good ten minutes, calling out his name. He wouldn't answer me. Now and then I could hear a brief roar of an engine revving up. I wondered if he'd found another generator and was just waiting until he was sure it was working before letting us in for another beautifully improvised wake. He never did. Still, the sound was proof enough that he was still inside and safe. When my hands and voice were tired, I took just a few seconds to debate between a dead friend and a live one, and then did the only thing that made sense, as unappealing as it was.

Rory had finished stuffing her bag with sanitary supplies, like the quantity could make up for the lateness of finding them, and stacked up some more of the plastic packets as a pillow under her sleeping bag.

She was lying on her back and didn't turn to look at me when I spread my sleeping bag next to hers, but she didn't turn her back either.

I swear I would have found the guts to say something sooner or later, but she saved me the trouble.

"I know," she said. "If I hadn't forgotten, he'd still be here. I know. Do you hate me?"

I thought about it, but not for too long.

"No," I said honestly.

"He *was* bitten," she said. "We all saw it, right?"

"Yeah, we all saw it."

"He was bitten *badly.* He could have lived for what? Hours?"

I wouldn't have insisted on explaining, but if she was asking, I didn't much feel like holding back.

"If you knew you only had hours left with Lis, you'd still want them, wouldn't you?"

I didn't mean to make her cry, really. In fact, I kept forgetting that it was possible. Even then, she hid it well, but it was several seconds before her breath was steady enough to answer.

"But more of us could have gotten bitten if I hadn't finished things fast! We had to contain it! What I did made *sense!*"

"Yeah, it did."

"So?" she sat up and looked at me with her getting-to-the-point expression. "Norman's a *guy!* Isn't he supposed to *get* that?"

I didn't mean to laugh at her either, God knew she'd gotten enough of that for one night, and there was nothing funny about any of this. It was just so ridiculous, the way she talked about him like some mysterious other species, that I couldn't help it.

"He's a *guy*, not a Vulcan."

Rory didn't laugh. "You know, there are plenty of other aisles to sleep in."

"Sorry, it's just, for someone who can have such an effect on them—"

"Yes," she snapped, "I *do* have an effect on them. Without being a dorky little suck-up who uses the word 'Vulcan' in casual conversation! Without having to resort to finding the ones who've never *seen* a girl before!"

There were plenty of things I could have said, all of which

would have made things worse, but that wasn't what I wanted. I didn't want to take the crushing feeling in my chest out on her.

I mean, I *did* want to, but it wasn't what I wanted most. I wanted to make things better. I really did. Maybe I couldn't always speak, but damn it, if it killed me, I was going to listen, really listen, this time.

I took a deep breath, paused a little longer to show that I wasn't just continuing the stupid argument we'd been having, and said, "Why do we keep doing this?"

Rory paused long enough to leave her old tone behind too and shrugged. "I don't know. Why do we?"

"I asked first."

She sighed and lay back on her makeshift cushion. "It's up to you, I guess," she said. "They—he's *your* friend. No one's going to help me without you, so I guess you can talk to me however you want."

This wouldn't have been so bad if she'd still been yelling, but it's harder to ignore things like that when they're said in such a level, serious tone. Besides, hadn't I just told myself that I wasn't going to ignore them this time?

"That's . . . not true," was the only answer I could think of.

"No?" Rory stared off in the direction of the locked stockroom. Even on her, even after too much time, I could recognize the look of a person preparing to say something without being entirely sure of wanting it to be heard. I went extra quiet to encourage her. "I was really starting to think that he liked me."

My stomach got way tenser than it should have, even with my oldest friendship out in the open, on the line.

"Norman? You're kidding, right? He's nuts about you!"

"*Me*," she emphasized. "I was starting to think he actually liked *me*, as a friend, not . . ." She trailed off, gesturing down at the body I could never help envying even when I pitied the rest of her.

"He does like you," I repeated firmly, though it made my stomach feel even queasier. "If you like him back, please, seriously, do everyone a favor and let him know."

"Why, so you can take him from me, too?"

I tried to find a way, but really, how do you answer a question like that? I just ended up waiting for her to elaborate.

"You know you would."

"So . . . you *do* like him?" I asked.

"Um . . . ew."

I tried to be offended on Norman's behalf, and part of me was. The rest of me was distracted by the rush of relief in my stomach.

"Don't tell him I said that," Rory added even though she'd pretty much said that to his face a thousand times. "Don't get me wrong, I get it now, what you see in him. You were right, he's not a total jackass *all* the time, and I guess I do like him, but not like that. But what if I *did?* What then? What do you think would happen if I told him? If I *kissed* him?"

"What do you mean, 'what would happen?'" I asked. My stomach was tensing back up and making me irritable, but I tried to be patient. "He'd sing Halle-fricken-lujah! What do you *think* would happen?"

"Yeah, I know, but who would he go to, to sing it with?"

"Oh," I said. "Yeah, at first. That's just because he doesn't know you like he knows me, and that's because you haven't let him! If you just—"

"I know, I know," Rory brushed me off. "Put myself out there. Invest the time. Be a friend first, blah, blah, blah. Been there, done that. Didn't work."

It wasn't until then that I figured out that we weren't actually talking about Norman.

"You mean Mark?" I asked. His name was still taboo except for extreme circumstances, but I figured this qualified.

"I mean Mark. I mean the guy I was friends with for eleven years of my life. The one who liked *me*. The one who *knew* me. The one I thought I could have something with. The one who, after two weeks of knowing you, suddenly couldn't talk about anything else!"

The one I killed.

I didn't say it, didn't say anything for a little while, trying to absorb, trying to think of something that wouldn't plunge us straight back into all-out war. I've already admitted that I *did* know Rory wanted Mark, but he was really, really cute. Lots of girls wanted him. I honestly didn't know how serious she was about it, I swear. But I *should* have known.

"I'm sorry," I said, but I wanted something more helpful to say, too. "Mark was cool." That wasn't a strong enough word. "He was special."

"You have no idea."

She was probably right about that.

"But eleven years goes back a long way. Maybe you were just too much like a sister or something by then. And just because it happened that way once, with one guy—"

"He wasn't just one guy!" Damp sinuses. "He was *my* Norman!"

That almost wasn't fair. Connecting that name with the name

of a dead person, the way that knocked the air clean out of my lungs, it had to qualify as below the belt. At least it made me give up the lost cause of saying something useful and go back to, "I'm sorry."

In order to convince myself to spread my arms, I basically had to decide that I didn't care if she hit me, how hard, or where. She didn't.

She did stay rigid for a few seconds after I pulled her close to me, but finally, she hugged me back, pressed her eyes to my shirt, and let slip something I'd never heard from her before: a real, chest-heaving sob.

"I want Lis back," she sniffled.

"I know. It won't be long now." Her tears made her fine, blonde hair cling to both our faces, and she still smelled like vanilla.

"I want just one person I know for sure loves me. Is that so much to ask?"

"No, of course not."

"I miss Mom, and Dad, and Carol, and Josh."

"I know." I wanted so badly for her to stop. I didn't want to remember the names of her stepmother and half brother. I didn't want the weight of dead people I'd never even met suddenly becoming real to me.

"I want my family back!"

I wanted to shush her before I could feel her words, to scold her for always being the one trying to drag the rest of us back down into the Unspeakable Past.

But I'd decided to listen, and I'd known going in that it would hurt.

"Me, too," I said, and the next thing I knew (whole truth), I was sobbing, too.

I wanted to go back an hour, a week, two weeks. I wanted Hector to challenge me to paintball, The Eagle Scout to crane his neck to see if we were breaking any rules, Claire to ask me why I played a game that stung like hell. I wanted my own mom and dad, coming to pick me up in that cramped little Prius, laughing and gasping at all the right parts of my stories afterward, telling me to enjoy being young, that I had so much life ahead of me. I wanted my computer and a double-double and to be in a place that didn't smell like decay. I wanted *people,* enough people that I didn't have to be sleeping-bag-close to all of them or worry about how long they would live. I wanted to take things for granted again. I wanted to go back to how things were before, wanted it so badly that I don't know how long it was before Rory and I were finally able to breathe, loosen our grip on each other, and look at the way things really were again.

"So," Rory sniffed, her voice going back to normal, "what do we do now?"

"Ugh," I groaned. "Don't ask me. I'm sick of 'what now.'"

I was. I was sick to death of it. That was part of what I wanted so much to go back to, having someone else to tell me "what now."

Luckily, by then the sky had gone pure black and the only real option for the immediate "what now" was to try to get some sleep, so that's what we did. The last thing I said before we turned off the flashlight was possibly the lamest making up line ever, but it was true.

"I do love you, you know. Even if you are a pain in the ass to try to hang out with."

"Yeah," Rory snorted into her sleeping bag. "Back at'cha."

I'll take a real hangover any day over the next kind of morning after.

Rory and I both stirred and stretched ourselves awake a little after sunrise, dressed and made use of the bottles of water, tubes of toothpaste, and fresh toothbrushes on the shelves. We didn't talk. There was nothing to talk about other than yesterday that didn't seem silly by comparison, and yesterday itself was too big and difficult and awful to tap into.

We sat on the floor of the protein bar section, eating our breakfast out of the foil. When I felt the extra figure standing calmly over us, slim and shadowed, with its head cocked slightly, thoughtfully, to one side, my first half-awake thought (whole truth) was that we'd stumbled into the metaphorical storm shelter of *another* dazzlingly gorgeous local survivor boy for us to fight over. When I turned to look at him properly, it was just Norman, waiting silently for our attention.

It wasn't really my fault I needed a double-take. If I hadn't known him so well, he might have been hard to recognize at all.

He was still in costume, but he had turned it inside out, muting the colors to the palette you see in those period movies that always win "Best Costume."

Always *won* "Best Costume."

His face was still painted, but strictly in black and white, in a sort of Gothic harlequin design. It still had a smile, though. A small one.

His wrench and the strap of one of our spare duffle bags hung from his left hand like he'd shifted them there out of the way. The mallet was nowhere in sight. That wasn't all that was strange, though. He was too still. I'd never seen him that still unless he was hiding, waiting to jump out at someone, and that couldn't be the case when he knew we'd already seen him.

There was silence while Rory and I stood up to meet him, more to level any advantages of position than out of welcome, and it continued for a while afterward as we all tried not to look at each other too much.

"I'm sorry," Norman said first. "Rory, I'm sorry if I scared you, and I'm sorry—" He almost gave up twice that I counted before finally continuing, "I'm sorry for trying to blame . . . on you, I'm sorry—"

"I'm sorry we lost him," Rory cut in. "Really sorry."

There was a very, very awkward handshake after that. I was relieved by it, of course. I just think there's a very narrow window of time when two people say hello for the first time, and maybe another when they say goodbye for the first time, when they can have a handshake that has a chance of not being awkward, and those two didn't have either situation going for them.

"I . . . uh," Norman held up the duffle bag which offered no information other than that it wasn't very heavy. "I'm going to . . . I need to do a kind of . . . memorial service. I know a place, it's not far, won't take more than a few hours on the scooter."

The pizza boy's scooter. That was what had been making the engine noises the night before. It wouldn't carry much, but Norman was an expert with them; they could cut through places no other vehicle could, and there were sure to be more like it nearby if we looked. We were so close to New York City that they might be all we would need later for a quick, in and out rescue mission.

After a detour.

I nodded and reached for Suprbat and the evil bunny bag. Norman looked at Rory with that same strange, steady stillness. "You're welcome to come."

I knew he meant it, all of it, the invitation itself, the olive branch that went with it, and the refusal to acknowledge the option of not going at all.

It might have been the first thing he ever said that Rory really understood. She'd offered us all a very similar invitation not too long ago.

"No, thanks. I think you guys could do it better alone." It wasn't a snub, it was a gift.

Norman nodded and put an arm around my shoulders with an unfamiliar weight.

I held back a moment before he could steer me into the stockroom, long enough to dig through my bag for that forgotten paintball helmet. He tried to duck me at first when I reached up to slip it over his rough, disheveled brown hair.

"You wear it," he said. "I'm the one with the catlike reflexes, remember?"

"You're also the one who knows how to drive that thing," I reasoned. "What am I supposed to do if something happens to you in the middle of God knows where?"

He surrendered and let me fasten it under his chin. As soon as I let him go, he sidestepped into the children's section and ripped the plastic off of one of those bicycle helmets that are always next to the basketballs for some reason. It was a little on the snug side, printed all over with a '90s bastardization of the

Spiderman logo, and too cheap to protect against more than a fall from a tricycle onto grass, but I let him put it on me anyway. It couldn't do any harm, even if he did spend a little longer than was healthy pushing my hair behind my ears, adjusting the strap, probably examining the cheapness of the Styrofoam lining.

"There," he said. "At least I won't look silly alone."

If there's a harsher, more definitive test of Norman's unfailing talent for making me smile, I never want to know what it is.

"Since when are you afraid of that?" I asked.

I may not quite have his gift, but I like to think I've returned that favor enough of the time.

We gave Rory one last wave before heading back to where the scooter was parked, and she waved back, looking half sad, half annoyingly knowing, almost the way Hector had been looking at us for the last few days. I made myself stop thinking about that pretty quickly.

We wheeled the scooter as close as possible to the fire escape before arranging ourselves on it. It was the only door we could be sure would lock behind us to keep Rory safe, and with no power, there would be no alarm.

Norman took the controls, looking comfortingly practiced at it, and I slid on close behind him, arms locked around his chest for dear life, left hand on right elbow, right hand clutching Suprbat as if it were a bolted-down railing. I could feel his lungs fighting me, all those small, hidden but sturdy muscles that gave him his almost superhuman speed and balance trying to expand with his breath, but I couldn't find the nerve to ease up, and he didn't complain.

It felt silly, being as scared as I was. Did I mention the almost superhuman speed and balance? There was probably nowhere safer to be on the road, or in the whole zombie-infested world, really, than clinging to Norman's back. Mom had always threatened to report him for driving unlicensed if she ever caught me riding with him in the old world, and I'd secretly been only too happy to use her as an excuse not to, but we had ridden down my driveway in my old go-cart together a hundred times, and that had to be more dangerous than something that actually had brakes.

Of course, there hadn't been anything actually trying to kill us back then.

Rationally, I knew that the chance of getting trapped in the middle of an infestation in a shuttle with limited supplies was just as lethal and more likely than being grabbed off a scooter that could slip through anywhere. Irrationally, when Norman reached for the bar latch of the door, I knew I was really, really going to miss that casing of steel.

"Pay attention," he said in the few moments when we could still easily hear each other. "By this afternoon, you're going to be teaching *her* to drive one of these."

Then the door was open and latched neatly behind us, and we were zipping forward through a blur of screams and rubble.

CHAPTER EIGHTEEN

TAKE THAT, YOU PICKY DEAD BASTARDS!

Riding on a scooter was nothing like riding in a car. That much, at least, was exactly the way I expected it.

There wasn't much conversation. It required too much effort. There was no rest, either, and certainly no boredom. It was more like one long, high stakes game. Really long. Really high stakes.

Norman made it look surprisingly easy, weaving between the wrecked and abandoned cars, dodging around anything that moved, but it was sort of like watching a well-played game of Tetris. No matter how good you are, it doesn't mean you can drop your focus for even a second. It wouldn't even have taken a crash. If we'd gotten cornered and had to slow down, we would have been swarmed in minutes.

At first, I was more worried about the closeness of the asphalt, absence of seatbelts, and the unbroken roar of the air rushing past us than I was about the zombies. Norman could keep the scooter on the road (or the sidewalk, when necessary), but there was only so much he could do to keep me on the scooter. Even if I'd been wearing a real helmet, there were plenty of other ways the road could undead-ify me if I slipped off and hit it.

I would have been happy to bury my face in the back of Norman's t-shirt and keep my arms locked for the whole ride, no matter what terrible muscle cramps it gave me, but I only had a couple of miles to get almost comfortable with that before it stopped being an option.

"Cassie?"

I could barely hear him at all through the air, but I could make out the syllables in the vibrations spreading from his skeleton into mine, so I made myself look up and squint against the wind.

The interstate was at ground level on its way out of Cherry Hill. That was part of the problem. It hit a choke point just as it was angling down to the water again, no side streets to cut onto, just thick trees on both sides. I've seen zombies do inhuman things to reach people, but when there are no people around, I guess they tend toward the path of least resistance because the crowd that was gathered in front of us by the bank, at the end of the downhill slope, was intimidating, to say the least.

Swerving around the usual, city-level peppering of zombies is one thing. A solid mass of them, closed in on both sides, is another. The scooter was faster and stronger, so we might have been able to bowl straight through them; though, with so many hands, one could easily catch hold of a bit of hair or clothing and pull us over into that shrieking, writhing mess.

"Cassie!"

I was looking at them, but what Norman wanted me to do about them, exactly, I had no idea.

All the undead eyes that still functioned among that horde were fixed on us, the sound of their screams hurt even through the howling of air in my ears, and they had begun to march up to meet us, ready to converge around the point of the inevitable collision. We were going too fast to make a U-turn, even.

"Cassie, you have to swing!"

I could hear the words, but I couldn't quite process the meaning. Swing what? Suprbat? I couldn't do that. I didn't have access to my arms. They were the only thing keeping me alive. Then again, they weren't going to be able to do that for much longer.

"Cass, please, for the love of God."

I could feel panic pulsing through his ribs. He swerved hard to the left to avoid the epicenter of the crowd, leaving the road for a moment and crunching twigs and pebbles under the tires.

"*Now!*"

I held the scooter between my legs like a horse, sure that I'd topple over backward as soon as I let go of Norman's shirt, just like I'd felt about letting go of the saddle horn back in my first year at Western Summer Camp with the Girl Scouts. I couldn't remember the counselor's name, but suddenly, I could hear her, clear as day, telling me to stop thinking and do it anyway.

Think about something else. Think of campfire songs for tonight!

"*Black socks never get dirty,*" I sang, and did it anyway. "*The longer you wear them, the blacker they get.*" Just like on a horse, I did somehow catch my new center of gravity, and as soon as I had it, I leaned all the way over to the right. In a motion a lot like the one I always imagine Suprbat getting confiscated for in the first place, I held it in both hands and hit the first zombie, clean to the side of the head, knocking it flat.

"*Someday, I think I might wash them*"—two more went down—"*but something keeps telling me*"—and another two—"'*don't do it yet.' Not yet, not yet, not yet.*"

The eighth zombie broke my stride when I broke its shoulder instead of its skull on the fourth "*yet*," but it didn't matter. We'd made it around to the bridge, and in a few more seconds, we were far out of reach.

"Uh, thanks," Norman called out. I felt a nervous laugh in his diaphragm when I wrapped my arms, a little less crushingly, back around his middle.

"Don't thank me," I shouted back. "Thank the character-building teachings of the Girl Scouts of America!"

That made his laughter turn real and easy, so maybe I was holding up my end of things okay.

There was something very unsatisfying about crossing *back* over the Delaware bay, after all the work we'd put into reaching the east bank the day before. The fact that it had narrowed to barely a river once we got away from Delaware itself didn't make things any better. It could only be a good thing, of course, our new freedom of movement. I just couldn't help thinking that it could have been an even better thing a day earlier. The New Jersey/Pennsylvania border wasn't the last formidable cluster we had to pass, and the nerve-wracking effort of the task never lapsed, especially once those dark clouds started to sprinkle, making our eyes sting and the roads go slick. The fact that it had become a two player game somehow helped. At least I could occasionally channel my nerves into some nice, constructive violence.

I was having trouble imagining what a whole day of this kind of travel was going to be like. For the time being, at least, Norman had calculated well, and in spite of the above average infestation on the streets of Philadelphia, it took us barely more than half an hour to find the building he was looking for.

He didn't shout to announce our arrival—there was no point in sounding more human and edible to the surrounding area than necessary—but I knew when he started circling, and on the second pass, I found a chance to look away from my next batting target just long enough to read the plaque on the front wall.

Curtis Institute of Music.

Somehow, I'd always expected the school of Hector's dreams (the one he hadn't been able to resist mentioning in every single conversation ever until the rejection had come and all mention of the pursuit of music had ended) to be a little more . . . prepossessing. I'd pictured ivy-covered walls and wrought iron gates and a sprawling, green campus. It was just a building, square and brown like all the ones around it, across from an unremarkable public park.

"We're going to have to jump," Norman finally called on the third circuit, nodding at the metal awning over the entrance of the restaurant next door.

I nodded and held Suprbat at the ready. He braked exactly as hard as he could without skidding on the wet street or sending us flying over the front, though my elbow did collide pretty hard with the small of his back.

We came to a stop precisely on target with all the head start we could hope for on the closest zombies, just a scant few yards.

Norman set the kickstand, dismounted right between me and the closest one, split its head into two jagged pieces with the wrench, jumped up to catch the awning, swung himself up to crouch on top of it, and reached down for me in a single, seamless, fluid motion.

It's funny how, when you're around someone enough, you forget to be impressed by even the coolest stuff they can do. It's even funnier how sometimes, without warning, you suddenly remember to notice again.

I waited to clobber the next zombie that reached for me, a quick girl who looked like she'd been a school athlete before someone had shoved broken glass in her neck, and then shoved Suprbat in my bag and jumped up to reach his hands. I had to kick another set of teeth away from my ankle while I hung there, and the layer of moisture coating everything made me sure for a moment that I was going to slip and fall. After a couple seconds of struggle, Norman managed to hoist me up high enough to get a good grip on the edge and pull myself on top with him before any more of them could get too close. We were going to have to set a good lure to get the scooter back later, but neither of us cared just then. Norman leaned over to the nearest window of the Institute's main building and smashed every last bit of it out of its frame so we could both climb, one after the other, into its unattainably exclusive halls.

"I was expecting something a little bigger," Norman panted as we both unbuckled our helmets, wrung out the hems of our shirts, and waited to catch our breath. "But this is okay, perfect, actually. We'll just have to do everything from indoors."

I nodded before asking, "Do what?"

I imagined us giving a eulogy in the assembly hall, wherever that was, maybe finding a piano and seeing if we could pick out Hector's song by ear, to know that it had been played in that place, just once, whatever the admission board had said.

Norman held up the spare bag and, with a wicked grin, the first real smile I'd seen on him since the soda cans came down, pulled open the zipper.

Inside were a shelf's worth of shaving cream bottles, a real goose down pillow, a double-wide carton of eggs in a Ziploc with most of the shells still intact, and about a dozen and a half rolls of toilet paper.

I cannot overstate how much better that was.

"Hmm," I said. "Where to begin? Decisions, decisions."

Norman didn't have that problem. He dropped the bag, took the first roll of paper, backed all the way into one of the grand, wood-paneled walls, and pitched it to me over the giant, ostentatious crystal chandelier.

"This is for Hector Zane!"

I caught it and pitched it back, looping it over one of the ornate rafters. "Greatest guitarist and songwriter never to be chosen by you picky, dead bastards!"

"Best post-apocalyptic dance party entertainer!"

"Best paintball partner ever to watch my back!"

"Best yearbook editor!"

"Listener!"

"Alibi!"

"Peacemaker!"

"Best friend ever not present today!" Norman threw so hard that the roll bounced off three corners of the room and then down an especially grand staircase. We went down to find it, but not right away.

The Institute felt a lot bigger on the inside with all its floors and concert halls. When you first walk into a thousand seat auditorium faced with the task of thoroughly trashing it with nothing but its small share of what fits in one duffle bag, there's actually a moment when it looks pretty daunting. But then you get started, and, well, you'd be surprised how fast and economical destruction can be if you really get creative.

We chased each other up and down the staircases, through the halls, around the theaters, the dining hall, the studios, throwing and catching, kicking and smashing and splattering all the way.

"This is for how he tried to save Kim."

"This is for bringing the coffee."

"This is for teaching me to play Magic."

"This is for the time he didn't tell about the washing machine."

"This is for the Vanilla Coke incident."

No one, under the circumstances, could have resisted the allure of a good ceiling fan, and when we found one, we weren't about to try. If you think the lack of power to get it spinning stopped Norman, well, what memoir have you been reading?

He inched his way up one of those over-decorated columns as easily as if it had been lying on its side, swung across on the rafters like they were monkey bars, and set it spinning by hand. I climbed on top of one of the piles of furniture we'd overturned to get a better shot and threw half a dozen of the eggs and most of a bottle of shaving cream up into the blades.

Plenty of it hit Norman's outstretched arms before it could reach the over-polished walls, and about half of it hailed right back down on me, but neither of us cared by then. In fact, Norman chose that moment to let go of the ceiling, somersault cleanly back onto his feet, and take a kitchen knife to that feather pillow before the blades had time to stop spinning.

In the end, we climbed onto the roof with the last of the toilet paper rolls, just to make sure, from a safe height, that the place would have the proper, TPed look from the outside, whether anyone would ever see it or not.

The rain was coming down in drops the size of blueberries by then which made it hard to get that good long streamer effect without the stuff disintegrating—that didn't stop us from trying, sprinting and throwing back and forth, tossing the broken ends over the edge to flutter in the cool, rising breeze, leaving channels of feathers and bubbly egg whites in the puddles behind us as the mess slowly washed off our clothes. The rain seemed to fall slower than usual, and clearer. I could see each individual drop as it passed by in front of me, feel each one hitting and instantly soaking through my hair and my shirt, icy cold but with no impact on my body temperature.

"This is for always knowing what I meant."

"This is for being the reason I know you."

Norman came up with that last one, for the record.

It was right at that moment when Norman and I held our hands together, like we had in so many games before, to throw the last roll over the edge, when I finally solved Hector's riddle. I recognized that feeling in my chest, the distortion of time, the vibration in all my senses.

The Chase.

I know, I know, it was about time. It was hard to distinguish through all the normal, everyday happy feelings that come with having the best friend ever, but it was always there. Judge me if you will for how close this revelation came after the one about Norman's sanity not being as airtight as I'd once imagined; tell me I have some hardwired, chromosome-deep weakness for what's dangerous and bad for me. Maybe you're right. Though, if the worst trouble it ever gets me into comes in the form of a scrawny little clown named Norman Kaminsky, who happens to be able to take down a hungry corpse just as brutally as I can, I'd say I've got a pretty manageable case.

Oh, and finish up scolding me A.S.A.P., if you would, because

I swear, this next part really did go as smoothly and awesomely as I tell it, so you'll want to pay attention.

We looked up at each other from where the roll had landed on the street below, I studied that painstaking harlequin makeup job, which was actually pretty hot when I looked at it right, and without choking, without mumbling, without wasting a moment considering alternative phraseology, I raised my voice over the rain.

"Will you please wipe that ridiculous smile off your face so I can kiss you?"

Norman smiled for real under the design and reached out to brush waterlogged feathers out of my hair. "Can't," he said. "This is really good paint."

I laughed, the way only he could ever make me, and kept laughing until I could breathe again. "Screw it," I said, and kissed him anyway.

That feeling I'd had before, the one I recognized, that subtle, humming distortion? I'd always thought it meant that I was in one of the biggest, most special, most important moments.

Nope. Turns out that feeling was a little like simmering water. A hint of something. A prelude.

This time, right around the moment when Norman kissed me back, I buried my hands in his sopping hair and he threw his arms around me as tightly as he had whenever there had been an excuse before, but for longer. Finally he held me in the complete, shameless, wholehearted way we'd imitated and substituted a thousand inadequate ways, and the simmer hit a rolling boil, bubbling over with a new texture, a new chemical makeup, a new nature.

This was not just one remarkable, unforgettable moment

suspended in nothingness. This was not just something to reminisce over in the smaller, plainer moments; it was something that would redefine us. This was a borderline, and after it, for better or worse (richer or poorer, in sickness and in health and all that jazz), nothing was ever going to be the same again.

Would it be unforgivably corny to call the new feeling The Catch?

Yeah, I guess it would.

Never mind.

CHAPTER NINETEEN

BUT WE'VE STILL GOT A JOB TO DO

It was early spring in New England.

With that taken into consideration, it's a miracle we weren't fighting a downpour every single day. But I do my best not to take that into consideration. That way I can remember how, on that rooftop, it felt like the rain was for *us*. It amplified everything for those vital few seconds, the way it forced us to shelter in one of the dorms for two hours afterward, waiting for the fireworks to dry out, reenacting that first kiss and recounting every earlier opportunity we would have taken if we'd had any sense.

And maybe it wasn't just the rain. Maybe *everything* was for us, everything that led us to be in that exact place at that exact time, feeling exactly the way we felt. We were practically the only people left to enjoy anything after all.

Yeah, I know, it's pretty messed up, a little crazy, and unconscionably selfish to even entertain the thought that the end of the world could be worth it just to bring Norman and me together. Plus, it assumes that we could never have figured it out any other way, and I can't honestly bring myself to think that poorly of us. But I try not to take any of that into consideration either.

It just makes it so much easier to accept everything else,

everything that's happened and everything that's been lost, when I think about the rooftop and the feathers and the rain and tell myself that they're all part of one big package deal.

Norman wasn't kidding, by the way, about paying attention to how to drive the scooter. Even if we'd been able to fit both of us plus Rory and the essential luggage onto the one we had all the way into New York, we'd have been stuck once we actually found Lis.

So as soon as the bottle rockets dried out and the rain let up enough for us to shoot a few to light up the far side of park, thinning out the crowd on our side just enough to risk opening the door from the inside and dragging the scooter in, Norman set me practicing laps around one of the auditoriums.

My balance isn't bad—not as paranormally good as his, but not bad. I still had trouble for a while, not wobbling one way or the other into the seats or the wall. He promised it would get easier when we got outside and had more space to go faster. The words "faster" and "outside," outside being where the zombies were, didn't mesh well with the word "easier" in my imagination.

When we were bracing for the road again an hour later with me in the driver's seat, I'm sorry to say that wanting Norman to myself a little longer was only second or third on the list of reasons that I really, really wanted to find some way to keep stalling. I didn't, though. The rain had kept us there about twice as long as we'd planned already, and when the sun cut through the clouds, it was high and bright enough to remind us with excessive persistence that it was getting pretty close to noon and there was still a long day of real, forward travel ahead of us.

It was comforting for the first few miles, having Norman

hanging on behind me, more comforting, in fact, than I liked to admit even though it's mostly okay to admit things like that when the guy behind you is actually your boyfriend.

Boyfriend. It was going to take me a while longer to get used to that word, and Caleb hadn't sped things up any by throwing it around early. I was already starting to wonder if I would ever have time to say it loudly or often enough. It sounded weird, yes, but I liked it. I really liked it.

Norman was on the small side for a guy, well, his upper torso was, I mean. But that layer of him folded around me felt like more protection than the child-sized Spiderman helmet could ever hope to offer. For one thing, it took the edge off the teeth-chattering cold that came with the rush of open air over wet skin and clothes, which I couldn't help noticing once time started to settle back to normal. Steering and balancing even felt more intuitive with the subtle, automatic shifts in his posture to follow and mimic with every turn. And, of course, it was much easier to stay focused on the road knowing that he had Suprbat hooked into his easy, no-singing-required acrobatic instinct, guaranteed to flatten anything that tried to touch us.

But like when I'd thought I might just barely survive riding with my face shielded between his shoulder blades, this crazy, zombie-eat-human world wasn't about to let us get by that easily. Painfully unromantic as it felt, we needed a second scooter, and as soon as we could get onto an above ground freeway far enough from ramps on both sides to give us a decent buffer zone from the downhill-loving zombies, I stopped and stood guard. Norman checked a gorgeous, smoke-colored Vespa, the kind of scooter his father would have drooled over, for keys and the fuel level.

I almost didn't want that first scooter we found to start just so we could ride together as far as the next one worth trying, but it did, and I knew that was technically a stroke of luck even if it didn't feel like one. It even came with a couple extra helmets, the freeway-designed sort with the face guard and everything.

We made sure we were ready to drive and swing at the same time, knowing the crowds that waited ahead. It was a lot harder than just doing one or the other. We stuck close, Norman just barely leading the way. I think he didn't like having to turn around too far to see me.

I knew how he felt. He could ride, he could fight, I never let him out of my sight for more than the time it took to beat my way around the edge of a bottleneck cluster, and I was still terrified that every single passing moment would be one that ended the fragilely perfect happiness I'd had for just that last few hours.

It was so inescapably possible, maybe even probable, that I would simply continue to lose absolutely everything in huge, sudden batches, over the course of weeks or months. Of course, I'd been vaguely aware of that trend of things all along; it was just suddenly a lot harder to accept it and put it far enough out of mind to allow me to function.

Hormones. They're a bitch.

We *did* make it back, though, thirty-six nail-biting minutes after getting the better of the Delaware Bay for the second time before lunch, to that pharmacy in Cherry Hill.

And Rory was there, waiting for us.

Not that I was seriously worried she might get overrun or go crazy with waiting and decide to go on without us, never to be seen or heard from again. Honest.

She was even keeping vigil by the front, and when she heard the engines of the scooters, she rolled up a section of metal shutter and threw open the door just long enough for us both to roll straight in instead of having to go over the roof.

I didn't park quite as smoothly as Norman did. I knocked over a rack of hairclips, nothing useful or messy, at least, and Rory had to break a zombie's hand in the door before she could get it locked again, but other than that, it was a pretty textbook entrance.

She had everything we'd brought in from the shuttle packed back up and ready along with some extra lighters, lip balm, and a comprehensive new first aid kit. An assortment of all our favorite snacks (or what had been our favorite snacks before we'd had to start living on them) was set out for lunch, and two separate maps were spread out, each with several possible routes already traced for discussion. You could tell she'd had time to prepare every detail at least ten times over and couldn't possibly be any more urgently ready than she was to get down to business, but it seemed to me we had some pretty significant news to deliver before all that.

I hesitated for a moment after unclipping the new, sturdier helmet and shaking out my hair, trying to decide how to present it some way that would thank her for giving us the time and space but assure her that we were both still behind her. A way that would convey as strongly as shouting from the rooftops of an actual, inhabited city that this was the biggest, most real and important thing, the farthest thing there had ever been from no big deal, but without making me sound like I was just on some manic drug trip.

Then Norman walked up beside me, slipped his hand into mine with our fingers all woven together, and smiled. He smiled at Rory so brightly that anyone watching would have sworn they'd been the kind of friends you could sing hallelujah with since the beginning of time.

Rory rolled her eyes, smiled back, and shot us a thumbs-up.

And that was that.

"So." She cleared her throat and pushed some tins of trail mix in our direction that had gone stale long before the dead rose to encourage us to eat and talk at the same time. "I crossed out all the tunnels, because, you know, darkness, crowding—"

"Say no more," I said, thinking of the way we'd seen the zombies gather in low points.

"Okay, well, the Brooklyn Bridge would get us into the city as early as possible, and from there, I kind of know where I am. I've even driven parts of it myself a couple times, so that might be an advantage worth considering, but the Washington Bridge lets us off closer to the latitude of the hospital, and the streets might be easier on the mainland side, for as far as that lasts. I'm just guessing, though."

I shuddered a little inside when the eyes fell on me again to make the call. I still wanted to pull away at the very first hint of "what now," ask why they would even want to hear from me on that subject after the mess I'd made of a simple safety sweep, but I didn't.

Peter could have done it better. I never doubt that. He would never have made the mistake I'd made the night before.

But I'm just as sure that, in any upside-down parallel universe where he somehow *would* have made it, it wouldn't have made the slightest difference to how hard he'd try the next day. Not in any universe.

"The streets will be hell anywhere near the city's escape routes. That's where these come in." I pointed to the pair of scooters.

I hope *my* face didn't go quite that pale the first time I was presented with the prospect of climbing onto one of them.

I helped clear space around the pharmacy's perimeter and then took the maps a few aisles inward to study while Norman and Rory practiced on the Vespa. It wouldn't be worth the time to get her fully proficient on it by herself, not with less than half a day's ride left there and back and the possibility of making it both ways before dark if we hurried. It was definitely worth letting her get a feel for it before going outside. If she could get the confidence to swing a crowbar from the back of one, it would make a huge difference to our chances.

Rory didn't learn quite as fast as I had. She'd never been that good with horses either, but she tried so hard to be useful, to be capable, getting right back up after every time a freak-out of an overzealous swing took her off the thing, that I couldn't be smug about it.

Well, maybe just the tiniest bit.

Give me a break. It wasn't exactly fun for me, stepping back and watching her share the little seat of a scooter with him, when I'd been so happy there less than an hour before, especially knowing that I was looking at a full day ahead of more of the same.

I could have made up some perfectly good excuse why Rory had to ride with *me* and no one would have questioned it. I wasn't as strong a rider, Norman could dodge quicker, I needed to focus on recalling the route I was busy memorizing, I needed her swinging to protect me more, blah, blah, blah.

But if riding with Norman scared her that much, I couldn't ask her to ride with me. I couldn't reassure her when I didn't even trust myself to keep her safe. I could just see it, the same uncertainty that would monopolize so much of my attention was also almost guaranteed to make me turn or brake or hit a bump just a little too hard, right at some moment when Rory very bravely had all her strength and focus diverted to the closest zombie, and before I could even understand whatever reflex I'd been acting on, it would be over.

That wasn't going to happen. Not again. There was no way I was going to track Lis down now only to deliver horrible news. And it wasn't just for Lis. I wasn't going to lose Rory. Not then, not like that, not after Hector and Peter and everyone else. No hormonal rush of envy was going to change my mind on that point.

Norman would drive all the more carefully with Rory to consider and to fight for him, and I could cut the easiest, most direct path for them in advance once I knew where I was going.

In retrospect, it was a slightly selfish decision, maybe completely, but I was going to make damn sure if anyone had to fall short of making it to that hospital, it was going to be the one in the lead on the pizza scooter, Suprbat in hand.

Knowing what it was like to watch Norman ride through clusters of zombies, close enough to see but too far to reach, made the seating arrangement a little easier to swallow, too. That's probably the best thing you can say about zombies. They put everything else in perspective.

Leaving the pharmacy wasn't like leaving any of our other shelters.

There was none of that cold but tidy feeling that always went with packing up everything we could possibly need, looking back, and knowing we would never see a place again, that no one would ever know or care that we had been there in the first place.

This time we were prepared for a two way trip. We packed up

the bare minimum to carry on our backs, just two days' worth of food and water, hopefully overkill, heavy jackets, a necessity I'd quickly come to appreciate, maps, weapons, the first aid kit, although the odds of anything happening that would make it useful but leave us a chance to use it were next to zero.

I carried more or less what I'd carried since the beginning—Suprbat and the evil bunny bag filled with the remaining explosives, trail mix, and Peter's journal.

The rest we piled in the corner farthest from the blood, the melted ice cream, and the rain puddle under the hole I'd made in the ceiling, preserving it for later, wondering when, if, and under what circumstances we'd get to make use of it.

At least, I was wondering that.

It probably shouldn't have taken us as long as it did to sort things, especially not after Rory's prep work. Maybe I didn't need all the time I took with the maps either. My memory's not photographic, but it's pretty good. There was no way I'd ever absorb all the information jumbled on that paper, and the important details I could pick out were pretty well locked in within about twenty minutes. Rory probably didn't get much out of riding after the first fifteen, at least nothing that wouldn't take days more on top of that to become useful.

But after almost a week of racing from one coast to the other, resenting and ultimately conquering every setback and obstacle, once the end was finally within reach, no one really, completely wanted to take that next step onto the home stretch.

It wasn't just the question of whether or not we'd make it back to that temporary home base and the Graceland shuttle that could take us more comfortably west. We set off at the beginning of every day wondering to some degree whether or not we'd live to see the end of it. It was the certainty that this time, if we did, we would come back finally knowing how this whole rescue mission ended, one way or another.

When we couldn't stall any longer without being reduced to talking about why, we lined up by the fire escape once more, two scooters this time, me wobbling alone on the front one, hand ready on the bar of the door.

When Rory started to hyperventilate behind me, I resisted the urge to turn around to look and just pretended to spend a few extra moments adjusting my position.

Norman rocked the Vespa back on one wheel for a moment with a harmless, out-of-gear engine rev, holding Rory on securely by the hand she had twisted into the fabric of his shirt and landing back on the front tire with such control that it hardly bounced.

If it had been me, I would have laughed, even if it was only a half-mad, nervous laugh. It would have broken the tension, maybe even reassured me, but Rory screamed bloody murder, dropped the crowbar with an echoing clatter, and wrapped him in a two-armed death grip so tight that he actually choked while she returned to her terrified gasping.

"Sorry," Norman wheezed and patted her awkwardly on the hand. "It's okay. I'm sorry."

He sounded more shaken by guilt than suffocation, and after that attempt at encouragement didn't work, he looked completely lost for what to do next.

I dismounted to pick up the crowbar for her, but she wouldn't move enough to take it back right away.

It was hard to hear through her panic, but she was muttering something that sounded like, "This is it."

Like I said, the scooters were really the least scary part of that day.

"Hey," I said, "at least they still haven't been able to make *you* run for a therapist."

That made her look up enough to glare at me for joking at Lis's expense, like she was Unspeakable, or at least beyond reproach.

Like a dead person.

After a second or two, she faltered a little, and she didn't try to put the glare into words, but she didn't drop it either.

Nor did I.

"It must have been awful for her, watching the whole world fill up with disgusting things after running this far just to be away from one. I bet she really hates them."

I'm not sure where I got that. It had never occurred to me before to hate zombies. What they'd made the world into, maybe, in my lower moments, but not zombies themselves, not really. That would be like declaring a bitter rivalry with magnetic north, or asking an earthquake to the prom. They don't think or plot or feel vindictive satisfaction. You can see in their dead eyes that they don't. They just do what they do, and I trick and kill and hide from them because that's what *I* do. Sometimes it's scary, sometimes it's fun—it's never personal. But once I'd said it, I was sure I was right. Lis, who hated bees, snakes, spiders, and even rats with such a fierce passion, would despise zombies almost beyond consolation.

And whatever Lis felt, Rory could sympathize with.

I couldn't see Norman's face through the helmet's shield, but the angle of his head was apprehensive.

I pushed back my own helmet and went on.

"It's bad enough that they even have to exist, but so many of them, so close to her? Making everything dirty, getting in her way, stopping her from going home to a long, hot shower. That's the only thing that could make her feel better after a day like last week, isn't it?"

Rory didn't need any coaxing to get her to snatch back the crowbar the next time I offered it, although the I-don't-care-if-you-hit-me technique for making myself get close enough to her was a little more challenging that time.

"Just think about that beautiful cracking sound they make when you hit them," I said before taking my seat again.

That beautiful cracking sound. I wasn't sure exactly when I'd gotten so fond of it, but it was definitely the best thing for *me* to think about when I secured my helmet again, turned the key in the ignition, and gave the signal. I tripped open the door latch and wound up Suprbat in one hand, itching to connect it with the first sick, undead monster I could reach.

It was me against them, me almost literally against the world—just me and Suprbat riding for the lives of my two oldest girl friends and the boy I loved, and I was ready to kick ass.

Yeah, it was bullshit, but it was between believing that bullshit and becoming a gasping, gibbering mess. By now I think you can guess which one I preferred to give into.

CHAPTER TWENTY

IT'S A HELL OF A TOWN

Rory did well. After the first few shrieks, I could hear her cheering behind me as the bodies went down.

We all did well. You'd have to say so, considering what it was we were doing. If you've ever played Tetris on one of those glitchy old computers that freeze every so often and then jump forward to where things would have been if they'd kept moving, that's what it was like scooting further northeast into the infestation together on the wet streets.

My legs were sore, my hands were sore, my back was sore, my lungs were stinging, my heart seemed to be under the impression that I was maintaining my sensible sixty miles an hour without the aid of wheels and a motor, and the inside of my head sounded something like this:

Zombie! Oh yeah! Who saw the distance I got on that jawbone? Zombie, zombie! what road am I—zombie—on again? I didn't miss the turn, did I? Zombie! Did I?

Oh, thank God, there it—zombie—is! I've got it, no, wait, I didn't mean to lean quite that far! I'm not going to fall, I'm not going to fall, wow, I seriously can't believe I didn't—zombie—fall!

Who screamed?

Rory screamed!

Important scream? No, the happy kind. Good. We'll still have good news for Lis if we find her.

When *we find her.* When *we find her.*

Wait, that was the right—zombie—turn, wasn't it?

For an hour and a half.

I took us across the first bridges east over the New York state line and then into Brooklyn, so we could take the bridge of the same name into Manhattan. That combined with the fact that, despite being known as the *Manhattan* Psychiatric Center, the facility Lis's doctor worked out of was actually on an even smaller island just next to it, added up to four separate bridge crossings in just one direction. They weren't too difficult on the scooters, I mean, not too much more difficult than everything else was to do on them. There was a little extra incentive to drive straight. The second one, across the Verrazano Narrows, was more than enough to make me feel really stupid for ever holding a shred of hope that we could reach the coast in anything larger. That's where the islands really began.

All of New England is pretty crammed together, and the roads are too small, but as soon as you get onto the islands themselves, it's different. It looks like someone squeezed everything together from the sides so hard that it all leaked upward. Everything's taller than it should be. Everything.

I don't like tall things unless I'm on top of them. That much has been true since before the zombies. I like climbing. I like high ground. I like to see what's coming. Add the zombies to my natural tendencies, and most of New York was pretty uncomfortable.

We have skyscrapers in California, of course, but the only place I'd ever seen them really crammed together like that, so close that you can't see between them, was downtown LA, and I only ever went there a few times a year, usually for museum trips or if I had to visit my parents' offices for some reason. Even then, it was nowhere near as bad as New England. It's like the difference between wearing a straightjacket and wearing a straightjacket inside the locked trunk of a car inside one of those machines that crush cars into cubes.

That's why I was so glad to reach the highway along the coast.

The coast. That was one advantage to taking the eastern route. More of the coast. It didn't quite hit me at those last few bridges that the water we were crossing had become salty with leftover industrial smells and the constant background fumes of decomposition. When we did finally get close enough to recognize the ocean itself, it was a relief I didn't even know I needed.

I know it wasn't the Pacific, not quite the ocean I grew up with, but on that day it was close enough. They all share the same water anyway, that water so salty and deep and endless that even on a frigid, overcast spring day full of death, it still smells like life and summer and long days outdoors. It still moves with that same roaring melody that has been playing before there was even one living cell to hear it, and it will continue playing until the sun burns out or explodes and it freezes or boils away. Just breathing its closeness is like taking an internal shower.

Oh, and you can see over it for miles and miles until the earth itself curves out of sight. I'd never realized how much I loved that feature of the ocean until I saw it from Brooklyn. I know the escape from the claustrophobia was an illusion. I know we were just as fenced in by the water as we were by walls. I know the bodies that must have wandered into it made it just as dangerous, but I was ready to take comfort wherever I could find it. Even after we had to double west a little to cross the bridge, I was more than happy to keep following the water up the east coast of Manhattan toward the hospital. Bits of land interrupted the ocean view when we got further north, but at least there was distance in front of them, the illusion of space in between, which was more than could be said for the view to my left.

Zombies aren't nearly as good at getting out of water as they are at going into it, so even though we were just as confined as we would have been farther into the city, the flow of their attack was a little thinner coming only from one side. Unfortunately, it was from our left side, which makes them a lot harder to hit if you're right-handed. It was still the closest scooter travel ever got to peaceful.

Maybe a little too peaceful.

See, this is where we hit the hour-and-a-half mark I mentioned when my zombie Tetris train of thought was interrupted, but it wasn't because we'd already made it to the hospital. I was so lost in the sound of the waves and the steady series of skulls offering themselves to the training of my non-dominant hand that Norman had to call my name twice to draw my attention to the presence of something unusual. Once he had me listening, fully listening, I could hear them before I turned my head—the distinct pitches and rhythms of mechanical rumbling.

I wasn't being followed by one scooter. I was being followed by four.

For a split second, I honestly expected to see Lis there, newly and miraculously comfortable on something less stable than a Corvette, surrounded by other smiling, ragtag survivors. Of course, it wasn't her. Maybe I was dumb enough to think that out of all the people who had been in New York City when the chaos set in, the first few we found wandering it alive would *have* to include the particular one we happened to be looking for, but I was nowhere near lucky enough for it to be true.

I slowed down a little at first for a better look at them because I hadn't seen live humans outside my travelling party since Tulsa, and it seemed like an occasion worth acknowledging. It's like that old Oregon Trail game they used to have in the school computer lab—how you click the "talk to" button that shows up at landmarks even though you know the digital people probably won't have anything to offer except overpriced meat you'd rather hunt for yourself because, let's be honest, hunting was the best part of the game.

There were three men, two in their early thirties, one a little older, each with his own scooter, none of them wearing helmets or decent windbreakers, so I could see them in good detail.

All three were wearing what were supposed to be undershirts, all obviously new. Nothing used is ever that white outside of a detergent commercial. You could tell by the delicate skin of their arms that they'd spent their lives in collared shirts. The scooters looked like recent finds, too, especially the one on the right which was a shade of powder blue that Claire would have swooned over. The extra careful way they all tried to keep their front wheels steady told me they'd been practicing barely longer than I had. They all sat straight, legs spread farther than necessary, like they were imagining huge, impractical, intimidating motorcycles.

You know how people always say a face has "character" when it lacks actual appealing qualities? Well, whoever started that trend had never seen these guys. They didn't have either. They had that type of complexion that looks like it's spent so long under fluorescent lights that the artificial color has soaked in, the kind of hair that just sits there, generic, medium brown, and straight as a pin, waiting to get thin and grey with age. One had less than a week's worth of patchy stubble, the youngest-looking one on the blue scooter had what could almost be called a goatee, but not quite, and the oldest one had a mustache that could have been an illustration in an employee grooming manual.

I'm telling you this because it's the only way I could find to keep them straight. They were the sort of faces you can see every day behind the same counter or in the same hallway without them ever leaving an impression, forgettable in every possible way except, in this case, for the incongruous way they were all smiling.

They *were* smiling, but not in a way that said, "Welcome, fellow human."

It was a way that set my teeth on edge.

"Nice day!" the mustache called to us.

I had slowed enough to ride side by side with Norman and Rory. Once we fell in sync, we kept a pretty urgent pace, trying to hang on to some of the shrinking distance between us and them.

"Yes," I agreed, keeping my eyes on the closest zombie, in the way you agree with a homeless person who corners you on the street to avoid offering more conversation material than necessary. Like with most homeless people, it didn't work on this guy.

"It must be!" he exclaimed, pulling almost alongside us, close enough to look at Rory's exposed face. "Look who couldn't resist getting out for a drive!"

Rory didn't give any sign that she could hear him, let alone recognize him, except for holding the crowbar a little higher, making it very clear exactly how close it was possible to get to her without challenging its range.

He looked at Norman and then at me, at our tinted helmets, anyway, and said, “And I wonder who else we have!”

Norman sped up and closed in on the guardrail to stop the guy from catching up again on the same side, and I filled in the space to their left. I couldn’t have planned better for the next zombie to wander by at exactly the right distance for me to lean left and take an unnecessary swing at it, giving the guys behind us a nice demonstration of my own range, along with a fresh, twitching speed bump to swerve around. I sure wasn’t complaining about the opportunity.

It didn’t unseat any of them, though it gave us a few extra yards.

“Hey!” the stubble called when he caught his balance. “Aren’t you going to tell us what happened? Did they take over your spot?”

He didn’t cross into my striking range. It turned out he didn’t need to. All three hung back far enough that I couldn’t see more of them than silhouettes in my cheap little rearview mirrors without taking my eyes off the road ahead and the zombies shambling over it. For a few seconds, I thought they were going to leave us alone.

Then I heard a sound that I’d never heard in person before, but I knew instantly what it was, too hard and heavy and pitchless to be a firework.

A gunshot. A real one.

The volume of it alone hit my chest harder than any paintball, so hard that for a moment I actually thought it had been on target. The bullet itself must have missed my left ear by a mile, judging by which of the oceanfront buildings ahead of me lost a chunk of brick at exactly that moment.

"What the hell?!" Rory shrieked beside me.

I was thinking pretty much the same thing.

You know that feeling you get, right when things cross over from kind of creepy to definitely, urgently, mortally terrifying? That pulsing, fever-nightmare, drug-trip feeling that you know will make you do things you won't feel properly until the next morning? Yeah, the more time you spend surrounded by zombies, the harder it is to feel that. This did the trick.

The next shot bounced off the concrete. I wasn't sure whether it was meant for me or Rory. I was sure from what I could see in the mirrors that none of the three guys had the skill to miss that closely on purpose.

It's not that I could have told them how to do any better, how exactly their grips should have looked or anything. I don't know the first thing about how to handle a real gun, but I *do* know how to tell a noob from a vet no matter what the game is. I can recognize the stiff, self-conscious way a person holds an unfamiliar toy or controller from across a darkened, fog-filled arena.

The guns these guys all fumbled out of their pockets were just as new to them as the scooters.

That didn't mean they couldn't get lucky, especially at that range. I was blocking them from pulling alongside the Vespa to get close to Rory again, but from behind it, they had a clear, wide shot at her back, if that was what they wanted. No matter how dangerously fast we tried to go, that wouldn't change. I was sure they wouldn't hesitate to match us. We were closed in by the water on one side, and they had a shorter path than we did to any given street on the other, so I did the only thing that seemed to have any chance of having an effect.

I slammed on the brakes.

A couple of shots went off, but the guys were moving too fast to really aim at me, if you could call what they did aiming. One managed to swerve around each side of me after Norman and Rory, and I took out the goatee who was stuck between them. He turned too fast and too late to avoid me and wiped out, hard.

Norman cut to the left in the borrowed time, and I could hear his motor leading the two behind him down the first alley that would circle back to me.

One of the zombies reached for me as soon as I was still enough. After practicing on moving targets with my off hand all afternoon, a two-handed swing solid enough to finish it off was second nature.

The goatee on the ground, on the other hand, was facing the same problem with nothing but a gun.

Now, in the world I knew, before zombies, when people used to imagine what it would be like to fight them in movies and stuff, guns were a pretty popular theoretical option. Norman and Hector and I actually discussed this pretty extensively back then, and it turns out our analysis of them was pretty much spot-on: They're not well-suited for the task.

Guns do a lot of damage to the very narrow spot they hit, but zombies don't go down just because of a lot of damage to places like their hearts and stomachs and spleens and stuff like live people do. And headshots aren't easy. Yeah, guns have range, but zombies don't. Taking down one particular zombie doesn't become a serious priority until it's within point blank range anyway, and once it is, you don't feel like lining up the perfect shot. You just want a solid, blunt, idiot-proof tool to get its head as far away from you as possible.

The biggest problem with guns, though? Reload time.

That's the problem the goatee was dealing with. I was dusting the dried blood off of Suprbat and angling my scooter inland while he was fumbling with the next clip, trying to outpace the nearest set of teeth.

The first zombie got its fingers into the neck of his undershirt just as that clicking sound announced that he'd figured it out. He fired immediately, right through its neck, but like I said, zombies don't care about things like necks. Not their own, anyway. The second shot managed to find the vital part of the zombie's head, but by then, that head had attached itself to the guy's cheek.

I should have been back on the move by then, but I stayed and watched him swat the fragments away, shoot the next closest zombie dead between the eyes like it would make up for lost opportunities, and then reach up to feel the ragged edges of the bite. As bland as his face was, it was capable of expressing that he knew what it meant.

It wasn't the first time I'd been the cause of a death, but it was the first time I'd kind of done it on purpose, the first time I wasn't completely sorry. I think that qualifies as one of those moments when you can't expect to be able to think with perfect clarity, so that's the excuse I'm taking for why I was still standing there with only one foot on the scooter when Norman and Rory made it back around to the road by the coast, with the mustache and the stubble on their tail.

Norman had pushed his helmet back far enough to look at me, frantically questioning. It was too late for me to be able to catch up with him fast enough to stay ahead of mustache and stubble. If he slowed down, all of the undershirt guys plus all the zombies in the area would be able to surround the three of us in seconds. And if he circled again, the undershirts would know his route, and with that advantage, they probably had just enough sense to corner him.

Years of paintball strategy told us to split up, act a little less like fish in a barrel, but without the promise of comparing scores over coke and pizza come dinnertime, it feels a lot different. I guess that goes without saying.

The goatee limped back to his scooter, set it back on its tires, pointed his weapon at me, and called me a word a lot worse than slut. He was close enough that he only missed me that time due to the Whack-a-Mole mallet bouncing off his head at exactly the right moment. I don't know why Norman included that of all things in what he brought from the pharmacy, and I didn't stop him to ask. I started my own scooter again suddenly enough to make the goatee miss me one more time, heading southwest, perpendicular to Norman's course. The mustache and the stubble had gained on him too much already while he slowed to wait for a sign from me.

"Baked potatoes!" I shouted.

Norman and Rory both nodded, and Norman dropped the helmet's shield back over his face. Still pointed in our separate directions, we both hit the gas.

TWENTY-ONE

HIDE-AND-SEEK TO THE EXTREME!

The mustache and stubble continued after Norman and Rory. The goatee picked me. Big surprise. I still didn't have a clue why any of them had attacked us in the first place, but since then I'd given that one, the one continually wiping the blood off his face as it replenished itself, plenty of reason to want me dead.

Level One: ride on a scooter.

Level Two: ride on a scooter while swinging a blunt object at flesh-eating corpses.

Level Three: drive the scooter.

Level Four: drive the scooter while swinging a blunt object at flesh-eating corpses left-handed while following a map of New York City from memory.

Level Five: do all of the above while also trying to ditch a pursuing gun-wielding maniac.

It's funny how each of those sounds impossible until you find yourself doing the one after it.

One plus to New York's layout is those neatly numbered streets. They're not perfectly intuitive, but they spared me enough of the fear of getting turned around to let me focus on knocking the dead pursuers out of my way and zigzagging fast enough to be really difficult for the live one to hit. I wondered if it had been naïve of me to assume that something as small as the zombie apocalypse would make it safe for three west coast kids reeking of sheltered wealth to wander New York alone (well, safe except for the zombies, I mean), or if this whole gun-wielding maniac incident was really as bizarre and improbable as it felt.

I'm still not a fan of the excess of skyscrapers, yet for that one round of Level Five, I was temporarily glad they were there, blocking the goatee's line of sight as much as mine. The zombies too, for that matter. The way they scream when something agitates them was the only thing making the sound of the pizza scooter even a little challenging to trace.

I just needed a place I could shelter from them long enough to take advantage of their help. Then, as soon as Norman had managed the same, Rory would be able to guide him to her old hangout on West Fifty-fifth, and I'd figure out how to meet them there.

Or was it West *Sixty*-fifth?

I couldn't remember just at that second. I'd let myself take too long a straight stretch, allowing the goatee to get close enough to bounce another bullet off the asphalt upsettingly close to my rear tire. I wasn't too worried about the difference between a couple of numbers just yet.

I waited until the last possible second to take a left and loop around a particularly tall, thin building with a bank logo on top, so the goatee had to slow a little to take the turn without scratching up another side of that powder blue paint job and possibly ending up with a matching limp for his other leg. In the few seconds I was out of his sight, I took another quick turn, to the right that time, and finally saw something promising.

The glass front wall of an apartment building's lobby had

already been shattered open. There were a few zombies milling around it, but I could see a door inside, other than the ones to the dead elevators. The office had a door. The office had a door, and it was closed.

I steered the scooter in through where the front entrance had been and all the way to the office, flattening two zombies on the way. I killed the engine and tried the handle, hoping it was only closed because zombies lack the sense to do things as subtle and delicate as opening a latch unless they do it by accident.

No such luck. It was locked.

I tore through the nearby desk left-handed with Suprbat raised in my right, half watching the zombies from the street pour in after me, half examining the contents of each drawer I emptied. I listened to the goatee's scooter getting closer, hesitating a street away, trying to decide which way I had gone.

The key with the tag that read "Manager's Office" turned out to be hidden under a green, three-ring binder right next to the blank space left by a stolen computer monitor within easy reach from the start.

A zombified, hunchbacked old man, mouth crusted with the blood of a kill at least a day old, had lumbered, shrieking, into the space between me and the door, and his thick glasses shattered all over the maroon carpet when I knocked him out of my way.

I pushed the scooter into the office first, knocking over a rolling desk chair, and squeezed myself in after it, closing the door most of the way behind me, far enough that none of the zombies could reach more than a few fingers in after me. I left enough of a gap to aim my last bottle rocket at the open front wall, pleaded with one of my lighters for a few seconds to hold a flame, and set it off.

Zombies who already have fresh meat within sight aren't distracted by loud noises, so I had to hammer for a few moments on the hands reaching in for me to force the door all the way closed, and even then it didn't stop them from clawing at the outside. The explosion of the rocket against the building across the street still drew a nice crowd of the ones that hadn't seen me. From my hiding place, I could hear them screaming at the wrong skyscraper.

It would have been hard for anyone to hear me over the sound of the zombies outside, even if I'd been calling out, but I pressed my hands over my face anyway to keep my breathing slow and calculated and silent, listening.

The goatee's scooter turned onto the street I'd come in from almost as soon as I'd secured my spot. It slowed in the section right in front of the apartment building with the zombies screaming their lungs out on both sides. There was one critical moment when the goatee could have seen the zombies scratching at my door before they saw him, when he could have guessed what they were after and followed their lead.

He was going to find me. That pulsing, feverish feeling said that it was a foregone conclusion. He was going to find me, and I would be cornered.

And then a shot went off, meant for one of the zombies out on the street, no doubt, and the scratching stopped, the ones who had been digging for me drawn away to more likely prey, dissipating any evidence of where I had gone.

Another shot shattered glass across the street, opening the way for the goatee to explore my false trail. I listened and waited for it to dead end.

Black socks never get dirty. The longer you wear them, the blacker they get.

I don't know how long the goatee took searching that building. I only know that I spent it kneeling on the floor of that office next to the dim crack under the door, which was the only interruption of the darkness, resisting the urge to waste any more lighter fuel just to look at more of the ugly maroon carpet, and I know that I'd silently sung every campfire song I knew at least five times over before I heard him outside again, swearing loudly enough to be understood over the screams. I could hear him trying to exhaust his rage at being a dead man walking (figuratively, soon to be literally) and if those curses and shots hadn't been sounding with *me* in mind, I would almost have felt sorry for him.

Finally, I heard him speeding off back to the southwest.

I started breathing out loud again after that. Louder than normal, in fact, sounding uncannily like Rory in my own ears, and it was several seconds before I was sure that I wasn't going to cry or puke. I hadn't felt that way since pretty early after learning that zombies were real. You'd think that once zombies can't do it to you, nothing can, but there's something different, something disturbingly personal about a real member of your own species trying to kick you out of it.

I sang the camp songs all over again, just to be sure, before starting up the scooter again and setting off to the northeast.

Everything I did felt excessively loud, like I was sending up a signal flare with every rotation of my wheels, every swing of Suprbat.

I followed Sixty-fifth Street all the way from Central Park to West End Avenue before I became certain that it was Fifty-fifth I was looking for after all. I followed the Hudson south to it, took a left, and tried again, still picking up every little cringe-worthy noise.

The sound of another human voice nearly startled me off the road.

At least, it did before I recognized the Five Guys logo hanging over Rory's head as she waved me down.

I jumped for the roof before the scooter had even settled onto its kickstand, before any of the gathering zombies could close in, not even wondering for a moment what exactly was in the rain gutter I grabbed onto. Rory was kind enough not to pay any attention to the sludge it left on my fingers as she took Suprbat and then pulled on my jacket collar to help me up.

Once my knees were planted on solid tar paper, I collapsed into her arms, trying to keep that teary nausea from rising up again. She didn't say anything at first, and I couldn't either. My vocal cords, still the only part of me prone to the deer-in-headlights effect, were scared rigid again, refusing to ask for the information my eyes were scanning for across the empty roof.

Then I felt a kiss on the cheek from behind.

I let Rory go and turned to reach for Norman. He must have been watching the back of the building for me from the other side of the giant sign. He reached for me, almost hugged me, and then tickled me hard between the ribs, right where I'm really, really, ridiculously over-sensitive.

"'Baked potatoes'?" he demanded.

"You . . . knew what . . . I meant!" I gasped as clearly as I could. I would have gestured at the meeting place we'd all safely found, but my arms were wrapped around my middle as a shield, and they weren't going to move any time soon.

"I didn't know *when* you meant," he said. "Where the hell were you?"

He finally gave up attacking my sides and crushed me to his chest so hard that this change didn't improve my respiratory capacity even a little. I thought about the dark, timeless hiding and the agonizing detour along Sixty-fifth and decided it was the sort of story that had a nice, long shelf life.

"Where did you guys lose them?" I asked.

"Broadway," Rory said softly, numbly. It was strange enough for me, seeing one of those standard, world-famous backdrops, one you see in every other high budget TV show, ruined and infested like that. I couldn't imagine how it would feel if it had been half of my home. "Norman took us under this semi that was propped up on one sidewalk. We were gone by the time they found another way around."

That sounded like Norman. It also sounded a lot scarier than a wheelie in a safely barricaded stockroom, but her tone wasn't complaining.

"So, what *was* that?" I asked the obvious question. "Did you know those guys?"

Rory shook her head. "Never seen them before in my life."

"Then what the hell was their problem?"

She shrugged. "How should I know? Maybe they thought they were the only people left alive and decided they wanted to keep it that way."

That was easily the lamest reason I'd ever heard for shooting at strangers, but I couldn't guess a better one.

"Whatever," she said. "They can't patrol the whole world, and if they want the city that badly, it's theirs." She sounded a little like a kid declaring that some toy was stupid anyway after having it taken away. I tried not to think about the places *I'd* never see again and how I'd end up redesigning them in my mind to make that okay. "We'll just find what we came for, and then we'll be gone before they even have to notice us again."

"Yeah," I agreed. "Let's just hope they like to sleep in." I took the evil bunny bag off my shoulder, fished out what little there was in it that could fit into the category of "amenities," and stopped when I realized that Norman and Rory's bags were still zipped. They'd obviously been waiting for me for some time, but they hadn't unpacked anything.

"What?" I asked.

"Well, we're *here,*" said Rory. "We're finally here. Lis is in *this* city, twenty minutes away, at most, considering that there's no traffic at all—"

"Except for the zombies and murder gangs," I pointed out.

"Those aren't going anywhere in the morning," she countered.

"No, but—"

"We can't stay here anyway! Two of the windows are missing. We can't barricade that. The roof's the only safe place. We don't have a tent, or blankets, or anything worth burning, and look at that sky!" She pointed at the clouds like I didn't know where to look to find sky. "It's *going* to rain again. I can't believe it hasn't started already!"

Even lying out in a downpour all night sounded like heaven to me at the time compared with getting back on that scooter again—its engine perpetually signaling my position, forcing my mind to fit shapes and distances together, drifting farther than an arm's reach from Norman and Rory, too far to keep reminding myself by hand that they were really there. Those clouds above us weren't just threatening; they were also already getting noticeably pink. My baked potato stunt had gotten us all to the same place without giving the undershirts any hints, but it had also taken us clear across the island from the Psychiatric Center.

"So we'll find a better building," I said. "This place is kind of full of them."

"Cass, please," Rory said. "I can't wait one more night. I can't. I know the way from here. Twenty minutes, I swear, and we'll be stretched out on hospital beds before we even need a flashlight."

Norman hadn't said anything. Not that that was unusual, but the way he held his closed duffle bag said more than his not-saying-anything usually did.

"You're on board with this?" I asked him.

"It'll take both of us to drive," he said, "so it's your call, but yeah, I'm feeling a little extra sympathetic to the difference a few hours of waiting can make today."

Ouch. How exactly do you say no to that?

I started stuffing things back into the evil bunny bag.

"Okay."

Rory hugged me, not the condescending way you hug someone to apologize for manipulating the hell out of them, the genuine way I would have wanted to hug someone right about then if they'd been able to offer me an evening in a securely fenced-in, functioning hot tub.

"Okay, okay," I said, "but we have to do it right now, and we're going as far around to the north as possible, so we can at least hope those guys like to stick close to where we found them."

"Thank you," was all she said.

Ever get that feeling, like your brain has accidentally zoomed out of the close-up view where it belongs, and you're suddenly aware that you're only living one little life out of billions like it, that yours is just one name on a really, really long roster? Maybe that was a trippier thought back when there were more than a handful of those billions of lives still actually in progress. It's still disorienting, kind of like trying to watch *Lost* starting with a random episode out of the middle of a season.

That's how it felt, watching myself riding scooters along the New York coastline with my friend, Rory, and my boyfriend, Norman, hiding from heavily armed thugs on our way to break into a psychiatric institute. Oh, and killing zombies. Can't forget the zombies. When, exactly, did they become the mundane part of the equation?

Did I space out because I was exhausted? Or because I was still trying to process the whole human-being-trying-to-kill-me concept?

Probably. But I didn't drift too far, never far enough to stop listening for any sounds of life that didn't belong, and whatever disconnect I could get from that task was probably a good thing anyway. It stopped me from doing stupid, panicky things.

Norman and I kept the scooters close so that Rory and I could compare navigation notes. We stuck to the north edge of the island almost all the way as planned with me just barely in the lead. The water made it harder to listen and hopefully harder to be heard as well, and again, the zombies weren't quite so thick there.

I didn't want to zoom in again when the last edge of the sun disappeared under the water, leaving only the last grace period of twilight. I didn't want to when we miraculously reached the road and the gate onto the adjacent island and had to hoist the scooters very loudly over it after the equally loud attempt at breaking the lock with the crowbar failed. I didn't want to when Rory cheered as if she *wanted* to alert the whole city.

I certainly didn't want to reclaim my one little chance at a life and all its associated concerns when we finally broke a window into the Manhattan Psychiatric Center's front office and found exactly what we'd found on the outside: a complete absence of any signs of recent habitation.

But I did.

I slipped back into myself and watched Rory go from loud joy and excitement to loud frustration and denial, tearing the office apart, prying open every door she could reach, calling out Lis's name. I called out with her.

I looked around the waiting room of the institute, our mythic promised land, the hope and purpose that every minute of our newly rebuilt lives had centered around, looking suspiciously like the site of an orderly and timely evacuation, and I searched anyway, just to stop it from sinking in.

That waiting room, at least, had definitely not been used as a shelter, and there was no particular reason for someone staying at the center to avoid it with the doors still secure like they had been. There was still the slim hope that someone might have settled further inside anyway, just to be safe.

Rory broke into the office with the name Defoe on the window, and Norman and I followed. It was as tidy as the waiting room had been before we got there, the desk perfectly aligned, all the drawers and cabinets closed and locked, except for the middle drawer of the filing cabinet, which was locked open instead, like some major neat freak had left in a big hurry.

From there, she started running down the halls, smashing

open the other offices, the patient rooms, what looked like a group therapy meeting room, screaming over and over again, "Lis! Lis! Lis! Lis!"

She repeated it so many times that it barely sounded like a name anymore, or a voice, for that matter. Hers didn't change the way a voice does when it repeats the same sound, getting softer or lower or higher. It was the same, over and over; the same full, uncompromising force behind it every time, and I had to keep shouting along just to be able to hear what we were saying.

Rory and I made one circuit of the first floor's main hallways, climbed a flight of stairs, and circled a matching set on the floor above. We were back at the beginning when my voice gave out, and I had to stop. Rory was ready to charge back up the stairs straight through to the third floor, still shouting with that mechanical consistency. I grabbed her elbow to stop her.

"Rory—"

"Let go! Lis! Lis!"

I couldn't yell, and without yelling, I couldn't lie to myself anymore.

"Rory, I'm so, so sorry—"

"Don't you *dare* start that! Lis!"

"Rory, there's no way—"

"Hey, guys?" Norman interrupted us from the door of Dr. Defoe's office. "You might want to come have a look at this."

I probably would have called it impossible before it happened, but that actually made her stop.

Norman held up one of the files from the clumsily secured cabinet to show us the name on the side.

Borealis Hart.

Before Rory could snatch it away from him, he opened it.

All the medical records and whatever else normally goes in a psych patient file was gone. There was just one folded sheet out of a prescription pad with a swirly, familiar scrawl on it.

"It was open on purpose," he said. "She left you a note."

CHAPTER TWENTY-TWO

OR WHAT YOU WILL

517 East 117th Street.
Love ya,
Lis.

"I'm working on it."

I don't know how many times I tried repeating those words. I stuck with them for a while after giving up "Try to get some sleep" as a lost cause.

The address in Lis's note was tantalizingly close, but with the stars already out, the rain falling, and no prep time for me to study the specific streets in question, I flat out vetoed any plan that involved leaving the institute before morning. Norman didn't hesitate to back me up that time. Rory didn't say she agreed, and she certainly wasn't happy, but she didn't really try to persuade us either, just hovered restlessly around me and the maps I had spread out on the floor. She knew it was the best decision; she just couldn't make it herself and feel like a good sister. So to be the good friend, I had to play the bad guy. It wasn't a fun arrangement.

"It's, what, two miles away?" Rory ranted over me. "How hard can that be to figure out?"

"It's about two miles away from *us*," I agreed as patiently as I could, "and about three miles from where we ran into those nutjobs. Remember, the reason we had to take the scenic route to get here in the first place? If they've got anything resembling a territory, this is going to be inside of it."

"So what's wrong with sneaking in while they sleep?"

"Did those guys *look* like they keep a curfew? We have no idea what their habits are like! And we have no experience traveling in the dark. We don't know that about them. If we go at a time we're used to, we might have an advantage."

We went on like that for most of the evening, while I plotted every detail of our course, Norman chiming in occasionally, on my side but in his cheery, lighthearted, good cop voice.

When I put the maps away a little while after midnight, we did finally shut the lanterns off and go quiet. Norman was perfectly still in his sleeping bag beside me, but his breathing never reached that slow, deep-sleep rhythm. I spent a lot of time staring at the pitch darkness, switching back and forth between open and closed eyelids. There was no visible difference. The dark had never bothered me at all before. In fact, I used to keep my alarm clock under a pillow to blot out its light-up display. That night wasn't different because of the obvious creep factor of spending it in a place one step shy of an abandoned insane asylum. It was just too much like the office at that apartment building. It was too featureless and hard to measure. I would have given just about anything for a self-illuminating clock to pin it down with.

Parts of time must have slipped by me. Though I was never aware of sleeping, dawn came earlier than I expected it, and as tired as I still was, my thinking was clearer than it would have been after a real all-nighter.

We ate and cleaned ourselves up as much as we could with

what we'd brought, not talking much except to go over the plan one more time, the exact route, the need for silence, the empty promise to cut and run south if anything went wrong, the meeting place if anything separated us, a more convenient one chosen by Rory this time.

I'd told Rory so many times that this would work, that it would be worth the extra time needed to do it right, that by the time we were back on the wet, briefly-sunny road, I almost believed it myself. I almost believed that nothing terrible could possibly find us as long as we stuck to the plan. I was almost surprised when I heard the voices again and the purring of scooters that didn't belong to us.

In my own defense, there *wasn't* a safer route than the one I picked. The undershirts didn't intercept us along the way. They were circling the exact parking lot we needed. Behind them, I could see the address, 517, painted on the side of a Costco. There probably wasn't a better time, either. Judging by the strained look under their eyes, they'd been there most of the night.

It was just two of them, the mustache and the stubble. The goatee probably wasn't dead quite yet, unless they'd decided to put him out of his misery, but he also probably wasn't capable of anything but raving in some cool corner of a secure hideout anymore.

"I told you they'd be back," the mustache shouted to the stubble before turning to us. "Hey! Hey, I'm talking to you!"

That would have been more than enough reason for us to turn tail, run for cover, and see if we couldn't rethink this whole thing, if it weren't for the figure on the rooftop.

It was backlit, impossible to see clearly, though its movements were far too healthy for it to be the goatee. It could have been another undershirt if the figure hadn't ducked so violently when the first shot went off. It didn't come up again, but after it had been gone a few seconds, there was a light behind one of the outside vents, the right color to be a flashlight beam. It looked like someone had retreated into the roof itself.

Wherever Lis had sent us, it wasn't abandoned this time.

Instead of trying to pass them to the south, I turned to the east, and Norman followed me, cutting behind the Costco, hoping for some way to shake them off and come back.

I was planning to get back to the coast and circle around a few blocks, but I misjudged the turn, and instead of the next through street, we ended up in an alley, which dead-ended at the mouth of a parking structure. I could feel its corners setting us up as a kiddie-level shooting gallery. It was too late to double back, so we were forced underground.

There were lots of cars left in it, at least. That much made it harder to get a clear shot. That and the darkness that got thicker the deeper we went, cut with shadows that moved as fast and suddenly as our headlights. Even better, it was enormous, with two full helixes circling downward in a sort of figure-eight instead of just one.

We didn't need a signal. Norman took the left helix and I took the right one, and like finding the simple rhythm of one of those arcade driving games, we started to race, the pace quick, smooth, and steady, listening for the engines behind to split up to follow us.

Like he always did in those games, Norman established a solid lead in a couple seconds, getting some nice distance ahead of both undershirts and me. I heard a shot just behind me, much closer.

One lap.

Two laps.

At the end of the third, Norman and Rory were already a full floor below me. The undershirt that had picked them, the mustache, looked at me across the middle aisle when he caught up to my level, and I looked back at him with the stubble closing to within a couple yards of me, waiting to see if he would turn and come after me. Instead he just fired a half-assed shot that missed me by a mile and kept going.

That's what I was hoping he'd do. As soon as he overtook me, I cut across the center and started circling Norman's side, heading up instead of down.

The stubble was too close, and he missed the turn and had to stop and double back in the middle of a lap instead.

I could easily have made it outside before he could get me back in range, but it wouldn't have helped.

Norman and Rory were still a good distance ahead of the mustache, but their progress wasn't toward another exit. They were headed toward the eighth level, the bottom level, at an alarming speed. And the bottom level wasn't just a dead end. It was a screaming, clawing mess.

Thanks to its inclines, most of the structure was pretty much zombie-free, with the occasional few stumbling in from above after the sound of us. Most of those wandered over the edges of the lanes and fell as soon as they spotted one of us on the opposite side.

The basement, on the other hand, had collected more zombies than it could hold. Hundreds of shrieking bodies that had wandered wherever the slope took them when there was nothing to chase all packed together like flies in the bottom of a pitcher plant.

That's where Norman and Rory were headed.

Norman wasn't unaware of this or anything. He knew he was closed in, and he had slowed enough to keep the mustache on his tail while expanding his pattern onto the full figure-eight track. That was going to give him a few more turns before falling into the flytrap, but not many.

Losing the stubble wasn't really on the table, so I opted for forcing a little breathing room from him, just enough to let me think clearly for a few seconds.

He was on track behind me, on the upward slope. I hit the brakes to let him gain on me.

I waited until I could hear him turning onto the same between-levels stretch I was on. I waited three more seconds. And then I ditched the pizza scooter against the inner railing and jumped.

I fell barely a story, and I rolled just right, like out of a tall tree; I still left a hell of a dent in the roof of the minivan I landed on, and the sore, rattled feeling in my ankles and shoulder almost made repeating that same move seem like a bad idea.

So I did it again before I could give it enough thought to change my mind.

That time I landed in a convertible, with the gearshift digging into my hip so hard that I could picture the inevitable, softball-sized, purple bruise already. Whoever it had belonged to had done enough riot looting to save me the trouble of trying to rip off one of the hubcaps or side mirrors. Sitting in the backseat, on top of a bunch of more expensive junk, was a jade green bowling ball just my size. I grabbed it and held it out over the next set of railings.

I didn't really care whether the stubble decided to try following me or went around the long way. Both options had about an equal chance of turning out well for me.

He picked the latter.

The circuit took a slightly different turn on the seventh level before going into the basement itself, passing right under the center well I'd been jumping through. I had one chance.

I watched the path of the two scooters below me, trying to get in sync with it like you can with older arcade games, seeing where things will be as clearly as where they are. I refused to think about the sound of the third scooter or how many more turns it had to take to reach me. I didn't think about why Norman suddenly cursed when he passed the sixth level, when he'd known how close to screwed he was long before then. I just kept breathing and tweaked my aim, my timing, to within a few degrees of perfect.

Norman took the last curve before the target stretch, and when he crossed the line a few feet before it that I'd measured out in my head, I let the ball go.

Norman and Rory's heads, pressed together against both slipstream and gunfire, crossed out of the ball's trajectory with maybe a fifth of a second to spare.

The nine pounds of polyurethane landed squarely on the mustache's front tire with what a person might have called superhuman accuracy if they'd been watching from the sidelines. Whole truth be told, I was actually aiming for the guy's nose.

Oh well, it knocked him off his wheels either way.

I would have liked to watch Norman get himself turned back around, but by then I had to duck really fast and roll under the ridiculously oversized SUV beside me to get out of the stubble's line of fire.

The pizza scooter was still at least two floors above, and I was going to have a major disadvantage going uphill on foot. I was in the process of working out a way back to it until Norman shouted out, "Here!"

I had no idea what might be there, all I knew was that he was shouting it from the sixth level, three below mine, and that was somewhere I could get to.

I jumped the first level from the low end of mine, so it was just a few feet, ran down the next incline into the far corner and down one of those tiny, concrete staircases, counting the landings.

I realized when I stumbled out of the first door and joined Norman and Rory along the adjacent wall that we were right about where the unexplained profanity had happened.

There was a door, riddled with bullet holes, surrounded by some painted-out space where more parking slots would normally go. It had a peephole on the inside, warped on our side to make it impossible to see in. A loading dock. It took a few moments for my internal compass to catch up after all the spinning. Once it did, I was sure it belonged to the Costco.

Norman hammered on the door.

"Let us in!" he called out. "We're alive, let us in!"

Just being alive didn't seem to be a good enough reason to trust us anymore, but I couldn't think of a better way to ask.

The stubble was far behind and seemed to have lost track of

exactly where we were. He was still winding his way toward us at a searching pace.

Norman knocked again.

The other engine started again below us, first with a crunch of broken plastic, but it shook free after a few seconds. Somehow, both the mustache and his scooter were still alive and kicking. The sound of him excited the zombies from monotonous grunting to fresh, sharp, identifiable shrieks, closer than before. They were climbing up.

Closed in on both sides, the three of us stared at that door. The only person we'd seen in the Costco had been on the roof. Even if he or she would have risked helping us, there was a good chance there was no one inside far enough underground to hear us.

The moustache took the last turn before the one that would bring us into view.

He was going to reach us first.

We stared at the sealed door, then at each other, and Norman took my left hand and squeezed it. I stuck Suprbat in my bag and reached for Rory with my right.

Then something inside moved. It sounded like a box tipping over.

Norman's hand was halfway to the door once more, but Rory pushed him aside and pounded on it with both fists, the crowbar shifted to the crook of her elbow, her face positioned right in front of the peephole.

"Please!" she cried out. "Please, don't let them—"

The door opened inward so suddenly that Rory stumbled forward through it and almost fell.

Norman and I scrambled in after her, dragging the Vespa,

fighting the wind resistance to get the door latched behind us as quickly as possible.

The loading dock was stacked to the ceiling with crates and roughly disassembled metal shelving arranged as a barricade a few feet in from the entrance. As quickly as we'd made it inside, whoever had opened the door for us had already disappeared into the structure, roosting somewhere like a squirrel in a tree before we could get a close look.

"Um, thank you?" Norman called to the many dark corners in front of us. The few battery lanterns glowing from somewhere inside made the shadows look deep, sharp, and spiky, even more so than in the parking lot.

"Stay where you are!" someone shouted from inside. It was a male voice, mature and well-used, like a teacher's or a salesperson's. "Hands where I can see them!"

Rory hung the crowbar from the strap of her bag, and we all raised our hands in the same confused, placating way.

"It's okay," said Norman, "We're not—"

"Step away slowly!"

None of us moved. "Away from what?" Norman asked.

"Not you, just her!"

Norman's voice was enough to identify his gender, but between our helmets, our jackets, and the awkward vantage point of the man talking, it would have been hard for him to guess any of our other qualities. Only Rory's face was exposed, so she had to be the "her" he meant. She took a tentative step forward, squinting into the dark. Norman held her back by the shoulder.

"Why?" he asked warily.

Deeper parts of the barricade were creaking with shifts of weight, and as my eyes adjusted to the level of the light, I could make out the outline of the man and several others perched above us in the structure.

"We don't want to fight," the man said. "So just hand her over and get out. Easy, now."

He reached a hand out of the dark in Rory's direction, inviting her closer. He was old with an impressive silver beard. He was the sturdy kind of old that doesn't look like it'll stop someone from climbing mountains and generally kicking ass. Other figures came further into the light around him, and before I could see their faces, I could see that they all had weapons, no real guns and nothing very useful for zombie-fighting, but lots of knives and broken glass and a couple of what I was pretty sure were police-issue Tasers. They were all pointed at us. Suddenly, I wished all three of us were still out in the parking structure, holding hands and waiting to see if it would be lead or teeth that got us in the end. I wished we could just have been cornered by the psychos and never had to know that there were more on the other side.

After the thrill and relief of believing we'd won, it wasn't fair to have to come to terms with being completely screwed all over again. It definitely wasn't fair to be left with just enough time to consider the possibility that none of the psychos had a mysterious, psychotic reason for wanting us dead. Maybe in whatever New York had become after the riots, having one of the last faces as pretty as Rory's was all the reason people needed to kill off your friends and invite you into abandoned warehouses.

"*Now,*" the man repeated.

Pointless as it seemed, I started to reach for Suprbat and for the clasp of my helmet, to finally wipe some of the sweat out of my eyes and give this whole surviving thing one last solid try, but Norman signaled for me to leave it, and after a moment of thought, I did. I'd never be pretty the way Rory was— the dazzling, undeniable, natural way that keeps working whether you're trying to be charming or not—but it seemed possible lately that even adequate good looks might be more dangerous than a little sweat.

Rory's mouth was open in shock, and it sounded like she was trying to find the breath to say something. She took another tentative half-step forward. Before she could get any further, Norman lifted the crowbar from her bag, stepped firmly in front of both of us, ripped off his own helmet and jacket, and threw them down with force equal to the frustration and disappointment built up in the back of my own throat.

I would have advised him against it, too, if I'd had time to think about it, giving up that non-descript look and showing off the small, gawky sixteen-year-old underneath.

His pronounced, angular features had only ever marked him as something separate from the beautiful people of Oakwood High, for better or worse, but with a look of pure determination, they aged him about ten years instead. Add in the complete mess of hair, stubble, and harlequin paint that had run wild over the course of two days of neglect, exertion, and awkward scooter gear, and he looked absolutely terrifying.

His voice echoed fiercely off the concrete walls. "If you want something from us, you come down here and take—"

One of the Tasers went off with an electric *pop*, hitting him just under the collarbone and knocking him off his feet. He and the crowbar hit the ground with an earsplitting *clang*, a crackle, and another noise, like he was trying to scream through closed teeth.

I raised Suprbat, not sure exactly what I was going to do with it except make sure that nothing more could happen until he got up again, and then, finally, Rory spoke up.

"Dr. Defoe?"

I heard the words, but I still couldn't put together why Rory would be moving *toward* the man with the outstretched hand, the one whose associate had fired the first Taser and was aiming the second one at me, so I held her back and tried to keep her behind me.

"Let go and step away," the man ordered. "All we want is Lis."

"Lis?" I repeated.

"I'm . . . I'm not Lis," Rory choked out.

One of the figures in the back climbed a few shelves closer, and this one I recognized, too, from the background of a few major school functions. Rory slipped out of my grip and ran for the barricade at the sight of him.

"*Dad!*"

Rory's father was speechless for a moment. Then, with a tearful, giddy, disbelieving grin, he confirmed, "That's not Lis."

The others lowered their weapons as he climbed down to meet her, and they were both crying by the time he was close enough to hug her. I was beginning to consider letting my guard down enough to check Norman over properly when the crash of one of the overhead vents swinging open made me jump and try to defend us against the shadow of one of the supporting concrete pillars below it.

A second effortlessly pretty girl climbed out of the vent and down onto the barricade easily enough to make it clear that she did this every day. She scanned the scene below like she was looking for hints to make sense of the last few snippets of overheard conversation, and cut in.

"*I'm* Lis."

CHAPTER TWENTY-THREE

SO WHAT DID YOU DO THIS WEEK?

"You found her!"

"I can't believe it! You found her!"

Funny, it had never occurred to me to think of Rory as the one who was lost, not until the Costco survivors all descended on Norman and me in a downright hero's welcome for bringing *her* home. And since Lis is the one who spent their separation with other family, I guess they were right. It started with the strangers, but after a long reunion group hug, the Harts gathered around us as well.

Lis squeezed me the way you do in elementary school when you really believe that if you just hold on tightly enough, the world will never be able to pull you apart. She smelled different, and I could have sworn she'd gotten stronger in the week we'd spent apart, but it was *her*.

"I'm so sorry I bailed on you for killing him!" she said, and I couldn't figure out if the spasm in my lungs was from laughing or crying.

"My girls," Mr. Hart kept repeating. "Both my girls." He spent a few moments trying to remember my name.

That's okay. I didn't know his either, except for the one he shared with his daughters. I did pick it up after a few hours of listening. It's David. Kind of a boring, dad-ish name for someone who's got the beautiful genes stamped all over him, in a past-prime way, but it probably gave him less trouble as a kid than Aurora and Borealis, so what do I know?

"Cassandra?" He snapped his fingers when it came to him. "That was you on the news, wasn't it? Ground Zero?"

"Cassie," I corrected.

"Cassie. Always knew you were good company for them. And *you,* that was a very brave thing you did for her!"

"Uh, yeah, just give me a sec," Norman said from the ground. He was shaking pretty badly, and his knee had started to swell slightly where the crowbar had hit it when he fell.

"I am *so* sorry," a woman who had climbed out of the shadows right next to Dr. Defoe, the one with the tasers, gushed over him. "We thought you were more of *them.*" She looked at the loading door we'd come in from. "We couldn't find Lis, and then we thought we saw her out *there,* so—"

"I was checking the rain buckets!" Lis said, exasperated, still clutching Rory and sniffling. "I'm gone for twenty minutes, and this is what happens?"

"We thought *they* had you!"

I thought back to the way the undershirts had first looked at Rory, like they knew her personally. "I think they thought so, too," I said.

"Oh, yeah, sorry," the woman said. "Oh! Maria, by the way," she introduced herself. She was curvy, maybe seven or eight years older than we were, and almost as many inches shorter. Her eyes were made up in a style that looked like she had been aiming for Goth but then decided it was too much trouble. I instantly pictured myself sitting next to her in some college classroom if I'd ever had the chance to get to one.

"And this is Chris." She pointed out a man about her age who was a few feet up the barricade behind her and having a much harder time getting down. I couldn't tell if he was waving at us or trying to block the dim light out of his eyes. I did recognize the symptoms of crippling nicotine withdrawal from my mother's many flirtations with it.

Dr. Defoe pulled back the leg of Norman's jeans to examine the bump. It looked painful, but everything was still where it was supposed to be.

"Tylenol," he prescribed in a much more comforting tone than the whole hard-ass thing he'd been trying for when we'd still been a possible threat. "It would be better if we had ice, but it'll be—Get down!"

Everyone else in the room responded to the sudden hail of bullets against the door so automatically that they were all flat against the floor before I was even aware of hearing it. Maria was even quick enough to pin both Norman and me under her in the process.

When the noise stopped, I looked back at the door for the first time from the inside and saw all the little, circular, raised dents, some old, some new, from the impacts. It didn't look like anything had gotten through it yet, but it was only a matter of time.

"So, uh," Norman was the first to speak. "Did we interrupt something here?"

"Kind of," said Maria. "Let's walk and talk."

She helped me get Norman steady on his feet and then led the way up into the barricade through the few strategically placed gaps and footholds, and back down the other side into a cramped little access staircase next to a dead freight elevator. She was a remarkably quick climber for her build.

Everyone started the climb up into the Costco itself. The

undershirts would probably figure out what level we'd moved to soon enough, but it might at least give us a few minutes of peace.

"Okay, we got the part where there are a lot more zombies than people, so you're sheltering in here," I prompted, "and somehow you got those psychos really, really pissed off at you. So you can start there."

Maria waited for another wave of noise to pass downstairs before she told us, "That's not just a psycho. That's our boss." She clapped Chris on the back sarcastically, like this was a great accomplishment they shared.

I probably laughed a little louder than I was supposed to, but I had just gone straight from bracing for death to seeing Lis alive and in person, so cut me some slack.

"What were you before?" I asked. "Discount hit men?"

"Cashiers," said Chris. "Right here. That was the manager."

"The one with the mustache?" I guessed.

"Yeah," said Maria. "His name's Steve, and this place is his *baby.* The other one is Rob. He was Steve's favorite shift supervisor. Steve's got a brother somewhere that he brought in after the zombies. He had two, but one of them got eaten."

"Um, both of them, actually," I admitted.

"Oh," said Maria. "Good. Oh my God, are those *cashews?*"

We had just climbed out onto the store's ground level, so it took me a few moments to answer her question.

I'd only been inside a Costco a couple times before, but it's not a place you forget. I was expecting the same giant maze made of giant shelves full of giant versions of packaged goods, just without those sample-prep stations and the constant crowd of people shoving each other and yelling in five or six different languages, give or take.

Instead, it looked even bigger than I was prepared for, because it was almost empty.

Most of those giant shelves had been taken down and reassembled as more barricades around the perimeter with a few smaller structures left on the inside, placed in a way that made them look a lot like lookout towers. The meat section had been cleared out, probably dumped somewhere as a tiny addition to the stench outside.

Cheap deck chairs and cookware surrounded a charred space of concrete that looked like a designated fire pit. Sheets of packing burlap lined with underwear that had never been unfolded were laid out like sleeping bags. A single, no-name-brand scooter stood against one of the barricades. Almost all of the produce was gone, too. Just some apples, coconuts, a few bags of carrots, and some dried-up looking oranges were left. The rest of the carefully arranged piles of food were made up of things like gallon bottles of mustard and imitation maple syrup, half-pound shakers of cinnamon and chili powder, and one fifty-pound bag of rice. At least, it would have been fifty pounds when it was full.

Once I'd taken a moment to process that, it was a little easier to figure out why Maria was shutting off her flashlight so quickly even though the sunlight was barely enough to see by. She looked at my bag like it was spilling gold all over the floor instead of crumbs from the ancient can of trail mix that had burst open when I hit that minivan.

I handed it over without thinking about it. Once Norman and Rory caught up, they joined me in looking around.

"It's not much," David apologized.

"The looters really did a number on it," Maria added, "but it's more comfortable than it looks."

"Are you kidding?" Rory laughed. "Who cares?"

She didn't care, of course, not about little things like food and sleep, not yet, and no one could blame her. I could feel the others watching Norman and me, waiting for us to agree.

"It's great," I said, just like I was supposed to. "You have . . . so much space."

"Yeah, I can see why you're attached," Norman added, "but under the circumstances, do you think it's worth—"

"You know what?" Defoe asked the group in general, in his natural, handling, cheering, youth-shrink voice, "I think the occasion calls for a warm lunch. What do you say?"

No one disagreed, but you could tell by their guilty faces that he was suggesting a special, almost reckless indulgence.

Then he called out into the massive room, "You two hear that?"

There was a creak of metal, and two kids, a boy and a girl, maybe eight or nine years old, came racing out of the barricade like it was nothing but the biggest, coolest jungle gym in the world.

The girl ran straight into Defoe's arms the way only a daughter or maybe a granddaughter would. Based on the immediate encore of the Hart family reunion, I guessed the boy was the Hart half brother. Josh. As much as I hadn't wanted to, I *did* remember his name. No one asked where his mother was. There was only one answer David or Lis wouldn't have volunteered already, and there was no point dragging that into the moment of celebration.

Norman and I looked at the kids, the one scooter, and then each other, and I knew he was as busy as I was piecing together why these people had stayed so long in a place the undershirts wanted so badly.

Chris and Maria quickly built a conservatively sized fire, selecting pieces from a stack of broken wooden shipping crates, measuring lighter fluid out of an only slightly oversized two pack by the capful.

We pooled our resources, and by pooling our resources, I mean Lis added the trail mix to a thin rice soup, light on the carrots and heavy on the soy sauce and powdered ginger. Rory jumped in to help her mix and watch it as if they'd been doing this together every night since the end of the world. While we waited for it to simmer and then sipped our shares from a set of matching Christmas mugs, all painted with a scene of Frosty the Snowman, we ignored the occasional sounds of attack from outside. We told our story, and listened to the others, mostly Maria, tell theirs.

She and Chris had been there from the start, working their registers when the riots broke out, when the place was stripped almost bare by the survival-style looters—the kind who'd bypass the big flatscreens up front and go straight for the bottled water and the batteries. They had been there when certain other misguided survivors, including the Defoes and the Harts, had run from places like the Psychiatric Center to the ransacked warehouse that had seemed, at the time, like the closest, safest place.

They had all been there when the manager, the one who had waited for the dead to rise the way ordinary people wait for their lotto numbers to come up, had declared himself the benevolent, unquestioned overlord of Costco East Harlem. They had all taken part in forcing him and his accomplices out through the roof access fire escape at knifepoint, never expecting them to survive to join the siege outside in living form.

It was a gripping tale, especially the way Maria told it, with all the right gestures and character voices and dramatic pauses. We listened the way we would have listened to the best ghost stories if the Scout camping trip had gone according to plan. Afterward, we spent the day playing glow-in-the-dark Frisbee, all ten of us, in the huge, empty space. Well, Chris only joined in a few rounds, "to see if it'll stop the shakes," in his own words. Apparently, it didn't, but he made a good audience for the rest of us. There was a pack of emergency signal lights that could only flash a little slower than a strobe, not much good for working by, but they were so bright that a few seconds of one could charge the Frisbee for a nice, long round.

We were together, alive, and even though Chris and Maria hadn't known any of the people being reunited in their old lives, they seemed so genuinely happy, the way people look when they read *Chicken Soup* books—so glad just to be reminded that sometimes heartwarming things do actually happen.

Nothing whatsoever could be wrong in the world.

Right.

Well, it was a nice break to feel that way, so we went with it. We waited exactly as long as it took for the little kids to fall asleep between their respective parental figures, and Chris and Maria to spread out to their own space, before Norman and Rory and I gathered our assigned bedding around Lis's.

"So how deep a creek are we up here, exactly?" I asked her.

Lis didn't stall. "Deep," she said.

Please don't think that, if we'd known, we would have done anything even a little bit differently. We wouldn't have. And don't think that we were less than ecstatic to find not only Lis but so much of the family alive and surrounded by such nice company. It was better luck than we'd hoped for.

But this was *not* the mythic safe haven we'd all been picturing at the end of the road, whether we'd admitted it or not. We'd been planning for a two-way rescue mission, and the return trip had been cancelled without being replaced by a practical alternative. We weren't out of the woods yet, not by a long shot. You don't get all the way across a post-apocalyptic wasteland the size of North America without learning to notice problems like that.

"Does anyone have an escape plan?" I asked.

"Sometimes Dad and Defoe argue about it when they think no one's listening, but no, not really."

A week ago, Rory and Lis would have whispered closer to my ear, or raised their voices to that nasal pitch that guys can't stand, to shut Norman out of the conversation for being a dork. They would have found some way to shut me out, too, if we didn't have such a long, tight history together. Not anymore, though. Even without the freshly shared adventure that had broken the wall between Norman and Rory, Lis was already addressing him just as much as Rory and I were.

This wasn't Oakwood High where there were enough of us to form whatever factions we liked to fight our own separate battles. It wasn't Tulsa Zoo, either, where everyone with legs long enough to reach a gas pedal could all fight the same one together. There were adults here, *parents,* real parents, which is like being around adults squared. It's such an acute case of adulthood that it actually becomes contagious and infects the surrounding, milder adults like Chris and Maria, the kind who might actually level with you if they met you alone. They were happy enough to tell us the campfire version of the local story, but if one of us asked them a question with more than one arguable answer, we probably wouldn't get an answer at all.

I could feel in the ready way Lis answered all my questions how glad she was to have anyone with her at the kiddie table other than actual kiddies.

"How many scooters?" I asked.

"Two, including the one you guys left downstairs."

"How many people here have driven them?"

"Just Chris and Maria," she answered.

"And Norman and me," I said. "Fuel level?"

"About half."

"Same," Norman added.

"How long do you think the supplies will last?"

Norman and Rory and I had always been ready to move on before having to make those kinds of calculations, but Lis's answer was only a little way off from what I'd already estimated.

"With all of us? Three weeks, maybe, if we're careful, and lucky, and if the rain keeps coming."

"How long do you think *those* guys can last with fuel and bullets and everything, the way they go through them?"

Lis shrugged for the first time. "They picked that stuff up after they were kicked out. They have access to . . . well, everywhere. They could be bluffing with the last of what they found already, or they could have a bomb shelter stash or something for all anyone knows. Or more."

"If they had the Costco, do you think they'd forget about the rest of us?"

Lis laughed a little, a much more serious laugh than all the giggles we'd shared in the old world. "For about five minutes, maybe. They want this place, but Steve and Maria . . . it's seriously personal between them."

"How many exits does this place have? The two of them can't surround us, can they?"

"No, but so what? They've got the zombies to do that for them."

"And no one would want to risk moving the kids, right?"

"Hey, *I'm* not into taking that risk," said Lis, and for a moment she looked exactly like the Lis I knew, all soft, fragile sweetness—the kind that can only exist if there's someone else, someone with a harsh, abrasive edge like Rory's, perpetually guarding it from being stepped on. Then she swatted a fly on the back of her arm like it was normal, like it wasn't the sort of thing that usually made her curl into a ball and threaten to puke unless someone could get it away from her, and the flashback was over. "Anyway, where are we going to go with two scooters? Or does someone get stuck driving the forklift?"

"Four scooters," I said. "You forgot to count *theirs*."

Lis laughed. For a long time, she laughed at me, and Norman and Rory didn't look too far away from joining in. And when I say a long time, I don't mean the way a few awkward moments can feel like eternity. I'm talking about *hours* going by before we really got back to talking seriously, and even then, Lis started in a humoring tone, but at least we talked, mostly because it was easier than sleeping. Before morning, the four of us had hammered out almost every little detail of a plan.

Every detail except for the one about getting anyone to listen to it.

CHAPTER TWENTY-FOUR

At Least Foxes Don't Eat Grain

Time for a fast-forward.

Trust me, if you'd been there, you'd have wanted to fast forward, too.

You'd have wanted to skip past the awkwardness of slipping as much of the plan as possible into the conversation over breakfast the next morning whenever we were sure Maria and Defoe were both listening, Maria because she wanted to fight, Defoe because he wanted to escape.

You wouldn't want to linger on the way they listened with averted eyes, afraid to hear any serious idea that Rory and Lis were involved in without David's written and notarized permission.

There was nothing about our desperate efforts worth describing, no brilliant, eloquent motivational speech that brought everyone around.

It was during lunchtime of the third day. A bullet finally pierced the front door, ricocheted off the far back wall, and came to rest between everyone's feet, right in the column of sunlight it had cut on its way in.

That was what started people beyond the four of us seriously considering the idea, and by considering it, I mean openly bickering about it.

Pretty much the same thing.

Here's the plan we had:

Lure the undershirts in through the front door to the outside of the barricade. Yeah, I know they had names, but I'd been calling them the undershirts for long enough that the habit was hard to break. Two scooter drivers would escape out the back, each carrying two of the underage non-scooter-drivers. The two other non-scooter-drivers would wait by the back exits while the two other scooter drivers would hide in the front barricade, close that nice, pulley-operated front door, and then use whatever means necessary to force the undershirts away from their scooters through the barricade's climbing paths. Those two scooter drivers would then take the scooters, escape out the front, circle around to pick up the non-scooter-drivers before the undershirts could notice them, and then we would all meet up at a designated point far to the north.

Here's what people found to argue about:

"How do we know how far *their* scooters will get us?"

"How far are we going to get without them?"

"Do we really have the right to strand them here?"

"What right do they have to strand *us* here?"

"Why not wait to see if we outlast them?"

"What if we *do* outlast them? If they don't come back, where's our ride coming from?"

"How old are you again?"

That part was Chris. Don't be too mad at him. He could barely sit still and focus long enough to argue at all by then.

Norman didn't cut him much slack for that, though. He ran out of patience for that question after the fourth or fifth time and buried his face in his hands.

"Oy," he muttered, then straightened up quickly to make sure he hadn't rubbed off any of his paints. "Do we need to go over what we had to do to get here again?" he asked.

"No," said David. "You put my family back together, and I'm grateful, but I'm done seeing them terrorized. Rory, Lis, and Josh are going to be the first ones out the back, or that front door's not opening."

"So is Chloe," said Defoe, "but she's not going anywhere without me."

"We don't have enough drivers," Chris pointed out, though no one needed him to. "You've never driven a scooter, Doc. You don't even drive a car."

Yeah, apparently, in New York, there are actually people other than children and epileptics who lack that skill. Go figure.

It's kind of like one of those logic word puzzles, isn't it? Like the one with the fox, the chicken, and the bag of grain, where you have to get all three of them from one side of the river to the other without them eating each other or sinking the raft? Don't bother looking for a pencil, though. There's no right answer to this one that doesn't involve people sitting on the handlebars.

Well, except for Rory's solution.

"I can do it," she said.

I might have contradicted her, or Norman might have, if there weren't so many people listening.

"I can drive Lis, and she can carry Josh, and someone else can do the same thing with the doctor and Chloe. Problem solved."

It wasn't going to be easy. Anyone who'd done even Level Three scooter riding would have known that, but she wasn't going to worry the people who hadn't, and we weren't going to blow her story.

"Why didn't you say that in the first place?" Chris snapped, louder than was necessary.

"I . . . don't know," Rory lied. "But I know how the brakes work and how to balance and everything."

I guess that was true enough. I'd spent less time riding than she had before I went solo, and I'd survived.

"I just, well, I haven't driven the Vespa before." That was true, too. "So once we get it upstairs, I just need a few laps to get the feel of it, just to be sure."

She caught Norman's eye, asking him for the quickest and hopefully most figurative of crash courses. He gave her a nod.

There was a moment then when I swear I could feel the dice rolling. We all could. We could feel the very strong possibility that someone might still veto the whole plan and keep us there in the dark, waiting to starve to death or be hit by a lucky ricochet.

I was actually glad at that moment when another spear of light punched through the door, the bullet skidding off into the barricade and out of sight.

Then the dice were off the table, the riders were off to whatever imitation of personal space they had to pack up anything worth taking, and the drivers were on our way downstairs to drag the Vespa up and settle one last little thing.

"So," said Chris. "Who's it going to be?"

"You're in no condition to do the stealing," Maria told him immediately.

"Are you up for driving the Defoes?" I asked him.

"Sure, yeah, I can do that," he said. Then he looked at Norman and me like we hadn't been right in front of him for days already, like he was noticing our ages all over again. "But shouldn't one of you get dibs on—"

"No," said Norman. "We're not splitting up. That's *my* condition."

I tried not to show how relieved I was that he'd been the first to insist on that.

"I could spend the rest of my life on some rooftop waiting for her to find someone to get directions from," he added. My sense of direction was a little better than his, and we both knew it, but Chris and Maria didn't need to know that his reasons were less than a hundred percent practical.

"Fine," said Chris. "No one's gotta twist my arm."

"Okay," I said, "that leaves two of us to steal, and one of us to wait with David."

"If we're going to take those bastards down a peg, *I'm* taking a front row seat," Maria declared.

"Hey," I said, "it is *our* second scooter, our fireworks—"

"Stop that," said Maria. "Right now. I mean it. *I* get to be there to tell Steve he got played, or I'm not playing at all."

"Okay, okay."

Norman and I looked at each other for a long moment over the seat of the Vespa while it was lodged in one of the sharp turns of the stairs, knowing that in a few hours, one of us would be helping Maria open the roll-down shutter to face Steve and Rob, the mustache and the stubble, up close and in person, one last time, and the other would be left hiding in the dark with nothing but a signal light, waiting for a ride, safer, but utterly helpless to influence the outcome.

I started with the best argument I could think of, which wasn't much of an argument at all.

"Your leg—"

"It's a *bruise,* Cass. You've seen me handle worse."

"But where it is, it could affect your range of motion."

"Maybe a little," he agreed. "But I could *lose* a leg, and an eye, and most of my fingers *and* drop cheap acid all on the same day, and I'd still be the best rider here."

I wasn't going to claim that he was wrong about that.

"It was my idea," I said.

Cheap shot, I know, but I had to try it. It didn't work.

"Flip you for it," Norman offered in a firm, take-it-or-leave-it tone.

I nodded, thinking that was the best I was going to get, and he felt automatically for the non-existent pockets of the inside-out costume. We hadn't had much reason to carry change around recently.

An idea struck me before he could ask Chris or Maria if they had any coins left.

"Rock, Paper, Scissors?" I offered, and he agreed.

Now, out of all the humiliating, incriminating, soul-baring pieces there are of the whole truth, this is the one I came closest to keeping to myself, the one I tried hardest to come up with a reason why it didn't count, but of course I know it does.

That's sort of where the whole "confessions" part of this story comes in, isn't it?

This one doesn't involve stupid excesses of tears or petty jealous feelings or failures of physical accuracy. Those are all proud memories by comparison, shining demonstrations of strength and moral fiber.

The whole truth is that Norman favors Scissors. *Heavily*. The whole truth is that I knew before I suggested it, before we raised our fists, that I wasn't going to open mine on the third beat, and that my chances of getting my way were a lot closer to ninety-five percent than fifty.

I didn't smile when I won. I didn't joke or rub it in. I wanted to apologize. Not badly enough that I would have offered him best out of three, not for all the KFC and double-doubles there had ever been in the world.

Norman *did* force a chuckle.

"Hey, it's okay." He shook me by the shoulder a little, like he was trying to loosen up my expression by hand. "You win. It's Rock, Paper, Scissors, not Russian Roulette."

I wanted something more. I wasn't sure what, exactly. I wanted something to make it okay, something more than an agreement to *call* it okay, before I collected my winnings. Even if there had been a way to do that, we didn't have the opportunity to find it.

Once the four of us finally got the Vespa set on its wheels on the main floor, miraculously still in one piece, we didn't even really get to catch our breaths before jumping into the rest of the preparations.

Maria and I divided up the remains of my fireworks stash and the open two pack of lighter fluid and tore down some of the front of the barricade to make one of the openings easier and more tempting for the undershirts to climb through. Norman quickly helped me transfer everything heavier than Peter's journal from my bag to his, and Chris reluctantly agreed to leave us his lighter and pick up another on the road. I knew I'd had two when we left the pharmacy, but if that was the only thing I'd lost in the chaos since then, I figured I'd gotten off pretty easy. The meeting place was set, all knowledge of the area and the possible routes checked and double-checked among all the drivers. Norman and Rory took the Vespa aside for the quietest hour of private coaching they could manage, thankfully during the loudest, most distracted hour of debate over what was really necessary to bring along.

I'd been hoping to steal Norman away for at least a few minutes once Rory graduated to solo practice (which she did remarkably smoothly; determination does amazing things), but Josh and Chloe got to him first. I guess when you're nine, restless, nervous, and being ignored by your families while they deal with the life-and-death situation that has you restless and nervous in the first place, you naturally go straight for the guy in the clown costume. He'd gone with the Harlequin design still for the last couple of days, a simpler version of it, but still a sign of mourning. Given the circumstances, I guess it was close enough to a clown as far as the kids were concerned.

He spent most of the rest of the prep time helping them blow up a bag of those long, thin party balloons, which wouldn't have interested any kind of looter.

At the same time, Norman kept one eye on anyone sorting supplies. Anything heavy or ungainly that made the cut to be brought along, he volunteered the space in his duffle, including the two cans of kerosene that had been saved since the riots because between his body and mine, ours was going to be the least overloaded of the scooters once we got going. He kept the crowbar and gave Rory the wrench. It was nice and manageable for her to swing while driving since Lis would be occupied with Josh. Chris and Maria took the sturdiest bars of metal they could from the shelving, and I shoved Suprbat to the bottom of my bag, out of the way, more for comfort than for the short ride around the building when I might actually need to use it.

When the gunfire started, right on schedule, announcing that our window had opened, Lis was the one who asked the inevitable question, "Are you sure about this?"

And it was her dad she stuck with the job of saying, "No. Do it anyway."

Rory and Lis both tried to hug me as if they weren't even sort of wondering if it was for the last time—when they hugged Norman, too, it kind of shattered the illusion.

"See you at dinner," they told their dad in that freaky twin unison they'd barely used in years. They gathered Josh up between them on the Vespa at their designated exit, in the opposite corner from Chris and the Defoes.

Even though we were going to be in the same building the whole time, I really wanted to say *something* meaningful to Norman before getting things started. I looked at the pile of rejected supplies on the floor where he'd packed his bag, and I was almost glad that something kind of important had been forgotten because it gave me an excuse.

I picked up the rainbow-colored box of face paints and brought it over to him.

"You could use a touchup before curtain call," I said.

He took the box and opened it to the mirror.

"Yeah, you're right."

He opened one of the individually wrapped wet wipes in the side pocket, the specialized ones that smell like nail polish remover, and started cleaning off the design.

He always rushed that process, even when we weren't on such an urgent deadline, so I'd learned to value the glimpses of his real face. He hadn't shown it at all in front of me, never mind anyone else, on the few mornings since he'd become my boyfriend, since Hector had died. I took the opportunity to look closer this time, memorizing him all over again. It felt like he'd aged years instead of days since the last time.

I absorbed as much of him as I could before he picked up the colored paints to cover himself in the old, coulrophobia-inducing, zombie-worthy layer again.

Only he didn't.

Instead he gathered up the colors, two at a time, and pitched them through one of the broken back windows, just below the ceiling. Some made it, others smashed and splattered against the wall.

I didn't ask the question, but I guess my face did because he leaned close and whispered the answer.

"Because whenever this ride finally lets off, parts of it have already been even more awesome than the birth of a zombie clown."

Then he kissed me, perfectly and completely, right there in front of everyone, without tickling or tackling, as if there weren't a captive audience right there, as if there were nothing at all but us. When he pulled away, I almost wanted the moment to end in a truly tasteless punch line to make me feel a little sturdier around the knees when we turned to take our places at opposite ends of the warehouse.

I climbed into my perch in the barricade across the main doorway from Maria. When she looked over to see if I was ready, she was grinning like we were about to open an extra-large

Christmas present instead of a potential deathtrap. I took one breath—a long breath, but only one—to remember that Norman was a safe-ish distance away and well-hidden before I gave her a nod. We each took one of the chains attached to the big, rolling front door, and pulled.

CHAPTER TWENTY-FIVE

THIS SHOOTOUT BROUGHT TO YOU BY THE LETTER F

I'd set my fair share of traps before. They're one of those things that actually translate pretty well from games to reality. If anything, they're easier in real life because people are *expecting* them in games.

Even so, we did it right. We opened the door a crack, enough to make it look like a tempting accident. We waited for the sound of the scooters to pass by close enough before shouting out.

"It happened again!" I started. "Were you watching? Who was watching?"

"Just help me get it closed!" Maria snapped back at me, and we both rattled the door up and down a little, to make it look like someone was trying to pull it shut but couldn't figure out what it was getting caught on.

"Are you pushing or pulling?"

We kept the squabbling up at a nice, natural pace while we waited for the scooters to stop, a few gunshots to clear away the closest zombies, and two pairs of living human hands to grab the bottom of the shutter.

"We got them!" Steve shouted to Rob. "Pull!"

I clicked off the dim lantern, and Maria and I held the chains for a few more seconds to put up a convincing struggle, then dropped them to retreat one shelf higher into the barricade, thoroughly hidden in the shadows, even when the door screeched open a good seven feet, letting in sunlight.

Steve and Rob charged in, guns blazing, almost literally, and screeched to a stop in front of the barricade. For a few seconds, they both scanned the dark, looking for whoever they'd been hearing or a way to push in further without going on foot.

There wasn't one. I had made double sure of that.

We had them, and it was so, so tempting to slam the door shut again right then, but I followed the plan. I lit the first string of firecrackers and dropped it between them and the exit. I reached one hand down to hold the chain, in case they tried to go around and get back out. They didn't. They just ducked and covered behind the scooters when it went off. The zombies outside must have been ambling in our direction anyway after the noise we'd made with the door, but after a few seconds of the constant volume of the firecrackers, half a dozen poured inside at full speed, shrieking as loudly as their varying degrees of internal decomposition allowed. I waited for the last body, a huge one in a formerly white business shirt, to make it inside before I pulled up on the chain. Maria followed my lead, trapping all the different things that were making me so uncomfortably nervous together with a metallic *slam.*

Across the warehouse, the other drivers heard their cue and slipped out through the emergency exits with nothing but two quick ignition purrs. Then it was just Norman and David left waiting for us.

Go on.

Yeah, I heckle people in my head when I'm anxious. Try to tell me you don't.

The gap's right there. Climb through to where it's safe.

Steve and Rob stayed and fought on the door side of the barricade longer and harder than I'd hoped, but not much better. With their headlights on, even with the door closed, there was decent light, but between them, they still managed to spend eleven shots and only finish three of the zombies.

One of the ones they missed completely, a woman in a supermarket apron with a pair of kitchen scissors lodged in her stomach, lunged at Rob. He managed to knock it down and drop the front wheel of his scooter on its head a few times until it squashed out of shape.

I hated to admit it, but it looked like they might actually beat the whole infestation without having to escape, as clumsy as they were at it.

That was okay. We could give them plenty of other reasons to get out of the entranceway.

I picked out one of those really flashy backyard fireworks from the bottom of the evil bunny bag, the kind that sends off multicolored pinwheels in every direction. Caterpillar's Pipe, the label on the side said.

I lit it and let go.

Don't just scream, I thought at them. *Get away from it. Go inside.*

Clusters of sparks hit the wall on one side and the barricade on the other, leaving deep scorch marks on everything they touched in between.

Maria followed it up with a shower of broken bottles and a squirt of lighter fluid, carefully aimed away from the scooters' tires, which made the last two zombies' clothes go up in flames.

That might finally have done the trick, I'm not sure, but it *might* have, if she hadn't burst out laughing over the girly little yelp Steve gave when the bits of glass went down the back of his undershirt.

But to be fair, it was a *really* funny yelp.

He squinted up into the shadows, one hand shielding his eyes from falling bits.

"Hello, Maria," he recognized her and finally started climbing the barricade, but not in the way we'd planned. He was climbing *up* instead of through.

Hey, you didn't think I'd waste time explaining the plan in advance if anything had actually gone according to it, did you?

He got just high enough, just fast enough, to be out of the bigger burning zombie's reach when it tried for him. The smaller one went for Rob and took his last two bullets. Last loaded ones, anyway. I almost shuddered out loud when he reloaded out of his backpack and I saw how heavy it was.

"Maria!" Steve called out again, and I could hear Maria cursing deeper in the shadows than before.

Rob backed all the way into the barricade, away from the ash and heat coming off of the big zombie, before finally shooting it down, strafing around it, and climbing up after Steve.

Steve found a flat section of shelving to crouch down on and do a reload of his own. He fired once, straight up, in Maria's general direction, and she emptied another box of glass over the edge on him.

In case I haven't made this clear enough, I don't do real guns. Not my thing. They're not like traps. Games and nerd events teach you a little about them, angles and lines of sight and which kinds you're allowed to get wet and stuff, but that's nothing. Strategy is completely different without the word "Rematch."

But I'll admit it, in that one brief instance, I was kind of aching for a ranged weapon. The scooters were right there, unguarded on the floor. I could have been on one of them in seconds. The only problem was that Steve and Rob weren't getting out of the way so Maria could join me, and in a game, I could have fixed that. They were so vulnerable, hanging there, never looking up at me.

No one ever did.

I sifted through the real life stuff I did have and took the heaviest, most aerodynamic thing within reach, the knock-off Swiss Army knife in the evil bunny bag, and threw it as hard as I could at the back of Steve's head.

It was on target. It didn't stop him, but it did make him turn to see where it had come from. I ducked out of sight behind a sheet of plywood, so he sprayed a whole clip blindly into the gap a few feet to my right.

Any sturdiness I'd been able to breathe back into my knees was completely gone in those few seconds. I gotta hand it to him for that.

Not so much for the fact that those seconds also allowed Maria to swing down behind him from the level above and tackle him to the ground, the ground, in this case, being about twelve feet away.

Rob aimed down at them, but there was no way to separate the two targets, rolling across the concrete, both moving like they hadn't quite taken inventory of their injuries yet.

"Get off of me!"

Okay, I had to Mr. Rogers that up a little, but that's the gist of what Steve shouted.

"Or what, you'll fire me?"

I could smell Maria's hair burning when he pushed her up

against one of the flaming corpses, which I'm guessing he thought was really witty.

The scooters were *right there.*

I climbed down as far as the pulley chain once more and yanked on it with my full weight. With no one pulling evenly on the other side, the door made an even more horrible sound than it was supposed to, a grating, crunching squeal, and it only lifted from one corner, but I was able to winch it just high enough for one scooter and one rider at a time to squeeze out through the side closest to me before it jammed.

Rob aimed unsteadily at me from the other side of the entranceway, and Steve raised his empty weapon in my direction, too, out of reflex, so I backed out of the light and shifted between levels a couple of times, hoping they'd lose track of me.

The first thing I considered shouting was, "What are you waiting for? This is the closest you'll ever get to stealing your boss's car!" but for obvious reasons, that seemed like it might hurt her chances of pulling it off, so instead I shouted the second most persuasive thing I could think of, "Bring my friends' daddy home." I took another strand of firecrackers, my second-to-last one, and threw it onto that big, zombified businessman's pyre.

Steve and Maria came apart when the strand went off next to their heads, and Rob was too busy shielding his eyes from the flashes to take the opportunity to shoot.

Maria understood my message, and she went straight for Steve's scooter and dragged it to the opening I'd made in the door. She stopped there, though. I don't know if she was hoping to understand the rest of my plan first, or if she just wanted to find something worse to do to Steve before parting ways with him, but I had to shout again for her to go before she finally did.

I watched for David's signal light and listened to his exit opening when she circled around to pick him up, but only out of the corner of my eye (and ear). Most of me was busy climbing behind as many silhouette-obscuring bits of scrap as I could, searching what was left of my bag, and trying to decide what exactly the plan was that I hadn't told her.

It was just Norman and me left then.

Rob fired another volley into my side of the barricade, and I know I felt shots pass me on both sides.

I lit another Caterpillar's Pipe and threw it, but Steve was ready and swatted it out the door with his gun before it went off.

"Who's there?" he called out, reloading at the same time. He didn't need to hurry anymore. I wasn't going to attack him head-on.

Quieter than I'd ever had to be in the trees or the smoke arena, I started inching my way around, across from the door, over to what had been Maria's side. I just had to get down, get to the scooter, and get out while they were still focused on the last place they'd spotted me.

It was *right there.*

"Chris?" Steve guessed. "You still on your feet up there?"

I was halfway across. Then three quarters. When they moved, I moved. When they spoke, I tested the next beam to see if it would squeak.

One more sheet of metal away, one more box flat. I was only about four feet off the ground by then, so I could land silently once I got close enough to the scooter.

Two more paces would have done it.

"Hey, Chris!" Steve called. "Is this what you want?"

He turned back to Rob's scooter, ripped the keys out of the

ignition, and threw them as hard as he could in the direction he thought was away from me.

Actually, they skidded along the floor right under me.

I knew before I'd finished reacting that I'd reacted wrong. I gasped out loud and reached out, down the front of the barricade, to catch them. It was too late. They kept skidding until they collided with God-only-knew which support strut of the makeshift mess behind me.

Steve grabbed my outstretched hand and dragged me out onto the open concrete like a ragdoll.

Rob made an uncertain sound somewhere out of my range of vision.

"What?" Steve snapped. "It's not like we were planning on *leaving* any time soon."

Rob made the sound again, so I guess he wasn't making it over the keys.

Then I realized that this was the first time since they'd broken in that they'd seen me up close, the first time either of them had ever actually seen my small, pale, freckled, fifteen-year-old face.

"Steve?" Rob said cautiously. "You okay, man?"

I hadn't looked in a mirror recently, so it's always possible that I'd gone through the same sudden, premature aging I'd seen on my friends, something in the way we held our features rather than how they were shaped. The difference might even have been dramatic enough on me that in that narrow streak of sunlight and the dim glow of the corpse fire, I could have been mistaken for a peer of Chris and Maria.

I think it's a lot more likely, though, that Steve wouldn't have noticed *anything* about my face, even if it were green with orange stripes and warts the size of Skittles. He was too busy looking at my jacket. It was open, showing off more of my underdeveloped frame and my I Heart Utah gift shop T-Shirt than of itself, but it was the same thick, dark green windbreaker I'd been wearing when I knocked the goatee off his scooter.

Okay, I *did* kill this guy's little brother to stop him from killing me because he thought I was someone I wasn't who had tried to kill *him* for taking part in a hostile takeover that probably involved killing more people. Here's where I guess I should say something deep and tragic and profound about how no matter how few living people are left, or how much death is out to get us, we still find reasons to try and kill each other ourselves, but . . .

I got nothing. Sorry.

Anyway, that's when Steve slammed my head into the floor, harder than the hit that killed Mark. In my case, being aneurism-free, it just hurt a lot, made my vision go sparkly, and kind of killed my interest in tallying up the score.

I head butted him right in that tasteless mustache, which made him curse and made my vision go even *more* sparkly, though not sparkly enough to blur out the shape of the gun he pointed between my eyes.

For what it's worth, I didn't close them.

If I had, I wouldn't have been able to see the flash of Norman's signal light.

"Hey, Bossman!"

Even with a concussion, I could tell by the position of his voice that he'd left his pickup point.

Steve, Rob, and I all turned our heads to look at him, visible for only half of each second, standing on the inside of the barricade on the far side of the warehouse, perfectly framed in the gap Maria and I had widened on our side, the strobe light held under his chin like a ghost storyteller in one hand, a can of kerosene in the other. Next to him was a pile of what looked like every flammable object left in the building, every bit of wood and cardboard and burlap, along with everything remotely comforting that no one had volunteered to carry, the candles and razors and towels, all leaning right against the shelving. I couldn't remember how much of that section of the structure was wooden, and from that distance, it was impossible to tell, but if there was any chemically possible way for the whole place to go up in flames, this was what the setup would look like.

"You want this dump?" Norman shouted, turning the kerosene over on top of the pile. "It's yours! Leave her alone, and there might even be something left of it!"

He picked up one of the strips of shipping cardboard and held the end of it to what could only be my missing lighter.

"Shit!"

Steve dropped his grip on my collar and scrambled, finally, through the gap in the barricade and across the building's main floor, hell bent on keeping those papery sparks away from the accelerant.

Several things went through my very fuzzy head at that moment. The clearest thing was how embarrassingly naïve it had been of me to think that Norman would agree, without a fight, to a plan that centered around sitting still and being quiet and *not* having a certifiably insane plan B up his sleeve.

The second clearest was about the keys.

I rolled myself up onto my hands and knees. Rob aimed down, and he could have had me, but he hesitated.

It looked like he'd only just added up how completely his friend had lost it, whatever "it" he had once had. He might even have been trying to apologize to me—I didn't stop to make sure. I just flattened myself under the barricade and crawled as far as I could into Maria's side before he could change his mind.

Steve *didn't* take up the habit of hesitating, and I heard him fire another whole clip across the room and replace it before he'd covered half the distance.

"Careful!" Norman warned him. "You might make me lose my grip!"

I dug into my bag for my lantern once I'd crawled too deep to see, and I tried to focus on moving forward, sweeping it back and forth to look for reflections off of any sharp little bits of metal that didn't belong, but I couldn't help turning my head to the left to check on Norman.

He was hanging from the barricade on his side by one arm, holding the burning cardboard right over the pile with the other. Steve fired twice more, and Norman swung himself side to side and back and forth between four different levels, less subtly but much more quickly and easily than I could have.

"You *are* aiming for me, right?"

Rob had climbed through and was following after Steve, to help or to try to stop him I didn't know. Ahead of me, up against a load-bearing six-pack of picture frames, I saw the little ring of keys.

Steve was shooting more slowly, and Norman was laughing his endless, manic laugh.

Bang.

"Ha! Almost broke a window that time!"

Bang.

"Oh, come on!"

Bang.

"Please, I've seen imperial storm troopers shoot straighter than—"

Bang.

The laughter stopped, and I looked up again in time to see the blood spreading down Norman's chest before he fell.

It was only about ten feet to the ground, but the torch fell, too, fluttering a few feet to his left and onto the bonfire, which caught in one blinding roar.

"Shit!" Steve repeated, and he and Rob both went straight to trying to put it out with vinegar and corn syrup and kitty litter, as if any of the junk in it could possibly matter.

There were a couple of seconds when I couldn't move. Okay, maybe four or five, crouching in the dark, trying to get my brain to accept enough data, and only enough data, to do any kind of useful processing.

The keys.

I shuffled forward the last few feet to grab them and then rolled out on the warehouse side so I could run back around through the big gap.

Steve and Rob were both too busy to waste a shot trying to stop me.

A couple of zombies had wandered in through the entrance since I'd left it, but one of them had gotten tangled in the pulley chain already, so I only had to finish the other one before taking Rob's scooter and ducking outside. At least it reminded me to have Suprbat ready.

One eye on the next zombie and one on the next possible emergency exit, I started my circuit of the outside as planned.

I was sure Norman would have made it back to his pickup point by then if he'd had to drag himself there by one finger. He was going to turn his signal back on under the door like we'd gone over, to let me know where to slow down, and he'd open the latch from the inside to join me.

I turned the new scooter tightly around one outside corner, then two, and measured my way in my head to where I was absolutely sure his exit had to be, scattering skull fragments every few seconds along the way.

There was no artificial light coming from under it, just lots of black smoke, but there *was* a decent-sized rock sitting not too far away, a little smaller than a cantaloupe. It looked like it had been ripped up and thrown by a rioter not too long ago.

I stopped, stepped off the scooter, and tried to lift it.

The zombies started to converge as soon as I was in one place, screaming, drawing more in around me, and I screamed, too, with the effort of lifting the rock into one of my arms while swinging Suprbat with the other because, really, what more harm could it do?

The moment I could steal two seconds without being consumed, I smashed the rock against the door handle as hard as I could, then shifted it back to the crook of my arm so I could make up the lost time with Suprbat. I had to do that three more times before the handle finally broke so I could pull the thing open.

The rush of escaping hot air assaulted every exposed bit of me and forced me to wait a few seconds, swinging Suprbat blindly, before I could look inside.

There was nothing to see but fire. I was right behind where the kerosene had been poured. The parts of the barricade that could burn had caught, and the flames were spreading around the perimeter. A few packing crate heavy parts of the structure had already collapsed completely.

Once they burned out, it would be the easiest thing in the world to walk straight inside, but with them still blazing, there was nowhere to go from that door.

I couldn't see Norman or his bags where they should have been waiting.

I had the wrong emergency exit.

I got back to the scooter and kept moving, and I was trying to figure out a way to do the same thing to each door, one at a time, but I'd had to ditch the rock to move on fast enough, and I kept feeling certain that I'd see the sign at the next door, the one after that, and then I'd circled almost all the way back to the front, and I knew I'd passed it by.

So I went around again. And again.

I was back searching for that rock to finally try dragging it onto the scooter with me when I saw it, a flashing, pure white, artificial light coming from under the next doorway, no orange or unpredictable flickering to it at all.

I'd only overshot by one door the first time around.

I slammed on the brakes, and when I'd swerved in close enough, the door swung open as slowly and weakly as if someone had just tripped the latch by accident.

Norman was lying on the floor, propped up on the overloaded duffle he'd volunteered to carry, steadily drenching it in blood and clutching the crowbar like he might actually try swinging it if a target got close enough.

I could barely hear his gurgling, hiccoughing gasps over the fire.

"Hi . . . Cassie."

First thing's first.

I took the crowbar and cleared some temporary space around

the scooter with a few wide, sweeping swings. I didn't care if I killed all the zombies in reach just as long as I broke them badly enough to let us get past them in a hurry.

Then I tried to pull his arm over my shoulder to help him stand, but the hole in his chest made such a horrible noise, like a broken garbage disposal, that even after all the horrible things I'd heard and seen already, it actually made me drop him. I wrapped the strap of the bag around him before trying again, twisted it tight, and dragged the whole bloody, twisted mess of him onto the scooter's footrest.

Suddenly, I was really, really glad he was so small.

It wasn't until a shot nicked the doorframe that I remembered that Steve and Rob were still there.

And they had done this to him.

I guess Steve had given up fighting the fire by then, and he was looking pretty pissed off about it.

I climbed into the seat of the scooter, pulled Norman onto my lap, did another sweep with the crowbar to buy a few seconds, and then took it to the door hinges.

One pull, then two, and the door stopped being attached to the doorway.

Steve actually stopped to look at it for a moment when it fell, maybe realizing how hard it would be to close again, or how big the holes were that had burned in the barricade so far, before I took my last string of firecrackers and an intriguing little cylinder called a Banshee's Orgasm, and threw them onto the nearest pile of embers.

"Have fun," I spat at him.

Okay, I had to Mr. Rogers the fuck out of that one.

Oh.

Oops.

Whatever.

I started up the scooter and gunned it. After a few seconds, when I heard, from almost a block away, how that last firework had gotten its name, I watched the impressive horde it attracted storming the broken door in those cheap, curved rearview mirrors.

Steve and Rob still had their guns, their ill-advised weapons of choice, with plenty of bullets, and the access stairway to retreat to if they were fast and smart enough. They'd survived being abandoned to what should have been death once before, so I don't honestly know if they or the zombies came out on top of the match I set up.

To this day, I don't care.

"Ca-ssie."

Norman's breath was still coming in those painful-sounding, wet, wheezing fits. He couldn't say a whole word all in one piece, and under the strap, his chest kept making that sick, sucking, draining sound.

I leaned forward and squeezed him between myself and the controls, telling myself it was to keep the pressure on, steering with one whole arm and defending with the other, trying not to feel the shape of the exit wound through my I Heart Utah shirt.

I'd say that has to qualify as Level Six of scooter riding.

"Prom-ise—" He cut off coughing and then tried to wipe the blood off his mouth but just ended up spreading it around.

And there I'd been, thinking I'd never have to see a terrifyingly red smile painted on him again.

"Don't let . . . me bite . . . you . . . unless . . . I'm here . . . to . . . enjoy it."

"I promise." I didn't argue to save him the trouble of more words. I knew he meant that I had to remember what to do in those critical thirty seconds after a life, but I figured promising not to let those thirty seconds start in the first place would have to be close enough. That's what *I* meant.

"How . . . much?"

I looked down for the first time at the gas gauge on Rob's scooter and measured it against the route to the meeting place and what I'd learned from the pizza scooter's impressive but not supernatural mileage.

"More than enough," I lied.

And *then,* away from the Costco, away from the guns and the fire and the extra thick hordes, listening to Norman choking on his own blood, *that's* when I got scared, almost too scared—scared enough that I had to do something to stop it from taking me off the road.

"Black socks never get dirty. The longer you wear them, the blacker they get.

"Someday I think I might wash them, but something keeps telling me, 'don't do it yet.'"

"Not yet," Norman choked back to me. *"Not yet, not yet."*

CHAPTER TWENTY-SIX

OR WHAT I GUESS YOU'D CALL AN EPILOGUE

Chris, Maria, and the Harts and Defoes all settled in Sleepy Hollow, a surprisingly peaceful spot for being in New England, even in those early days of the infestation.

There was another little group of non-psychopathic survivors holed up in a diner there when we were passing through, so it was sort of like fate. Three years later, they're all still there.

Josh and Chloe are twelve now. So far, they call each other "best friend," like Norman and I once did, and people try not to sound like panda breeders when they talk about them.

At least they can play outside now. Zombies are only a slightly bigger danger than wild animals since the first wave mostly rotted into uselessness. There aren't enough people left to die for their numbers to stay up, but the thirty second rule is still in effect, so it looks like they'll never disappear completely. Not until we do.

Maria's helping out with that. She clicked with one of the diner guys, and she's pregnant right now with his kid. They fight a lot, but they always make up enthusiastically.

And Norman, the coolest, bravest guy I ever knew—the coolest, bravest man I *know*—yeah, he's alive.

You could even say we're living happily ever after, if by "happy" you're not imagining anything fancier than "together and in love," and by "ever after" you mean "until the day one of us eats from the wrong dented can of Spaghetti-Os or reaches into the wrong dark corner without a psychiatrist handy to do something life-saving with a knitting needle."

According to Dr. Defoe (whose credentials I never fully examined while he was saving my boyfriend's life), Hector was right all along about shoulder wounds. A few inches higher, closer to the carotid artery and the thick, bullet-fragmenting surface of the scapula, and Norman would have gotten to tell him so in person.

But what we were *all* wrong about was never thinking to argue about the center mass at all. Where it hit, the shot went straight through Norman's right lung, but some impromptu surgery and a *lot* of antibiotics later, all it left was a couple of cool scars, a rib that can predict the weather, and a new, improved, more gravelly, and much sexier rock-and-roll scream when I can talk him into using it.

We visit Sleepy Hollow every couple of months when we're starved for the chance to work a crowd, but mostly we travel, just the two of us—sort of an extended, unofficial honeymoon. Always to the north or south, though, never far to the west. We say it's because we don't want to risk the desert again, but really, we just don't want to look backward.

I don't want to see my home again. I don't want to walk the USC campus and wonder what I could have learned in its classrooms. I don't want to know if the Hollywood sign is still there. I don't want to see if the fairytale-perfect paint has been allowed to fade on Sleeping Beauty's castle.

Learning to live a new life is more fun.

So far, we've been lucky. Healthy. We'll never feel completely safe, not the way we did in the glory days of our species, but if we're lucky for a few more years, learn a few more tricks to tip the odds of survival in our favor (sturdy shoes prevent so many problems that they're practically a cheat code, by the way), then maybe, *maybe* we'll follow Maria's example and see if we can't do our fair share to keep the party going for at least a few more generations.

That *is* kind of the point of writing all this down, after all, and keeping it in the deepest, safest pocket of my bag next to Peter's contribution.

Besides, it might be a nice excuse to make the trek to see Dr. Teach and the rest of the Tulsa crowd again.

For now, I've got a rather impressive stretch of abandoned beachside Miami all to myself and that same coolest, bravest man (who's getting a little impatient at the moment) waiting for me on this mansion's back patio, watching the inviting waves.

So, until the next truly earth-shattering story I bear witness to (i.e. hopefully never), this is Cassandra Emily Fremont wishing you good luck and a happy zombie apocalypse.

ACKNOWLEDGEMENTS

Thanks must go again to my amazing husband, Matt, for introducing me to the horror genre I now call home, and for all the support, brainstorming, and the patience and understanding that only a soul mate and fellow neurotic author could have. I wouldn't be the author I am without you.

A giant thanks to my agent, Jennifer Mishler, for picking me out of the slush pile to take that big chance on. Thank you for your faith in me, and in my work, and for everything you do to help it succeed.

Similarly, giant, sloppy thank you kisses to head publicist D. Kirk Cunningham, executive editor Christopher Loke, and everyone else at Jolly Fish Press who works so hard to make each book a success. You guys are finny and funny and oh-so delish!

Thanks to my parents for devoting so much time and effort to my education and for teaching me my love of books and learning. Thanks, Dad, for being the best English teacher I ever had. Forgive me for all the gratuitous violence and crude colloquial language. Please enjoy the motor scooters. Thanks, Mum, for putting up with a mathematically-challenged daughter and for all the long, tantrum-filled hours spent helping me scrape through my General Ed requirements so I could study what I love.

Thanks also to my little sister, Heather, for giving me five extra vicarious years of the young adult experience. Things do get better, I swear.

Thanks to my father-in-law, Scott, for all the enthusiastic free publicity, the expert coaching in the terrifying art of live interviews, and for helping Matt and me pull off the cross-country road trip that inspired much of this book. Also for the coffee grinder. One cannot overestimate the importance of good coffee.

Thanks to my sometimes critique partner, Emery Schulz. Even though I must brave the gooier, grabbier, toothier parts of my imagination without you, you forced me to step up my game as a writer without the use of a sledgehammer.

Thanks to the members of Boy Scout troop 137 and its short-lived sister Venturer crew in the year 2003 for a camping trip that thankfully didn't end the world, and to everyone else who, for better or worse, gave my teen years their unforgettable, tumultuous intensity. Thank you all for the inspiration.

Thank you to the authors of all the books that have made me laugh, cry, shiver, or feel warm and fuzzy inside, the books that have brightened my life and made me want to do what you do.

Finally, thanks to the online community of authors, readers, and bloggers for all your camaraderie and support. Nobody can do this alone. You guys are awesome!

F.J.R. Titchenell is an author of Young Adult, Fantasy, Sci-Fi, and Horror fiction. She graduated with a B.A. in English from California State University, Los Angeles, in 2009 at the age of nineteen. She currently lives in San Gabriel, California, with her husband and fellow author, Matt Carter, and their pet king snake, Mica.

Follow F.J.R. Titchenell on her blog at:
fjrtitchenell.weebly.com